Twisted Candy

Zane Menzy

DEDICATION

To all the ghost stories I have been told through the years.
This story wouldn't be what it is had I never heard them.

TWISTED CANDY

CANDY BOY BOOK NO. 4

CHAPTER 1

"Fuck you smell good, man." Levi smothered his face with Josh's briefs while stroking his morning wood. "I can't wait for you to get home."

He'd been sniffing these bad boys for the past ten minutes, inhaling every ripe whiff of Josh's ball sweat he could muster. They didn't carry the same manly stench like Mark's briefs had—a deceitful smell that Levi would forever associate with the best sex of his life—but Josh's scent was still incredibly alluring because it smelled like a promise of sexy things to come.

"As soon as you step inside, I'm gonna lick you all over," Levi whispered. "Gonna suck that big dick of yours until it blows in my mouth."

His horny commentary was interrupted by an inconvenient lump joining him on the bed. He threw the briefs on the floor in fright and found himself staring at Phoebe, Josh's cat. "I'm kind of fucking busy here, cat."

Phoebe didn't give a shit, she just sat beside him with displeased eyes, like she knew what he'd been doing and was totally judging him for it.

"Trust me, cat, Josh does the same sort of thing in here so don't look at me like that."

Phoebe continued staring and let rip a demanding meow.

"What are you after?" He frowned and glanced at the bedside clock. It was ten in the morning. "If you want more food then you're just gonna have to wait until Danny's gone."

Phoebe pleaded with her eyes, her lingering presence killing Levi's erection.

"Sorry, cat, but my butt ain't moving until I know it's safe to leave this room."

After Danny had passed out naked on the lounge floor, Levi had got up and filled Phoebe's bowl with cat biscuits before sneaking to Josh's bedroom to go to sleep. He had no intention of stepping a single foot out of the bedroom until he was sure Danny had left and gone home to pack for his birthday trip away with his father. Levi was glad the boy would be away for seven days. It would give them both the space they'd need to ignore each other and pretend like last night never happened.

The evening had been an evening of firsts for Daniel Candy. It was the geeky boy's first time getting drunk, his first kiss, and his first sexual experience. Under the guise of helping his younger stepbrother lose his virginity, Levi had fucked the boy's face and tight little arsehole in a steamy session that had been surprisingly hotter than he'd expected. The hook-up had been a first of sorts for Levi also since it was first time he'd topped another guy. It felt great to assert his dominance, almost as if he was reclaiming some of the pride Dwight had stolen from him.

Aside from an orgasm and the reclaiming of his pride, fucking Danny had also provided Levi with a heap of filthy pictures to accompany the story he planned to write and post to his blog. Forbidden Candy would be a huge hit with his followers. How could it not? Virgin straight boy getting fucked by his own stepbrother. Taboo shit like that was fucking gold amongst pervy fuckers around the world and Levi planned to cash in on their need for hot wanking material.

But Forbidden Candy hadn't just been about the money, it had also been a way for Levi to get back at Danny for being a narking little shit and dobbing him in for spending too much money. It was also a not-so-little *fuck you* to Levi's stepfather for deciding to confiscate his credit card and tell him it was time to get a job.

Your son is my job. Ha! Take that Mark, you dickhead.

Danny was Mark's pride and joy, and heir to the Candy throne. Father and son looked alike and acted alike; dark-haired, poor-sighted wankers who thought their shit didn't stink. Claiming Danny's virginity was like defiling the most treasured possession Mark owned. Levi had stolen something the Candy men could never get back—the honour of Danny's first time.

Mark was a conservative guy with old-fashioned values. He wasn't the type to yell "Faggot!" down the street at two men holding hands but he certainly was not the kind of man who approved of such things. He'd have a Chernobyl-sized meltdown if he found out his baby boy had let someone put their cock in his arsehole and then swallowed their semen.

Levi smiled to himself, imaging his stepfather's reaction. *That's right, Mark. I fagged your son out like the little bitch that he is.*

Despite finding it funny, Levi did feel a little bad for his stepbrother who would soon be waking up naked on a lounge floor, most likely with a pounding headache and an arsehole that would be feeling tender and sore. He figured it was safe to assume Danny's first reaction would

5

be regret, gut-churning, heart-breaking regret about what he'd given away so easily. Well, it didn't matter how much Danny would want things to be different, he would forever now be another one of Levi's conquests.

Phoebe's ears suddenly went low and she leapt from the bed and scarpered out of the room. "Crazy bitch," Levi muttered. He went to roll over and grab Josh's briefs from the floor but before he could reach for them, Danny's head suddenly popped into the room, his hair sticking out in ten different directions.

"Hi…" Danny said quietly. "I wasn't sure if you were up or not."

"I'm awake." Levi made sure he smiled back and kept his face steady. "Talk about ninja feet. I didn't even hear you coming down the hall."

Danny chuckled. "That's because I have socks on. I wish I was a ninja though." He stepped inside the bedroom and began pretending to wield about an invisible samurai sword. As Danny goofed around playing pretend. With only socks and underwear on, Danny's pale, slim frame was on full display—including the bright red lovebites running up the side of his neck.

"You seem awfully chipper," Levi said, trying his best to act like everything was normal. "I thought you'd have your head in the toilet bowl all morning."

Danny dropped his invisible sword. "I did. Didn't you hear me?"

Levi shook his head.

"It must have been about four in the morning. I spewed for ages but I went back to sleep and I just woke up feeling awesome."

"Really? You feel awesome?"

"I sure do." Danny grinned excitedly. "It's a good thing I do because me and Dad are flying out this afternoon for my birthday trek."

"That's right."

Danny walked over and sat on the edge of the bed. "Are you sure you don't want to come? I reckon you'd really enjoy it. Fiordland is one of the most beautiful places on earth. It's packed with wildlife and most of it is completely untouched. There are probably parts of it that no person has ever even walked on. Imagine how cool it would be to know your body is connected to a place no one has ever been before." It was the perfect set up for a virgin joke but Levi bit his tongue and let Danny prattle on. "You really should come, I reckon it'll be a blast. We can go Moa hunting!"

"You do know they're extinct, right?"

Danny snorted. "I was only joking. They were wiped out by about 1445 but there are some stories about people who believe they saw one much, much later. Did you know that in 1959 there was a woman called Alice McKenzie who claimed to have seen a moa in Fiordland bush in 1887, and again on a Fiordland beach when she was seventeen. She also said that her brother had seen one on another occasion."

"Somebody's a walking Wikipedia page."

"I just read a lot. That's all." Danny tapped Levi's blanket-covered leg. "So did you want to come with us? Dad's friend Geoff is flying us down in his plane so it's not like we need to ring and ask if there is an available seat."

"Thanks for the offer, buddy, but I think I'll give it a pass this time."

The excitement in Danny's eyes died a sudden death and he gazed down at the floor. "That's a shame."

Rather than just give the impression he didn't want to go, Levi fed his stepbrother a bullshit excuse. "It does sound a lot of fun"—*not*—"but I have to stay around here so I can try and find a job."

"I understand. That is really important." He lifted his gaze from the floor and looked Levi in the eyes. "What sort of job are you looking for?"

"I'm not sure yet but I'm sure I can find something."

"The supermarket in Greenmeadows had a sign up that said they were looking for staff. You'd be able to do night shifts there after your classes."

Typical Danny. Sensible and practical. Also fucking delusional. There was no way Levi would be seen dead working in a supermarket. "I'm hoping to find something a bit more... exclusive than that. Something that doesn't involve minimum wage and a hideous uniform."

"I'm sure you will find the perfect job. You can do anything," Danny said like he believed every word. His gaze bore into Levi's eyes and an uncomfortable moment descended upon the room as a tense silence snaked around them and squeezed.

Danny didn't even have to move his lips for Levi to know what he was about to say next—a question or comment about the sex. Levi's mind scrambled for something to say, something that would keep the conversation in the land of last-night-never-happened territory, but his mind drew a blank and before he could say anything, Danny said, "Last night was pretty crazy, wasn't it?"

Levi agreed with a nod, feeling resentful at his clueless stepbrother for not knowing that there were certain things you just shouldn't talk about.

"I guess it's one way to remember my birthday," Danny said.

Levi studied Danny's face, trying to gauge what he was thinking. Was he mad? Upset? Confused? It was hard to tell. Rather than ignore the situation, Levi decided to tackle it head on. After all, maybe it was best to calm

Danny down before he spent the next seven days alone with his father. Heaven forbid Danny let slip to Mark anything about what had happened.

"Are you okay, buddy?" Levi asked in a soothing voice. "I know it's different for everybody but I know some people can get upset after their first time if it didn't go the way they thought it might and…" Levi trailed off and scratched the back of his neck. "And I guess it's safe to say last night probably wasn't how you ever imagined you'd lose your virginity."

"It wasn't how I ever thought I would lose my virginity but I still think it was perfect."

"Really? You thought it was perfect?"

"Mmhmm. Obviously I never thought I'd have sex with a guy but I still think it was perfect because it was with someone I care about and someone who cares about me. That's what I always wanted. It made it special." Danny's face glowed with pride. "And you were right. I feel different. More confident. It's like… I know I'm a man now and I think other people will be able to see that."

Levi sat quietly watching Danny's lips' sharp movements, remembering it was those very lips which had been wrapped around his cock only hours earlier.

"I just feel so amazing," Danny continued. "And I have you to thank. So, thank you, Levi. Thank you for the best birthday present ever!"

"Uh… you're welcome."

"And thank you for my new outfits and the makeover," Danny said excitedly. "I can't wait to go back to school and show everyone the new me."

It was a bit hard to tell right now with Danny sat in just his underwear but he'd certainly looked like a new and improved Danny last night. The new clothes, stylish haircut and swapping of thick-rimmed glasses for contact lenses had all combined to transform the usually dorky-looking teen into a regular young guy who—to Levi's surprise—was actually quite good-looking.

Levi smiled. "I think you will find everyone will take notice of the new you." He looked at the hickeys on Danny's neck. "Have you seen your neck this morning?"

"No."

Levi smirked. "You might wanna have a look in the mirror then before your dad picks you up."

Danny stood up and walked to Josh's dresser, inspecting the damage. "Whoa!" He gently grazed a finger over the love bites. "I didn't know you gave me those."

Levi bit down on his lip. "Yeah, soz."

"Don't be sorry. This is great." Danny grinned his satisfaction at having a bad case of root rash. "I just hope they last until I get back from my trip so everyone at school can see."

"Considering you are going away for a week I'm afraid you're a bit out of luck."

"Damn." Danny rubbed his neck again, giving his lovebites one last look in the mirror before coming to sit back on the edge of the bed. "What should I tell Dad?"

"Anything you like as long as you don't tell him they're from me."

"I can tell him they're from Angie."

Levi raised a questioning brow. "Angie?"

"Angie Vickers. She's a girl from my school who I've had a big crush on since Year 10. I've told Dad about her before so he'll just think I was finally brave enough to go up and talk to her and ask her out."

It was highly unbelievable, Levi thought, but he also knew Mark would probably be desperate to believe it was true. Levi's stepfather had never admitted to being concerned about Danny's scathing unpopularity but on some level it must have bugged the man to know he'd fathered such a luckless wimp.

Danny's eyes pointed to Levi's phone on the bedside table. "What are the pictures like?"

"The pictures?" Levi replied, playing dumb.

"The ones you took last night."

"I haven't actually looked at them yet," Levi lied.

"Can I see them?"

Levi reached for his phone and handed it over. He was expecting Danny to ask if he could delete them. That was fine. He had already emailed them to himself anyway.

"I can't believe that's me," Danny whispered in a shocked tone. "I look so... so naked." He laughed.

"That's what naked pictures tend to look like."

"I know but I just can't believe it's me." Danny's mouth farted out a giggle. "Oh my gosh. There's even one of me here sucking your penis!" The fact he chose to say penis instead of cock or dick made him sound terribly... *terribly Danny*.

"Did you want me to delete them?"

Danny shook his head. "No, it's fine. I trust you."

You really shouldn't. "Thanks, buddy."

"To be honest I'm actually really flattered you even want them. I never thought anyone would want pictures of me like that." Levi's phone suddenly blared to life in Danny's hand and he quickly handed it back.

Levi looked at the name on the screen and answered the call. "Morning, Peacharoo."

Peach giggled into the phone. "Morning, poppet. Have I called you too early?"

"No. I'm awake... sort of."

"Good. What are you doing this afternoon?"

"Nothing much."

"Brilliant. You can come visit me later then. I want you to help me plan The Flyer Ball."

Levi rolled his eyes. "You mean you want someone to sit there and nod and smile and tell you how good your ideas are for an event you have probably been planning for the best part of a year."

"Exactly… but afterwards I thought we could go out for dinner."

"I hate to break it to you but I am a povo-arsed bitch, remember?"

"Don't let that bring you down, poppet. I will pay."

"If that's the case you better take me to Fidel's."

Peach laughed. "Sounds like somebody doesn't intend to be a cheap date."

"You gotta pay top dollar for the pleasure of my company."

"Spoken like a true manwhore."

They both laughed before arranging what time Levi should arrive at her apartment. The conversation carried on, pointless crap mostly but it went on for quite some time. Levi thought Danny would take the long phone call as a hint to bugger off back to the lounge but no, he just lingered on the edge of the bed like a bad smell. When Levi ended the call, he glanced at Danny who was staring at him strangely. "Have I got something on my face?"

Danny chuckled. "No."

"Then why are you looking at me like that?"

"I just like looking at you."

Levi rolled his eyes to the side. "Okaaaay."

"Sorry. I don't mean to weird you out. I just feel really close to you today."

"I guess that's to be expected after last night."

Danny kept smiling and staring, sending them back to the grips of another awkward silence. *Stop fucking looking at me like that. It's getting creepy.* Just as Levi was about to say something, a pulsating knock sounded at the front door.

"Who the fuck will that be?" Levi was about to roll out of bed and tell whoever it was that Josh was away on holiday.

"That'll be Dad," Danny said, getting to his feet. "I didn't expect him here so soon."

"I thought I was meant to be dropping you off?"

"You were but I wasn't sure if you'd wake up in time so I called him when I woke up and asked if he could come get me."

"You better hurry up and get dressed." Levi lay back down and closed his eyes. "If he asks where I am tell him I'm asleep."

"Okay. I'll see you when I get back."

"Have fun," Levi mumbled, not bothering to open his eyes. He waited five minutes before he heard the front door open and close. *He's gone!* Levi opened his eyes and sat up, reaching over the side of the bed to collect Josh's briefs and smother his face once again with his best mate's smell. Just as he gripped his meat and began to tug, Phoebe ran back into the bedroom and let rip another *fucking-feed-me-bitch* roar of a meow.

"Fine, cat. You win." He dropped the briefs on the mattress and rolled out of bed, marching in just his birthday suit to the kitchen, and fed the snooty feline two huge spoonfuls of jelly meat. He went and stood at the kitchen sink, gazing out the window. The sky was a depressing grey and it was beginning to rain. It was the perfect weather for just staying in bed all day, Levi thought. But now that he was actually up and out of bed, he knew he wouldn't be able to get back to sleep. Not when there was a story to write and vengeance to claim.

CHAPTER 2

Sat in his car, Levi squinted through the drizzle at the run-down house across the street. It wasn't the type of residence he usually visited. His friends all lived in much more desirable postcodes than this but it was where he had to be if he wanted his revenge. *The raping little fucker owes me an apology and I know exactly how he can say sorry.*

Levi had decided the best way for Kaleb Ladbrook to apologise for what he'd done was to agree to have sex on Levi's terms. Dark thoughts danced in his brain as he imagined forcing Kaleb to apologise on his hands and knees with his pants snagged around his ankles while Levi rammed his arse full of cock. If the kid was loose enough then Levi would shove his fist up there too. Anything to cheapen and humiliate him. It seemed fair.

Stepping out of the car, he pulled his jacket tighter around himself, then headed towards Kaleb's house. Bouncing up the front steps, Levi took a moment to wipe rain from his face before knocking on the door. His mouth was a stew of hot, nasty words waiting to fire out but when the door flung open, Levi swallowed them down. "Hi, is Kaleb home?" he asked the woman standing in front of him holding a cigarette in one of her pudgy hands.

The woman, Kaleb's mother he assumed, eyed him suspiciously. She appeared to be in her late forties and had a plump figure with hard lines that bracketed her lipsticked mouth. Her wrinkles were made harsher by her curly black hair that fell past her shoulders, framing her saggy boobs.

"He might be," she said between puffs. Her voice was a nicotine-soaked rasp. "And who might you be?"

"I'm Levi. He's friends with my—"

"KALEB!" she screamed at the top of her lungs like a screeching banshee. "Ya got a mate here to see you." And on that note, she walked away leaving the front door wide open with Levi waiting outside.

The sound of running thuds came from the other end of the house until eventually Kaleb appeared at the front door. He was bare-chested and covered in dried mud. A pair of rugby shorts hung on his hips and his feet were also bare. "Levi," he spluttered. "What are you doing here?"

"I was hoping we could have a chat."

"If this is about Danny's birthday trip, I told him last night that I couldn't make it."

"I'm not here about that." Levi eyed Kaleb's rugby shorts. "But on that note, I'm guessing this infected tattoo of yours can't be that infected if you're well enough to be out playing rugby."

"Yeah, you got me," Kaleb said with a broken laugh. "Don't tell Danny but the truth is I didn't really want to go."

"I can't blame you. Seven days hiking in mosquito-infested forest is not what I'd call fun."

"Exactly." Kaleb smiled, scratching at his chest. "So what can I do for you?"

Two younger kids poked their heads out of a doorway farther up the hallway, spying on the conversation.

"Is there somewhere we can talk in private?" Levi asked.

Kaleb frowned then looked behind and spotted his nosy siblings. "Sure. Follow me."

As they padded along the shadowy hallway, Levi eyed the scandalous tattoo on the boy's lower back. In red and yellow ink was the same *DS* he had seen on the naked male draped over Dwight's bed the week before. He had to control his anger so that he didn't kick Kaleb in the back.

At the end of the hallway, they turned into one of the bedrooms and Kaleb closed the door behind them. Levi glanced around the boy's bedroom which was quite bare aside from a single bed covered in crochet blankets and two sets of drawers. He figured the minimalist approach had less to do with style and more to do with lack of funds.

Kaleb sat down on the edge of his rickety bed, picked up a towel from the floor and proceeded to rub some of the mud from his shins.

While Kaleb's gaze focused on scrubbing mud off his leg, Levi sized the lad up. He was about the same height as Levi, five-foot-ten, and had shaggy blond hair and dull blue eyes. His muscular chest was hairless but his forearms and legs were covered in a golden fuzz of blond hairs. He was very much a *Blondie*. Despite his obvious muscles, Kaleb didn't carry the intimidating build most rugby players had, he was more trim and toned than he was broad and muscular. Definitely nowhere near the size of someone like Lucas Maxwell.

Kaleb glanced up and asked, "What did you want to talk about?"

Levi suddenly found himself at a loss as to how to word the reason for his visit. He ummed and ahhed, wondering the best way to broach the subject. In the end, he didn't have to. Kaleb did it for him.

"Are you here because of Dwight?"

Hearing Dwight's name made Levi's tummy somersault. "I am."

"How did you find out it was me?" Kaleb dropped the towel on the floor.

"That's not important. What I want to know is why you thought it was okay to rape me."

"Rape you?" Kaleb laughed. "Nobody raped you."

"Considering I didn't give you permission to be there, then yes, you raped me."

"Don't be stupid. That wasn't rape. Dwight told me you were gagging for it. And let's be honest, you were gagging for it."

"Look, I don't want to make a bigger deal out of this than I have to but you can't pretend like you're not in the wrong here."

Kaleb leaned back on his elbows, smirking. "Go to the police then. If you think it's rape then that's what you should do, but me and Dwight will both say it was consensual—which it was."

"How the hell is me tied to a bed consensual?"

Kaleb sighed like he couldn't be bothered having the conversation. "Why are you even here, Levi? What is it you want from me?"

"An apology would be a good start."

"Sorry."

"You could try saying it like you mean it."

"It's hard to sound like I mean it when I didn't do anything wrong to apologise for."

"Um, hello? What part of 'you raped me' do you not understand?"

Kaleb scoffed. "You wanted it. Shit, you even called me daddy while I fucked you. That sounds a lot like consent to me."

Levi's pulsed thundered. "I didn't know it was you!"

"You still called me it. Begged for my load." He smirked. "Which I gave you."

"Like I said. Rape."

"No it wasn't. You fucking loved my dick inside you."

"No I didn't."

Kaleb closed his eyes and began moaning "Daddy. Oh Daddy. Yes Daddy. Make me loose Daddy. I love your big dick Daddy."

Levi glowered. "Fuck up you little prick."

Kaleb smiled as if he found all the tension inside the room funny.

Levi took a deep breath. "Unless you want me going to the police then I suggest you learn how to apologise properly and pay me some sort of compensation for what you did to me."

Kaleb laughed. "You are dreaming. Do I look like I have any money?"

"I'm not talking about money."

"Then what sort of compensation are you talking about?"

"By letting me do to you what you did to me."

Kaleb snorted. "That's so not happening."

"It will if you don't want trouble."

"Bring the trouble. I don't give a shit." Kaleb got to his feet with a menacing scowl on his face. "You don't scare me."

Levi stood his ground, refusing to be intimidated by a school kid. "I should scare you."

"Why?"

"Because we both know you want to be a Fitzroy Flyer. I am the king of that fucking scene so it would be in your best interest to be on my good side."

Kaleb laughed right in his face. "Oh, man. You really are pathetic like Dwight says you are."

"Fuck you! I'm not pathetic."

"Yeah you are. Why would I give a shit about getting access to some lame-arsed group in Fitzroy when I plan on moving overseas to a real city."

It was Levi's turn to let rip a mocking laugh. "Good luck with that because from where I am standing you don't look like you have enough money to get a taxi to the airport let alone board a plane to go overseas."

"Danny's promised to take me with him when he moves to Sydney for uni next year. He said we can get a flat together over there."

Levi wasn't surprised to hear this. His stepbrother probably would be stupid enough to pay for Kaleb to move over and join him, desperate to keep the only friend he had. "You don't think maybe it's time to stop using Danny to pay for everything for you?"

"That's rich coming from you," Kaleb replied. "Danny's told me all about how much money you spend of his father's money."

Rather than defend his own habit of spending other people's money, Levi focused on Kaleb using Danny. "I'm not the one pretending to be friends with someone just so they can buy me new clothes or whatever the fuck else it is Danny pays for you."

"I'm not *pretending* to be his friend."

"If you're not pretending then how come you won't let him hang out with you at school?"

"Because I have a reputation to keep. If I hung out with Danny every day then that reputation would get ruined."

"I wonder how ruined it will be when everyone finds out the school's star jock is a gay rapist who lets men tattoo their initials on his back."

Kaleb returned with a threat of his own. "And I wonder what the Fitzroy Flyers will think when they find out you have a thing for daddy dick."

"Be careful what threats you make, Kaleb, because I am telling you now you will be the one who comes off second best."

"Look, man, I don't want to fight with you," Kaleb said, striking a diplomatic tone. "The truth is, I actually think you're really cute."

"If that's the case then you won't mind spending a night with me so we can settle the score."

"I can't do that."

"Why not?"

"Because I'm with Dwight now."

Levi frowned. "You can't be serious?"

"Me and Dwight are like a couple." Kaleb forced a smile then elaborated. "Well…sort of. He has said I can fuck other guys but he's the only one allowed to fuck me which is why I can't give you what you want."

"Do you know how mental that sounds?"

"It's not mental. That's why I got the tattoo. It's a way to symbolise that I belong to him now." Kaleb lowered his voice. "He owns me."

"No one can own you, Kaleb."

"Yes they can. Dwight owns me and according to him I own you."

Levi's eyes went wild. "Like fuck you do."

"It's true. I came inside you. That makes you mine."

Levi flicked his eyes to Kaleb's crotch, wondering for the briefest of moments if what the blond teen was saying was true. *Don't be stupid* he told himself. "That doesn't mean anything."

"But Dwight says—"

20

"Dwight says a lot of shit," Levi interrupted. "I've already dealt with him and now I am here to deal to you, so quit fucking about and just agree to what it is I am asking."

"What did you do to Dwight?" Kaleb said, managing to sound both soft and angry.

"None of your business," Levi replied. "Now what day do you want me to come get you so we can settle the score."

"I told you, Levi, I can't do that."

"And I am telling you now that you will."

They locked eyes like they were in a gun fight, waiting for the other to draw a pistol. Then Kaleb did—a gun made of flesh. He tugged down the waistband of his rugby shorts and exposed himself, yanking on his pale cock that wasn't entirely flaccid. He stepped forward and grabbed Levi's wrist, placing Levi's hand to his growing erection. The hot skin zapped Levi's fingers and, as if it was instinct, Levi furled his fingers around Kaleb's member, squeezing and pulling.

"That's it," Kaleb whispered. "Have a play with it." He pressed their cheeks together and licked Levi's earlobe, chewing lightly at it.

Levi's ears had always been his weak spot. Touching, licking, biting... all sent him over the edge. His breathing increased and he felt his own cock begin to come to life, pulsing and stiffening from the erotic nibbling. With one hand busy tugging Kaleb's dick, Levi ran his other hand down Kaleb's spine until two fingers brushed the top of his crack.

At that, Kaleb released a low growl and slid his mouth down the side of Levi's neck, sucking and biting at him with slobbery ferocity.

It was insane how quickly they'd gone from a near punch-up to a raw embrace of passion but Levi didn't question it, preferring to embrace the animal within. He pushed forward, eliminating the space that separated them, pressing their cocks together in an electrifying heat. Kaleb's mouth suddenly latched onto Levi's lips and he accepted the sweet slide of the boy's tongue into his mouth.

He had hoped to have Kaleb come to his house one night when everyone was out. Tie the boy to the bed and film the whole thing. He still intended to do that but a quick fuck right now wouldn't hurt. His finger stroked the length of Kaleb's crack and poked at his hole, hard enough that the fingertip went in for a second.

"Whoa there." Kaleb pulled away from the kiss. "What are you doing?"

"Fingering you." Levi glanced towards the small bedside drawer. "Have you got some lube?"

"You're not fucking me, Levi," Kaleb said. "I'm keen to fool around but I told you, Dwight's the only man allowed inside me."

Levi let go of Kaleb's dick, scowling. "Stop playing hard to get. Just drop your pants and turn around."

"Why don't you drop your pants and turn around."

"Because I'm in charge. Not you."

Kaleb sniggered. He casually put his cock away and sat back down on the bed. "Maybe it's best you just leave because you're never going to get what you want, unless of course you change your mind and want me to be the top."

Levi's blood was pumping from the sting of rejection. He wasn't used to being turned down, certainly not from someone less attractive than himself. He wet his lips and focused on keeping his cool. "If you know what's good for you, Kaleb, then you will do what I say."

Kaleb laughed. "Now who sounds like a rapist."

"You fucking owe me," Levi growled.

"I don't owe you shit, dude. Now I'm sorry if you feel like I got one over you, and maybe I did, but don't pretend like you didn't enjoy it. You were begging for my load that day so I gave it to you." He grinned, palming his crotch. "Every. Last. Drop."

What Levi wanted to do was run across the room and stab the smug shit but instead he used his words to do the slicing. "It must suck knowing Dwight would drop you in a heartbeat for me, even though you're the dumb fuck who let him tattoo his initials on your body."

Kaleb's jaw ticked. The comment definitely hit a nerve. "Dwight doesn't want you. He told me."

"Do you really believe that though?" Levi tilted his head in a condescending manner. "Let's be honest, you're not exactly the sexiest guy in the room right now."

"You might be good-looking but you're nowhere near as hot as you like to think you are. Not to mention you're a total cunt."

Rubbing his face, Levi weighed his options. He could stand here arguing until he was blue in the face, or he could just give an ultimatum and leave. He chose the latter. "You have one week to give me what I want or I'll show you just how much of a cunt I can be."

"That's no way to talk to your daddy." Kaleb shot him a shit-eating grin.

"Daddy this," Levi hissed and flipped him the bird. "One week, Kaleb. One week." He turned around and let himself out of the bedroom, stomping the whole way to the front door which he slammed behind him. He half-expected Kaleb's mother to come outside screaming at him but the wrinkled hag made no appearance.

As he sat down in his car, his phone vibrated several times in quick succession. At first he thought it was a text message but when he checked his phone he saw that it was a notification from his blog. He signed into his blog, hoping it was an update to do with the amount of new paid followers signing up so they could read the story he'd promised about Danny.

To Levi's disappointment it was just a message from Demon Dave. It was quite polite, and dangled the bait of offering financial help, but it also contained what Levi considered to be a thinly veiled threat.

Dear Candy Boy

I am sorry to hear you are struggling financially. That is never a nice thing. If your next story fails to bring you the income you need then I may be able to help. But you would have to learn to play nice and stop insulting me in your messages. I can be a wonderful friend if you let me, a not so wonderful one if you are rude.

Perhaps you could come visit me to discuss an arrangement that could work out great for both of us. You would be able to catch up with Shay while you are here. I am sure he would love to see his little prince. You could both "Hang out" LOL

Let me know what you think.

Yours sincerely and erotically

Demon Dave

"Fuck off," Levi muttered as he put his phone away. He doubted very much Demon Dave's ability to help him out with money. The dude was probably some crusty old fart who thought Levi would be impressed by a hundred dollar note. As fucking if.

Even if the guy had access to the kind of money that would make a difference to Levi's situation, he still wouldn't want to meet him because there was no way on this earth he would go near Shay Jacobs. Just seeing his name on the screen was like a polar blast; it made Levi shiver and cut him to the bone. The last time they saw each other things had been said that could never be unsaid, and things had been done that could never be undone. Shay was nothing more than a bad memory who lived on as *Twisted Candy*. Other than that, Levi's childhood hero was dead to him. And that's exactly how he wanted Shay Jacobs to remain.

CHAPTER 3

Sophie eased the car into the driveway, ignoring the rattling of the vehicle's motor which sounded like an expensive problem needing to be fixed. It had been making the horrible noise for about a month now but there just wasn't any money to take the car to a mechanic.

Climbing out of the vehicle, Sophie smiled to herself when she heard bouts of masculine laughter coming from the back porch. She had just come back from dropping Mia off at her parents for the night so her and Lucas could have a night at home drinking with an old school friend, Brad Kenny.

The tall, blond farm boy had been good friends with both of them at high school but when Sophie and Lucas dropped out after she had found out she was pregnant, Brad—like everyone else—had avoided them like the plague. Well, after nearly four years of keeping his distance, Brad was suddenly back in touch. He had been texting Lucas on and off the past two months and had finally arranged to come over that afternoon for drinks.

As she walked inside the house, another bout of hearty laughter erupted from the back porch. It made her happy to hear Lucas having fun, taking a break from the role of stressed out father and actually sitting down to have a drink with a friend their own age.

"Oh, man." Sophie heard Brad say. "That is too fucking funny. I wish I'd been there."

"Yeah, mate. I knocked that faggot until he was on the floor," Lucas crowed, laughing.

"Good fucking job!"

Sophie cringed at the word faggot. She didn't like it.

"Yeah, mate. I really got him good. When he was down on the ground, I grabbed him by the ghoulies and told him exactly what I thought of him," Lucas gloated. "I ain't usually one for grabbing a guy's cock but I grabbed his. Tiny fucking thing. I almost thought it was a vagina."

More laughter.

Sophie walked through the ranch slider door of the lounge and stepped out onto the patio where Lucas and Brad were enjoying a beer in the sun. "Who are you talking about?" she asked.

The guilty look on Lucas's face was enough to give away that she'd just walked in on a story she wasn't supposed to hear. When he didn't respond, she repeated the question. "Who did you have a fight with?"

Lucas tried to flash Brad a don't-tell-her look but he wasn't quick enough.

"Lucas was just telling me about how he punched over Levi," Brad said, chasing his comment down with a mouthful of beer. "You deserve a medal for that one, mate."

Sophie's gaze flew like a dart to Lucas's sheepish face. "That better not be true."

Lucas shifted his seat, lowering his voice. "He fucking deserved it."

"How can you be so stupid." She walked over and whacked him on the shoulder, hard, then sat down beside him. "For Christ's sake, Lucas. We don't have money for a lawyer if this goes to court."

"Chill, babe, chill," Lucas said, trying to calm her down. "This happened way over a week ago. Levi's too much of a fucking pussy to press charges."

Sophie wished she could have said she was surprised to hear Lucas had assaulted her ex-boyfriend but the truth was she wasn't surprised at all. Lucas had always wanted to hit Levi. Always. Even before Lucas and her got together, Lucas and Levi had never gotten along.

"Why on earth would you hit him?" Sophie asked.

Lucas swigged back on his bottle of beer. "He insulted Mia so I dealt to him."

"He insulted Mia?" Sophie frowned.

"I ran into him and Peach at a café and I was being friendly, you know, not rude, and so I got my phone out and started showing them pictures of Mia and he said he didn't give a shit about seeing pictures of our daughter. He called her a cum sprout!"

Brad snorted, trying not to laugh. Lucas shot him a snotty look and Brad quickly apologised. "Sorry, man. I just… I've never heard that term before."

"I have," Sophie sighed. "It's typical Levi-talk. Vulgar and hurtful." She fixed her gaze on Lucas. "So Peach was there?"

Lucas nodded.

"Bloody hell, Lucas." She whacked his shoulder again, harder. "How could you be so stupid!"

"What's the problem with Peach being there?"

"Because not only does Levi have a witness to being assaulted but he has the most vengeful and vindictive witness there is."

"Nar, Peach is alright," Lucas replied casually. "She's always been friendly when I've seen her around town."

"It's called being fake. Peach is the master of it."

"Peach is fake?" Lucas looked back wide-eyed. "Really?"

"Peach is more plastic than the chairs we are sitting on right now." Sophie grabbed Lucas's beer from him and took a sip before handing it back. "I appreciate that you did what you did because you felt you were sticking up for Mia but what use is that if you end up with a conviction."

Sophie's worry about Peach being present at Levi's beating ran deeper than the pink-haired gossip columnist's ability to be a grade-A bitch. While Levi was a typical male with the observation skills of a blind cyclops, Peach would have enough intuition to potentially spot who had gifted Mia her olive skin and pretty hazel eyes.

"I told you, babe, this happened well over a week ago," Lucas said. "If Levi was going to do anything then he would have done it by now."

I don't know about that.

Like a shark circling a surfer, a bad feeling swam in circles in Sophie's stomach. Levi wasn't the kind of person to let someone get the better of him and not do anything about it. Even if he were feeling kind enough to let this go—which was highly unlikely—then there was no way in hell Peach would let it go.

When Sophie had dumped Levi in favour of Lucas, Levi had been too hurt to do anything drastic. He disappeared from school for weeks and never spoke to her again, punishing her by refusing to acknowledge her existence. She had felt terrible at the time but had been grateful not to feel the wrath of his vengeance. But she didn't escape Peach's. While Levi moped about in heartache, the pink-haired monster had made sure Sophie paid for breaking Levi's heart, forcing all their friends to sever ties with Lucas and Sophie when news of her pregnancy became public. While Peach and Levi couldn't damage them socially anymore, Sophie knew that people with that much money could pay for cruelty to be dished out in unique ways.

"I want you to apologise," Sophie blurted.

"What?" Lucas sat upright in his chair like he'd just been shot. "No way, babe."

"Yes way. I want you to visit Levi and apologise."

"Piss off," he blurted before mouthing *sorry*.

Sophie could see Brad looked uncomfortable as he listened to them hover on the edge of an argument. She didn't care. This was too important. "You will go see him and you will say sorry, and you will ask him if there is anything you can do to make sure he won't press charges."

"I can't do that. That'll make me look like a pussy."

"You can and you will," Sophie said in her best stern mother voice. She glared at Lucas until he capitulated.

"Fine," he relented with a sigh. "I have to mow his family's lawns next week so I guess I can tell the fuckface I'm sorry while I'm there."

She stroked his arm. "Thank you, babe."

"Just for the record, I'm only doing it to make you happy," he said sulkily. "Not because I'm scared of him or nuffin."

Sophie couldn't help but smile at her man's masculine pride. "And that's why you're the best boyfriend in the world." She leaned in and gave him a kiss.

"I still think you did the right thing," Brad piped up. "Somebody should have punched that uppity prick in the face years ago."

Like Lucas, Brad had never been a huge fan of Levi's. But unlike Lucas, the lanky farm boy had never been openly hostile to Levi from what Sophie could recall. Few people had ever been rude to Levi's face, which is partly why she'd always admired Lucas for at least making his feelings known, even if his rudeness hadn't always been valid. There were lots of reasons to dislike Levi Candy but few people disliked him for the right reasons, Sophie thought. Most of the guys at high school had hated Levi for his wealth and good looks and all the attention he received from the girls. Attention Levi had loved to milk, much to Sophie's annoyance at the time.

The little she knew of Levi's actions after their breakup was that he had further damaged his likeability with all the guys in their social group when he'd begun a slutty bender of fuckboy freedom that had involved fucking way too many of their girlfriends. To the best of her knowledge not one of the guys ever challenged Levi about his disgusting behaviour, probably too scared to risk being blacklisted from the cult of popularity Peach had already started weaving around her beloved Levi.

Sophie had never understood the close bond between Peach and Levi, but Sophie knew that in Peach's eyes Levi could do no wrong. Levi probably only had one other *real* friend and that was Josh, the one male whose girlfriends would be safe from Levi's roving eye. Josh was also the only person from school to have known Levi in his Brixton days. Sophie had asked Levi plenty of times about what his life had been like back then but he never really answered the question and would just say something meaningless like "I prefer to live in the moment, not the past." You didn't have to be a rocket scientist to know that was Levi's way of hiding something. He was spontaneous, funny, and could be the life and soul of the party but he could also be riddled with dark moods that oozed secrets. What those secrets were, Sophie never found out, but she was damn sure they had a lot to do with Levi's need for control—despite his best attempts at playing the whole *I'm just an easy going guy* card.

"Come on, Sophie," Brad said, getting her attention. "You have to admit if there anyone in Fitzroy who deserved being punched over then it is Levi."

"I don't disagree," she said. "I just wish it wasn't my man doing the punching."

"It did feel good though, babe." Lucas grinned, wrapping an arm around her shoulder. "You should of heard the way he squealed when I grabbed him by the gonads. He screamed like a little girl."

Brad laughed while Sophie imagined how much that must have hurt.

"I reckon good on ya, mate," Brad said. "That dude is one of the biggest fuckwits I have ever met. He's in a couple of my classes at polytech and he barely turns up but the tutors keep passing him because of who his dad is."

"His stepdad," Sophie corrected.

"His stepdad?" Brad looked surprised.

"Didn't you know," Lucas started. "Cuntface Candy used to be Brixton scum."

"Not everyone from Brixton is scum," Sophie interjected.

"Most of them are," Lucas said defiantly. "And he is for sure. I can't believe you dated that dickhead."

Sophie sighed inwardly. If she had a dollar for every time she'd heard Lucas say that then she'd be about as rich as the Candy family. "I'm with you now so you don't have to worry about that, do you?"

"Nope." Lucas grinned, hugging her closer to him and giving her a big sloppy kiss. "You saw the light."

Sophie smiled at Brad. "Sorry for inflicting you with our PDA."

"It's fine. It's actually really cool to see how you two still dig each other so much."

"You betcha," Lucas said. "I still can't believe how lucky I am to be with Sophie. She's amazing."

Sophie wanted to blush. Lucas really could get mushy when he started talking about her. It was sweet mostly but probably not the best conversation for guests to listen to. "What about you, Brad? Are you seeing anyone at the moment?" she asked.

"I haven't dated anyone since me and Melanie split up last year."

"Melanie Hohepa?" Sophie asked.

"Yeah, we were together for nearly two years."

"Oh wow, I didn't know that," Sophie replied. "I guess that shows how long we have been out of the scene."

"You're not missing much," Brad said, his tone surly.

"Have you fallen out with the flyers or something?" Sophie quickly apologised. "Sorry, I shouldn't be so nosy."

"Nar, it's okay." Brad leaned back and pressed his mouth to the lip of the bottle, taking a swig. "I haven't had a falling out or nothing like that"—an overly lengthy pause hiccupped his sentence—"I just got over it, that's all. Same shit every weekend with the same boring-arse people."

Sophie didn't believe a word he was saying. She wasn't a big fan of the Fitzroy Flyers but boring was not something you could ever accuse them of being.

"Is that true? The Flyers are boring?" Lucas sounded surprised. "I look online sometimes at some of the parties they have and it looks fucking epic. I wish we would get invited to one of the parties."

Sophie wanted to tell Lucas to keep quiet and not make it so obvious how desperate he was to be part of that scene. That ship had sailed years ago, and after assaulting Levi in front of Peach the ship had more than sailed, it had sunk.

"Honestly, mate, you ain't missing much," Brad said. "You'd have as much fun just going to a normal old pub around town. The Flyers are all a bunch of try-hards."

Pot. Kettle. Black, Sophie thought. She didn't dislike Brad but he was one of the biggest try-hards she had ever known. Admittedly he wasn't sixteen anymore and he did seem a lot more laidback right now than what she remembered him to be back in high school, but back when they had been friends Brad was one of the worst culprits for peacocking his way around school, flashing his wealth and popularity around.

"I was looking at the Flyer's Facebook page the other night and it was saying they have the annual Flyer ball coming up," Lucas said, continuing to paint himself like someone who spent all his time online stalking the more exciting lives of others. "Will you be going?"

Brad shrugged, running a hand through his hair. "If I can be bothered then maybe, yeah."

"Oh, man. I bet it will be epic. I've seen the pictures of the last two they have had and those nights look like they go off!"

Sophie chuckled. "What Lucas is trying to say is; we have no social life."

Brad laughed.

"Do you think you could get us an invite?" Lucas asked excitedly. "You probably could, aye?"

"Babe, don't sound so needy," Sophie said.

"I'm not being needy. I just want us to have a night out where we can have fun with our old friends. Wouldn't you like that?"

"I think you will find that's what we are doing right now," she said, pointing towards Brad.

"Yeah, doofus." Brad grinned. "What am I? chopped Liver?"

Lucas laughed. "Nar, man. You're not chopped liver. You're the best steak going. I'm having a fucking blast catching up with you." He raised his bottle and motioned for Brad to do the same. They *clinked* their beers together. "Cheers for coming 'round, Brad. It really is great having you here."

"Cheers. I like being here." Brad glanced around the tiny backyard. "This is nice and chill. Just the way I like it."

Lucas managed to go only two more minutes before he brought up the Fitzroy Flyer Ball again. Even if Brad could get them invited, there was no way they could afford a ticket to that kind of glitzy event. Lucas's desperate need to get a ticket to the flyer ball was descending into cringeworthy territory but thankfully it was stopped by the noise of his cell phone ringing in the lounge.

"I better go answer that," Lucas said. "It could be work."

Sophie couldn't help but smile the way her man raced to answer the phone with an air of pride to his long strides. With Dwight away on holiday in Bali for three weeks, Lucas had been put in charge of running Dwight's lawnmowing business and his cell phone was now hooked up to receive all calls from customers ringing through to the business number. To most people it would probably just be an added hassle of a job. Not to Lucas. He loved the added responsibility and took it very seriously, desperate to impress the man he referred to as an uncle.

Sophie shot Brad a smile. "I'm sorry about Lucas harping on about the flyers. He just wishes so much to be included sometimes, that's all."

"It's all good. I understand."

"Please don't let it scare you off coming back to visit again. You've seriously made his week by coming around. We don't get too many visitors."

"Don't worry, I'll be back." Brad placed his empty bottle on the ground then reached into the box for a new bottle. "Did you want one?" he asked.

"Only if you don't mind."

Brad cocked an eyebrow, grinning. "I wouldn't offer if I minded."

"In that case, sure."

Brad hunched down again and pulled out another bottle which he handed her. "I really am enjoying being here," he said. "I wished I'd kept in touch all these years."

Sophie smiled. "You're here now so that's what's important."

They had just begun talking about Brad's course at polytech when Lucas reappeared, his face even paler than usual. He looked so jitttery, Sophie was expecting him to burst into tears.

"What's wrong, babe?" she asked. "You look like you've seen a ghost."

Lucas dragged a hand through his auburn hair. "That was the police."

Her heart sank. "Is everything alright?"

Lucas shook his head. "Uncle Dwight's house has burned down."

CHAPTER 4

It was sweltering outside, the Bali heat draping the land like a wet blanket that had just come out of the oven. Inside their five-star hotel suite, Dwight lazed back in on one of the lounge chairs, wearing nothing but his boxer shorts. Even though the air-conditioning was on, the near-naked look was the only way to feel comfortable in such atrocious heat. What wasn't comfortable though, was the boring conversation his son was inflicting on his ears.

Josh, also rocking the shirtless look, sat across from him in the opposite lounge chair. He was rambling on about his moral dilemma: *should he break up with Jessica or not?* For the past ten days he had been struggling with what to do about his sort-of girlfriend, going on and on and on and on and on and on about the girl and how he didn't think they should stay together.

To Dwight, the answer was simple. *Ditch the bitch.* But that wasn't how you worded things to Josh. Nope. The boy would have a shit-fit if he heard a man speak about a woman that way. Josh's mother had made sure she had raised their son to be the perfect little gentleman who was careful not to offend anyone. As much as Dwight loved his son, he wasn't a fan of Josh's constant need to behave appropriately. It just grew fucking tiring and boring. He wished Josh would live a little and make the most of his youth and good-looks.

Since they had arrived here Josh had been approached by dozens of flirty tourists at the bars in town but not once had he reciprocated the flirting. To Dwight this was the biggest moral crime of all; not taking advantage of the attention good-looks gave you. Meanwhile Dwight had managed to bag himself three women while he was here, two Australian backpackers and one Irish girl who claimed to be on a "spiritual journey around the world to discover herself." Well, she discovered Dwight's cock and that was all he cared about.

Much to Dwight's surprise, he'd also had a couple opportunities to fuck guys while staying here. He wouldn't have minded getting rough and dirty with another bloke but he didn't want to risk Josh walking in and busting him fucking some dude up the arse. It would be a cold day in hell before he gave his son any reason to doubt his heterosexuality.

"Dad?"

"Huh?" Dwight blinked; unaware he'd slipped into a state of such mindnumbing boredom that he'd totally not heard Josh asking him a question.

"What do you think I should do about Jessica?"

"I've told you what to do, Joshy. I told you the first day we got here. Send her an email and tell her you've decided its best you break up."

"I can't just dump her over email." Josh stared at Dwight with an incredulous look on his face. "That's terrible."

"And leading her on like you're into her—when you say you ain't at all—is a good thing?" Dwight glared back at his son, feigning as much concern as he could muster. "Come on, Joshy. It is for the best. We are here in beautiful Bali, more girls here than you can shake a stick at, and you haven't so much as even looked at one the whole time we've been here. Why deny yourself some fun when you are not even into the chick back home?"

"It's not that I'm not into her... it's just that she's not the one."

"Call it what you like, son, but you need to grow some balls and do the right thing and what better time to do it than while you're a thousand miles away."

"You don't think that's a bit cowardly?"

"I think we have different ways of pronouncing the word *smart*," Dwight replied, winking.

Josh paused for a moment then slowly nodded. "It would be the right thing in the long run, wouldn't it?"

"Of course, Joshy. I wouldn't steer you wrong. Just send the girl an email, be nice about it obviously, but you can't let her hold you back from living your life." Dwight felt proud of that little spiel. *I could be a fucking life coach with gems like that*, he thought.

"You're right, Dad. I'm gonna do it."

"You are?" Dwight was shocked. After days and days of this bullshit topic this was the first time Josh had said he would do anything about it.

"Yeah. It is for the best. It was silly of me to let her think we might be getting back together."

Dwight nodded. "Why did you get back with her?"

A guilty little smile pulled at Josh's lips.

Dwight laughed huskily. "Say no more."

"I know it's bad but she promised me a blow—"

"I get it," Dwight snapped, raising his hand. He felt bad for the way Josh looked back at him a little hurt and confused. He usually demanded every dirty detail about Josh's sexual escapades—which admittedly weren't all that dirty—encouraging the lad to talk with him like a mate at the pub rather than father and son. But after the whole Levi incident, it didn't feel right talking sex with Josh anymore. Not now they'd both put their dick in the same mouth The same mouth that had taken great delight in telling Dwight how Josh was the bigger man of the two.

The size of Josh's cock shouldn't have bothered Dwight, but it did. It bothered him so much that he had developed the bad habit of eyeing his son in a way he shouldn't. Not sexually—fuck, he hoped it wasn't—but in a competitive sense. More than once he'd taken note of his son's strong hands and long feet, trying to find some sort of proof to Levi's claim, but so far all he saw was his own features without the added seventeen years. The only noticeable difference between them was their chests. While Dwight's was covered in a healthy nest of dark curls, Josh's pecs were still a mostly smooth surface, but so had Dwight's been at the same age.

"Should I email her or call her, do you think?" Josh asked.

"How are you gonna call her?" Dwight frowned and sprawled backward in the chair. "That will cost a fucking fortune to call from the hotel."

"I have minutes on my phone."

"Your cell phone can call back to New Zealand?"

Josh nodded. "I paid for an international roaming package before we left."

"At least one of us is smart. And rich."

"You're the rich one, Dad." Josh glanced around the plush hotel suite. "I still can't get over how you paid for this holiday. I can't thank you enough."

Don't thank me, thank your faggot mate's credit card.

"This holiday has blown the old savings account a little bit but it's been worth it." Dwight shot his son a warm smile. "I can't think of a better way to spend money than on my boy."

"Thanks, Dad. I promise you'll get the best old folks' home there is when the time comes." Josh grinned.

"Fuck putting me in a home, just give me the bloody blue juice. I'd rather be dead than sat dribbling in a corner in my own shitty pants."

Josh snickered. "I'll keep that in mind. But yeah, thanks again for the holiday."

Using Levi's credit card to book a luxury 21-day holiday had been quite a big risk. To be more precise, it was a humungous motherfucking arsehole-twitching risk. Dwight knew that if he were busted for it then he would get jail time for sure—there was no questioning that. Five years earlier, when he'd last been in court, the judge had made it clear to him that anymore brushes with the law and he would go for a lengthy holiday behind bars. But just like Dwight had thought, Levi hadn't said a word about him using his credit card. The kid would be too shit scared to rock the boat in fear of Dwight releasing the contents of the video he had hidden back home of Levi tied to the bed getting fucked by two different men.

He had watched the video countless times before coming on holiday, giving his wanking hand a thorough workout. In fact, the only time during the holiday he found himself wishing he was back home was when he thought about that video, wishing he could be at home in bed and watching it on his laptop.

The video was hot on so many levels. It was hot because Levi was hot, of course, but what gave the footage its extra heat was how it was so fucking sadistic. It wasn't just a video of some young guy getting nailed in the arse, it was the destruction of Levi Candy. Blondie's young prick had corrupted Levi, leaving him nothing more than used goods. And that was perfect for Dwight. Until that had happened, Levi was getting dangerous because Dwight was finding himself too damn attracted to his son's best friend. And that was not allowed. Nope. Levi had to be cheapened, made undesirable to his heart, and Dwight's heart would never long for a man who had been claimed in such degrading fashion by someone else. Especially when that someone else was a clueless teenager who produced more erections than braincells.

Blondie, a wannabe dominant top turned Dwight's latest submissive bottom, was going to be quite the handy regular hook-up. The kid was desperate to impress, sucking back his annoyance at being used like a fuck-hole to try and win Dwight's affection. Boys like that were fun, as long as they were enamoured then there was nothing they wouldn't do for a man. Unfortunately for Blondie it wouldn't end in the relationship he probably was hoping for. The kid would be used as a convenient place to dump some cum for the next few months until Dwight grew tired of him and wanted a new toy to play with. Yep, sucked to be Blondie. But that wasn't Dwight's problem.

"I'm gonna go call Jessica now." Josh got to his feet and went to make his way to the bedroom, but before he got there the noise of a phone ringing blared through the room.

"Is that your cell phone?" Dwight asked.

Josh shook his head and pointed to a landline phone attached to the wall. "It's that phone." Josh walked over to it and answered the call. "Hello…. Uh, yep… I will just get him for you." He glanced back at Dwight. "It's for you, Dad."

Who the fuck could be ringing me here? For a split-second, Dwight wondered if maybe one of the backpackers he'd slept with was trying to get hold of him, keen for a repeat performance. But when he answered the phone, he was greeted by the professional tone of one of the receptionists. "Mr Stephenson. I have a Mr Maxwell on the line for you. Would you like to accept the call?"

"Umm…"

As if Josh had read his mind, he said, "If it costs, I'll pay."

Dwight nodded thanks to his son then answered the receptionist. "I'll accept the call."

"I'll put Mr Maxwell through right now," she said.

"Hello… Uncle Dwight?" Lucas's voice sounded like he was lost.

"I'm here," Dwight said. "What's up?"

"I have some bad news."

"If you've driven over something you shouldn't have and rooted the ride-on just call Paul at the mower shop and tell him to charge the repairs to my account."

"It's not that… it's worse."

"What's happened?" Lucas paused too long for Dwight's liking. "Just tell me what the hell's happened."

"I just got a call from the police to say that your house has burned down."

Dwight's eyebrows almost hit his hairline. "My house has fucking what?"

"Burned down. It's completely gone."

Dwight felt woozy, his knees went weak and for a moment he thought he just might faint. "When did this happen?"

"About a week ago."

"A Fucking week! My house burned down a week ago and you only bother to call and tell me now? What the fuck, Lucas."

Josh rushed over, worry etched all over his face. "Your house has burned down?"

Dwight waved a hand in Josh's face to make him be quiet so he could focus on what Lucas was saying.

"It's not like that, Uncle Dwight. I only found out today," Lucas said. "I had a phone call from the police just ten minutes ago and that's when they told me."

"Why the hell did the pigs take so long to get hold of someone?"

"No one knew how to get hold of you. They said they tried your parents but they didn't know what hotel you were staying at. It was only when the police interviewed someone who lives up the road from you who told them the name of your business that they rang the work mobile and spoke to me."

Lucas's voice just became pointless noise as Dwight broke out in a cold sweat, worried about what the police might have found at his house. "Do you know if the pigs have searched the property?" he asked.

"I dunno… I guess so."

Fuckity fuck fuck fuck fuuuuuuuck! He cut his eyes to Josh, somehow convinced that his worried-looking son could hear his profanity-laced internal dialogue. "Joshy, I might be on the phone for a while, so how's about you go downstairs and order us both some breakfast and when I'm done here I'll come down and tell you everything."

"I don't mind waiting," Josh replied, obviously dying to know exactly what had happened.

"Just go." Dwight softened his expression. "Please?"

Josh eyed him for a stiff moment. "Okay. I'll see you downstairs."

Dwight waited for Josh to leave the room.

"Hello? Are you there?" Lucas sounded lost again.

"I'm here," Dwight replied.

"I'm so sorry about your house, Uncle Dwight. Is there anything I can do?"

"Yeah, build me a fucking time machine."

Lucas laughed nervously.

Dwight pressed a hand to his chest. His heart was racing like a greyhound. "Lucas, do you know how much of a search the police did at the property?"

"I don't know. They didn't say."

"Fuck. Fuck. Fuck. Fuck. Fuck," Dwight cursed down the line. "This is not fucking good. Not fucking good at all."

"Do you not have insurance?" Lucas asked dimwittedly, proving that he was tiny in at least one part of his bulky body—his brain.

"It's not that," Dwight growled.

"What is it?"

"Fucking hell, Lucas, use your brain, son. Why would I—and you too for that matter—not want people on that fucking property?"

A two second silence was followed by a very sickly sounding, "Oh-ohhhh."

"Yes. Exactly."

"But it's hidden, isn't it? I mean, you said it was the perfect place because it's in the middle of nowhere."

"It was hidden in the middle of nowhere but when you have a fucking housefire that close by then it's a little less inconspicuous, don't ya think?"

"What do we do?"

Dwight sighed, pinching the bridge of his nose. He knew this probably wasn't the kind of conversation they should be having on the phone but he needed Lucas to take care of the situation. "I need you to go out there to see if everything is as it should be, and if it isn't you ring me back ASAP. Actually, just ring me back regardless. I need to know."

"Would it be okay if I go check it out tomorrow?"

"No it wouldn't. Why the hell would you leave it a day?"

"It's just that my mate Brad is here at the moment and we—"

"I don't care if you've got the Queen of fucking England sat with you, get ya arse out there." Dwight felt

45

bad for the way he was yelling so he quickly apologised. "I'm sorry for getting mad at you, son, but this is serious. We could be in a fuck tonne of trouble here."

"I suppose I could let Sophie entertain Brad for a couple hours while I go check."

"Exactly. Now get a wriggle on."

"I will. I'll go right now and see if everything's okay."

Dwight was about to hang up but then he remembered an important question. "Lucas, one more thing."

"Yeah?"

"Did they say what caused the fire?"

"No, but they said they were treating it as suspicious."

Dwight didn't need to be a fireman or detective to work out what had caused the fire. A certain someone must have found out that their credit card had been used to pay for a luxury Bali getaway. The rage he felt from knowing Levi had got one over him sent Dwight into a fit of deranged laughter.

"What's so funny?" Lucas asked. "Are you okay?"

Dwight stopped laughing and caught his breath, grinning psychotically. "Someone has bigger balls than I gave him credit for."

"Who are you talking about?"

"You don't need to worry about that, but I'm gonna rip his fucking balls right off when I see him next."

CHAPTER 5

Levi sucked on a cigarette as he peered out his bedroom window, watching the afternoon sun try and fight its way through the thick, grey clouds. It had been raining since he'd stormed out of Kaleb's house three hours earlier, and only now did it look like the sun would win its battle against the clouds.

He took one last hit on his cigarette, absorbing the nicotine before flicking the wafting butt out the window where it fell on the rain-drenched garden below. Slumping onto his computer chair, Levi smiled as he scanned the profile summary he'd just written about Danny. It was truly scandalous—even for Levi. Someone he'd referred to as his brother for seven years had been reduced to a list of stats for strangers around the world to view and pass judgement on.

Name: Lil d
Height: 5 ft 10
Hair colour: black
Eye colour: blue
Build: skinny/slim
Cock size: 5.5 inches uncut (has an upward curve)
Shoe Size: 10
Rating: 7.5/10

Perhaps the most shocking thing about fucking his stepbrother was how it had been way more enjoyable than Levi had anticipated. Danny carried just enough attractive traits to make the union of their flesh genuinely erotic and satisfying, and the taboo friction of his virgin arsehole had been immensely sexy. As far as Candy Boy scores go 7.5 was pretty respectable. Before the birthday makeover, Levi would have been hesitant to gift Danny even just a rating of 5 but it was amazing how much better he looked in decent clothes, wearing contacts, and rocking a trendy haircut.

He scrolled down the page until he saw the pictures he'd attached. There were lots. Every inch of Danny's pale, young body had been captured on film to be shared with Candy Boy's followers. You name the body part, and Levi had taken a shot of it. Toes, feet, legs, cock, chest, back. There was even a close-up of his pink puckered arsehole, taken right before Levi's cock had desecrated it.

Levi rubbed his dick through his pants when his eyes landed on the hottest picture of all. The one where Danny's drunk mouth was filled with Levi's ejaculating dick. That picture wasn't just hot, it was sinful. He'd used photoshop to insert a black strip over Danny's eyes so his identity could remain at least somewhat hidden.

There was only going to be one person reading the story who knew whose mouth it was filled with Levi's dick, and Levi doubted very much if Dwight would have the balls to show Mark such a scandalous picture, unless he wanted his credit card fraud exposed. Even if Dwight was that stupid, there was no way Danny would own up to sucking his own brother's cock. Of that Levi was sure.

Beneath the triumphant smile on Levi's lips was a twitch of guilt about what he'd done. Usually he didn't care who he hurt to get what he wanted but something about the way he'd used Danny, taking the boy's virginity and turning him into the latest Candy Boy star, didn't feel right. It was like he'd contaminated a piece of purity. Danny radiated innocence and was not the kind of person to wind up with nude photos online, let alone a picture of him with a cock stuffed in his gaping gob. Hell, Danny was so pathetically innocent that he still kissed his father goodnight before going to bed.

Rather than continue analysing why it felt so wrong—and risk unleashing an avalanche of guilt inside his frosty heart—Levi reminded himself that Danny had got what he deserved for narking on him about the credit card bill.

If I hadn't done it then I might not have found out who Blondie was his inner voice reminded him. A surge of anger flooded his veins as he thought about Kaleb refusing to apologise the way Levi had wanted him to. The anger had less to do with Kaleb saying no and more to do with why the boy had said no. Kaleb was being loyal to Dwight and that pissed Levi off to no end.

"I was wondering if you were home yet."

At the sound of the familiar voice, Levi turned, and his eyes landed on Danny, who was standing in the doorway all bright-eyed and fresh-faced with his hands behind his back.

"What are you doing here?" Levi asked, closing his laptop screen. "I thought you and Mark were supposed to be on your way to the South Island by now."

"I told Dad I didn't want to go."

"But you've been wanting to walk the Milford Track for years."

"I changed my mind."

"Just like that? Years of dreaming of going to your dream holiday spot and you just change your mind?"

Danny nodded, his hands still behind his back. He looked like a kid who'd just stolen cookies that he was trying to hide. He entered the room and slowly revealed what he was hiding behind his back. A big bouquet of bright blue and yellow flowers.

"Did you get those for your birthday?" Levi asked.

"No, silly. They're for you." Danny walked over and handed Levi the flowers.

Tied to the base of the bouquet was a tiny card that read: ***Thank you for last night. Love Danny.***

Levi placed the flowers down gently on his desk, trying not to laugh. If it was any other male giving him flowers then he would have wondered what the fuck they were playing at but this was typical Danny behaviour. He was the type to make a grand gesture of thanks for something he considered a nice deed, and although last night was simply about money and revenge for Levi, it had been a monumental occasion for Danny.

"Do you like them?" Danny asked.

"Uh… they're nice."

"I hope I haven't weirded you out."

"Nar. It's fine." Levi capitulated with some honesty. "Maybe it's a little weird but it's all good."

"Sorry."

"You don't have to say sorry. It's actually a very sweet gesture." Levi cracked a smile. "It probably makes sense to give flowers to the person who deflowered you."

Danny erupted with one of his walrus-like laughs, nearly keeling over as he clutched his tummy. He took three gasping breaths to try and speak. "Flowers. Deflowered. That's so funny."

"It wasn't that funny," Levi said dryly.

Danny's laughter began to die down to sniggers and snorts, until finally there was just a gormless smile on his face. "So what time is your date?" he asked.

"My date?"

"Yeah, your date. You got asked out by a girl for dinner this morning, remember?"

"That wasn't a girl calling to arrange a date. It was Peach."

"Who just happens to be a girl that called you up and asked you out for dinner. That makes it a date."

"No, that is a friend asking a friend out for dinner. There is a difference."

"So you and Peach don't…?"

"Don't what?"

"Have sex."

"Hell no. That's not what me and Peach are about. She's like a sister to me."

"But I'm your brother and we had sex."

Levi blanched but forced a laugh. "Yep. You got me there, buddy. That was a one-off birthday present though, so it doesn't really count."

"Was it really just a one-off?"

"Obviously. It's not like you would be in a hurry for a round two."

"Why not?"

What the actual fuck? "Are you telling me you want to have sex again? Is that what these flowers are really about?"

Danny frowned, seemed about to answer in the negative but then hesitated. "Maybe." He swallowed and lowered his voice. "Yes."

"I thought you were straight?"

"Maybe I'm not as straight as you think," Danny replied coyly.

Levi found that hard to believe. Danny may have agreed to having sex with him but he was more an easily manipulated and impressionable straight boy than anything else. "So you're telling me that you got off on last night?"

"I enjoyed parts of it."

Levi leaned back into his chair, studying Danny's face. "So then, what parts did you enjoy about last night, Mr supposedly-not-so straight?"

"The kissing. I really liked kissing you. That was nice."

"Okay but what about the actual gay stuff. Like sucking my dick or being fucked?"

"I liked it when you sucked my dick," Danny said enthusiastically. "That was awesome!"

Levi rolled his eyes. "Every guy likes their dick being sucked but that wasn't what I asked you."

Danny ran a hand through his hair before exhaling slowly. "If I'm being completely honest then I guess some of the other stuff wasn't as fun for me. Some of it hurt—a lot—but I could get used to it I reckon. But I mostly want to do it again so I can have a turn being the man."

"The man?"

"You know, the one who sticks it in."

Levi laughed, shaking his head. "That's definitely not happening."

"Why not?"

"Because I said so."

"But at the moment it only feels like I have lost half my virginity. I want to lose the front half."

Levi smiled bemusedly. "I can sort of get where you're coming from, but sorry, buddy, I'm the big brother in this relationship so that role is not up for negotiation."

"Big is the right word," Danny said with a botched attempt at a flirty smirk.

Levi stopped himself from saying *thank you* out loud. Being complimented about the size of his cock was an ego fuel he was rarely fed. In fact, Danny was probably the only person to ever compliment his size in such an honest way.

"Are you sure I can't do you?" Danny asked again, more than a hint of desperation straining his voice. "I really want to know how good it feels. I bet it's amazing."

"You don't need to have sex with me again to find out how it will feel. Pretty soon, when you're back at school rocking this new look"—Levi looked him up and down—"you'll have plenty of girls keen to let you be the man."

The words of encouragement looked like they marched in one of Danny's ears and right out the other. "Can I kiss you instead?"

"Say what?"

"Can I kiss you?"

"No," Levi said firmly.

Danny's voice trembled with wounded dignity. "It's because you think I'm ugly, isn't it?"

"It's not that at all. I just don't think it's a good idea. We don't want to make a habit out of fooling around."

"Was I that bad at it?"

"No. You weren't bad at all."

"It must be because I'm hideous then," Danny said in his best sulky voice.

"Don't be a dork. If you were hideous then last night wouldn't have happened, would it?"

Danny's gaze fell to the floor, down where Levi's bare feet were crossed at the ankle. The sad look on his face radiated an extra spicy flavour of guilt sauce.

Levi heaved an exasperated sigh. "If I kiss you will it wipe that poor-me look off your face?"

Danny lifted his head, grinning. "Yes."

Levi got to his feet and stepped towards his stepbrother so they were face to face. "Just one kiss though, right?"

Danny leaned forward, crashing his mouth into Levi's, their lips meeting in an anxious embrace. The boy was much more confident than last night, his tongue immediately invading Levi's mouth and sucking the oxygen from his lungs. After a few seconds, Danny's arms went around Levi and he began to kiss even more passionately, his tongue exploring Levi's mouth like wildfire.

The kiss deepened until, breathless, Levi finally had to pull away. "Someone is a good kisser. You must have been taught by an expert," he joked, trying to lighten the mood.

Danny's eyes were wide open, his cherry pink lips parted slightly. "My teacher was an expert at lots of things." He reached out and stroked a finger down Levi's chest, letting it descend until it landed at Levi's belt buckle. "He taught me how to kiss down there too."

"He did," Levi replied in a croaky whisper.

"And can I? Kiss you down there?"

"Danny you just said yourself that you didn't like doing that so why would you want to do it again?"

"I also said I could get used to it."

"But you're not gay."

"But don't people sometimes do things they don't like if they love a person."

For Christ's sake. Levi groaned internally. "We love each other because we are family"—words Levi never thought he would hear himself say—"You don't love me for any other reason."

"That's what I was thinking too but..."

"But?"

"But when we made love—"

"Sex! We had sex, Danny, not love."

"Sorry. When we had 'sex,'" Danny said, offering up dramatic finger quotes, "you made me feel more special than anyone ever has. I want to feel that feeling again. I want to feel it again with you."

This was not at all how Levi had expected their brotherly relationship to be after what had happened last night. He had assumed Danny would have kept a safe distance from him for weeks, if not months, but here Danny was asking for a round two. The kid was so hungry for experience he didn't seem to care who he got it with.

"You probably just need to go watch some porn and jerk off," Levi said bluntly. "Trust me, you will feel a lot better and realise you're not thinking straight. No pun intended."

"I've already done it three times today and I'm still not thinking straight." Danny grinned then commented quietly, "Pun very much intended."

Danny was oozing desire so thick and potent it was almost as if Levi could taste it in the air around them. He knew he had to do or say something to get his stepbrother out of his room before anything happened. Levi slipped into Candy Boy mode and proceeded to tell Danny the cold harsh truth. "Here's the thing, when I hook up with guys, I like to get a little freaky."

"What do you mean by freaky?"

"I don't think of the guy as my lover, I just think of him as a piece of meat. Someone I can use and abuse and humiliate. I make him suck me off, tell him to piss his pants in front of me so I can then mock him for it, then I make him kiss my feet and tell him to say thank you for the privilege." Levi yanked his stepbrother closer, forcing him to meet his eyes dead-on even though Danny was starting to withdraw with a grimace on his face. "If you want us to fuck, Danny, then let's fuck. But be warned, I'm going to fuck you like you're a hole in the ground and make you moan like a cheap dirty slut. Last night was me being kind but if we fuck right here, right now, then I am just going to bend you over the end of my bed and fuck you raw until I flood that tight little arse of yours with my load. Is that what you want? To be my slut? To walk around with a bleeding arse and my cum inside you?"

"Uh…" Danny looked horrified. "I-I don't want to be a slut."

"I didn't think so." Levi patted Danny on the shoulder. "This is why it is best we don't talk about last night or the possibility of it ever happening again. Not unless you're prepared to let me fuck you how I just described." His tone was crisp and utterly dismissive.

"I-I understand," Danny stammered. He hurried away, scuttling out of the room like a cockroach threatened with fly spray.

That solved the problem.

With Danny now out of the way, Levi decided to start getting ready for his visit to go see Peach. He strolled into his en suite and turned the shower on, stripping off all his clothes. As he waited for the water to heat up, he dropped a hand to his hardening dick, and he realised just how fucking close he'd just come to giving into temptation. *I definitely would have fucked him if he hadn't run off.* He shuddered at the thought.

He wasn't sure what was worse: Danny asking to "make love" again, or himself for wishing Danny had agreed to being fucked like a piece of meat. Neither were good scenarios. Danny may have discovered last night that the male gender wasn't a deal breaker when it came to sex but Levi had also discovered something equally eye-opening—he was actually attracted to his dweeby stepbrother.

Sort of…

There was definitely an attraction but it was diluted somewhat because whatever it was about Danny that was spinning Levi's wheels it had less to do with Danny and more to do with someone Danny reminded him of.

But who the fuck does he keep reminding me of?

He wasn't even sure if it was Danny's appearance or personality that kept triggering a faceless memory but something about his stepbrother was unearthing latent desires for somebody he used to know.

He closed his eyes and cast his mind back through the years and thought of all the men it could possibly be but no one stood out as the likely candidate. He began picturing Danny naked, slowly going over in his mind each part of Danny's young, skinny body for some sort of clue as to who it might be Danny was reminding him of. The only thing this achieved was sending hot tendrils of lust soaring through his body, and the insane need to be inside his stepbrother's tight passage again. He wondered if he should go tell Danny they could have sex again, that it didn't have to be rough or nasty.

I can just say let's "make love" like last night. Something lame like that will get his arse in here in a heartbeat. I can just fuck him in the shower and wash my cock when I'm done.

Levi's erection twitched and bobbed, nodding in agreement. He was about to put his briefs back on and go find Danny but his common sense prevailed and he thought better of it. He bit his lip, holding back the lust that raged through him. Rather than stoop to a whole new low, turning his stepbrother into some sort of convenient cum dump, Levi decided to take some of his own advice.

He had a wank.

CHAPTER 6

An hour after emptying his balls in the shower, Levi arrived at Peach's apartment with a bottle of wine tucked under his arm. He'd nicked it from Mark's collection in the cellar, too poor to stop off at the bottle store and buy his own. This whole being broke business was becoming a royal pain in the arse. Forbidden Candy would have to do incredibly well if he wanted any chance of being able to support himself and live a fraction of the life he was accustomed to. Unfortunately, as hot as the story was Levi wasn't confident it would boost his Candy Boy income to the level he needed.

After some small talk about their respective Friday nights, Peach began to tell him her plans for the annual Fitzroy Flyer ball. The ball was only in its third year of existence but already it was known as the pinnacle event for the city's young elite. Anybody who was anybody would be making sure they bought a ticket to take part in what would no doubt be an orgy of excess and wild times. Peach marketed the event as a fundraiser for charity but it was really just an excuse for her to exercise her power as queen bee of the social scene.

Each year she acted like she had left everything to the last minute but that couldn't be further from the truth. Peach was organised and meticulous by nature, and as Levi sat in her lounge, nodding along to her tell him about her latest concept, he could tell she had been planning this night for months, maybe even since the morning after last year's event.

"Tell me what you think?" Peach asked when she had finally finished sharing her master plan for delivering party excellence. "And I want you to be honest."

"I think…" Levi paused with a dramatic sigh. "It's fucking amazeballs!"

"You do?"

"I do."

"Thank God." She clutched her chest. "I was worried you might think it was lame since the whole fifty shades thing is so five years ago."

"It's not lame," Levi assured her. "Sex never goes out of fashion."

"That's true."

"Honestly, Peach, I think it's brilliant."

It really was brilliant. Peach had discovered that one of the gay saunas in town was closing down and the owners, in desperate need of cash, were open to the idea of hiring the venue out for private functions. The venue went hand-in-hand with her vision of putting on a BDSM-themed ball where guests could attend dressed kinked-up to the eyeballs.

"It is brilliant, isn't it," Peach said cockily. "It has tonnes of private rooms, a 3-level theatre, maze, steam room, dry sauna, and a large drinking lounge. It will need a bit of a makeover to make it a bit more hetero-friendly—if you know what I mean—but otherwise the place is perfect. Can you imagine how many potential scandals could happen in those private rooms? It will give me gossip to report on for months!"

Levi laughed. "Is that all you're worried about?"

"That's half the point of these events. I need people to do stupid shit so I can report on it and help drive sales of the paper." Peach always had an eye on what mattered most—money.

"How much will the tickets be?" Levi asked.

Unlike regular events hosted by member of the Fitzroy Flyers the annual ball was open to anyone who could afford a ticket. Actually, that wasn't entirely correct, Benson Bangers were forbidden from attending. It didn't matter if they tried paying double for a ticket, they would still be refused entry at the door, if they were stupid enough to try and attend and risk utter humiliation. Last year two of Wade Benson's conquests had taken advantage of the masquerade theme and managed to sneak inside but once their presence was discovered by Peach she had the bouncers promptly escort the two girls out of the party.

"I'm thinking 600 for a single pass, 1000 for a couple."

"Mark better give me my credit card back before then," Levi grumbled.

"Don't worry about that, poppet, you know I will give you a free ticket. How can it be the biggest event of the year if you're not there?"

"That's what I was thinking. You do sort of need me there." Levi grinned cheekily.

"Does your stepdad still expect you to find a job?"

Levi nodded. "I'm supposed to be looking but I'm sort of waiting for him to get over his little tizz and give me back the credit card. He usually gets over himself in a week or two."

"Speaking of work"—she paused to take a sip of wine—"how is my book cover coming along?"

"It's, um… it's looking good. I should have it finished next week."

Peach laughed. "You haven't started it yet, have you?"

"Not yet, sorry. But I can get it done for you by the end of next week."

"You don't have to be that quick with it, you can take your time."

"What sort of images do you want for the cover?"

Peach shrugged. "Surprise me."

Levi wished she'd give him more detail than "surprise me" but he wasn't going to complain. While neither of them would outright say it, they both knew this was less a design job and more an act of charity. He wasn't keen on pity but his pride came second to money, and until Mark returned his credit card, or Candy Boy returned a huge profit, then Levi would accept what favours he could.

They carried on talking about the upcoming flyer ball, swapping theories on who would hook up with who and any potential scandals that could unfold. When they'd polished off just over half the bottle of wine, Peach glanced up at the clock on the lounge wall, and said, "Shall we head to Fidel's soon?"

Levi studied the yellowish bruises still lingering on her face from Bobby's nasty fists. "I was only really joking about wanting to go to Fidel's. We can stay in if you want."

"It's a Saturday night. Surely you and I are overdue being seen out and about together."

"But aren't you worried about—"

"About this?" Peach pointed to her injuries.

"Yeah."

"The bruises are mostly gone now. It's nothing a bit of makeup can't fix." Peach uncurled her legs off the couch and got to her feet. "Just let me go get ready and then we can go."

As soon as she left the lounge, Levi pulled his phone out and logged onto his blog. He let out a sad little sigh when he saw Forbidden Candy was yet to boost his number of followers as much as he wanted. Just before he put his phone back in his pocket, it came to life with the sound of an incoming video call. His eyes lit up when he saw who it was calling him. He swiped the screen to accept the call. "Hey, man. How's it going?"

Josh's handsome face smiled back at him. "It's going good, cum bucket. What are you up to?"

Levi laughed, surprised to hear Josh call him cum bucket straight away. "I'm at Peach's place."

Josh's face morphed into a *oh fuck* look before putting on a cutesy voice. "Hi Peacharoo."

"It's okay. She's in her bedroom getting ready for town."

"Oh... so she can't hear us talking then?"

"Nope."

"So it's safe for me to ask you if you've been..." Josh paused like he was listening to an imaginary drum roll, "enjoying sniffing my dirty undies?"

"Yeah, man." Levi blushed a little. "I've sniffed them every day."

Josh laughed, but not nastily. "That's so fucking weird, but it's also pretty cool."

Levi's dick reacted positively to Josh's happy tone and smile. "Will you be wanting to see me sniff them when you get home?"

"I think you know the answer to that, cum bucket."

Levi's pulse quickened. Josh appeared to get a kick out of calling him that degrading name and for whatever reason Levi enjoyed hearing him say it.

"I might even let you do more than just sniff my underwear," Josh said seductively.

"Such as?"

"You'll have to wait to find out, cum bucket."

Levi chuckled. "Yes, sir."

"Sir..." Josh repeated back slowly, like he was tasting the flavour of the word. "I like the sound of that."

I thought you might.

It was Levi's turn to dip his voice to seductive levels. "Should I call you that more often? Sir?"

"You probably should if you want to see more of this." Josh suddenly changed the angle of his phone and gave Levi a full-body view shot of what he was wearing— very little. He was bare chested, bare footed, in just a pair of silk boxers. He left the camera dangling on the cock-teasing angle for a cock-hardening ten seconds before his face came back into view. He looked like he was about to say something filthy as fuck, but instead he blurted, "I broke up with Jessica today."

"You what?" Levi had heard perfectly well what Josh had just said but he couldn't quite believe it. "You broke up with Jessica?"

"Yep. I called her up and told her I think it is best we start seeing other people." Levi's smile did not go unnoticed. "Someone looks awfully happy about my tragic breakup news."

"Sorry." Levi smirked.

"It's all good. I figured you'd be happy hearing we'd split up." Josh slung him a mischievous grin. "After all, her loss is your gain."

"Is it?"

Josh nodded. "Now that I am single again, I am able to be a bit more, what you call, open to suggestion."

Levi was loving how upfront and sexual Josh was being. They'd never had a chance to finalize any sort of kinky arrangement between them before he left for his holiday, but it appeared there was definitely an arrangement to be explored.

"Does that mean you'll let me suck you off again… sir?" Levi knew he was pushing his luck but he wanted to test the waters.

"I told you, cum bucket, just wait and see." Josh hooked his mouth into a dirty smile. "Put it this way; I'm not ruling it out." He turned his phone around again and gave Levi another shot of his tanned chest and rock-hard abs.

"You're so fucking hot," Levi whispered.

Josh replied by slipping a thumb into the waistband of his boxers and tugging them down so that his curly brown pubes became visible. He didn't stop there, the boxers were pulled even lower until the base of his dick was on show. It wasn't erect but it wasn't flaccid either.

Levi swallowed, dropping a hand to his pants, rubbing his groin. "I am going to suck that hot prick so hard, sir. I'll swallow every drop you give me. I'll be waiting naked on my hands and knees inside your kitchen, ready to suck you the moment you walk in the door."

"Settle down, cum bucket." Josh laughed, flipping the phone back to his face.

Josh's laughter stung like a bee. "Sorry. I-I didn't mean to sound too full on."

"It's not that, it's just that I won't be walking in alone. Dad will be with me."

"Huh?"

"That's the other reason I am calling you. Dad's house burned down last weekend. I was wondering if you'd heard anything about it?"

Oh fuck. "Uh, err, nar." Levi shook his head. "I don't know anything about it."

"Was it not in the papers or online at all?"

"I haven't seen any mention of it," Levi replied, "but then I don't really read the local news."

Lies, lies, lies. It had been in the local newspaper and online. Levi had checked both regularly since burning the huckery house to the ground. The articles had been short, nothing too detailed, just reporting there had been a suspicious house fire out at Rapanui Beach. Thankfully the police didn't appear to have any clue as to how the fire started or who had started it.

"From what we've been told, Dad's house is totally had it. Burnt to the ground. Nothing left. Lucas rang him up this morning to tell him the news."

"That's not good." Levi feigned sympathy while nasty glee glowed in his heart. "Your dad must be ropeable."

"That's the understatement of the century. I can't tell if he's mad or sad or both. All I know is I have never seen him like this... so down and so prickly."

Good fucking job!

"He's downstairs in the bar at the moment drinking his sorrows away," Josh continued. "I'm half-expecting to have to go down there soon and carry him back to the room."

"That'll be a good work out for you. Build up your muscles even more." Levi hoped that comment might steer the conversation back to sex or gift him another video shot of Josh being a cocktease. He got neither.

"I've tried to tell Dad it's okay, that the insurance company will pay out."

"He has insurance?"

"Yeah. But it could take a while for that to all get sorted, so I've told him that until he can build a new place that he's welcome to stay with me."

"Your place?"

"He has nowhere to live so he has to find somewhere to stay."

Noooooo! Had Levi known burning Dwight's house down would mean he'd end up living with Josh then Levi would never have lit the fire in the first place. *That's not true. Burning that fucker to the ground felt amazing. If only the prick had been in it when I started the fire.*

"How long will he stay with you for?" Levi asked glumly.

"However long it takes for the insurance money to come through for him to rebuild."

"That could take months!"

"I know."

"Can't he stay with your grandparents?" Levi suggested. "He's their son, surely they'll have him."

"And he's my dad. I'd rather he stay with me." Josh threw Levi a displeased smile. "I know it might interrupt what *you* might want *us* to do but he is my father, Levi, and I have to do what is right by him."

"Of course," Levi replied, quickly backing off. "I didn't mean to sound like a dick. I'm sorry."

"Don't worry, cum bucket. I'm sure you and me can find somewhere private to do whatever it is we want to do."

"And what do we want to do?"

"Wait and see," Josh said sternly.

"Stop playing so hard to get," Levi said, only half-joking. "My balls are about to explode."

"Yeah? I make you that horny, do I?"

"Like you wouldn't believe."

"Show me how horny I make you."

"Say what?"

"Show. Me. How. Horny. I. Make. You." Josh's brown eyes glimmered with a potent mix of desire and power. He was clearly enjoying this.

Levi hesitated. He didn't want Peach walking back in the room and busting him on her couch with his cock out. *She takes ages getting ready though* his mind reminded him. That was true. Plus, he'd have plenty of warning with the sound of her high heels clopping their way back to the lounge. He cast a quick glance around the room before sliding a hand down between his legs. His fingers fumbled with the zipper of his jeans until the metal teeth opened in the form of a V. He reached inside the gap, through the hole in the front of his boxers, and freed his erection before flipping his phone around to show Josh the size of his arousal.

Levi could no longer see Josh's face but he could hear him emit a soft, throaty chuckle at the sight of Levi's erect dick. "Oh, man. You're hard as fuck. You really do have it bad for me." Another mockful chuckle.

Levi wagged his dick around. "Yep. I've got it bad."

There was a stretch of silence followed by a dry-voiced reply from Josh, "Show me your balls."

Levi fished a hand into his open zipper and scooped his balls out. He rolled his nutsac in his fingers, enjoying the shaved smoothness of his balls.

"Mmm," Josh mumbled. "I don't think mine have been that small since I was twelve."

Levi laughed, pointing his phone's camera back to his face.

Josh smirked at him. "I wasn't being mean. Just stating a fact."

"Gee, thanks."

"Don't get sad, cum bucket. You can't help having sexy little bitch nuts."

"You think they're sexy?" Levi said, trying not to laugh at the term bitch nuts.

Josh nodded. "If I had to play with another guy's balls then yours are whose I would play with."

Levi's heart skipped a beat. "Does that mean you wanna play with them when you get home?"

"You'll have to wait and see," Josh replied coyly. "But I do like looking at them for some reason."

That was a start, Levi thought.

"I never used to think my dick was that big but I'm starting to think I might be quite a good size. It'll be interesting to see our dicks lined up together, see how much bigger mine is." The usually humble Josh reeked of arrogance, but Levi let it slide since it was this sexual arrogance that was going to get him into Josh's pants.

"You do have a nice cock," Levi admitted.

"It's quite a bit bigger than yours, aye?"

"I suppose so."

"Only suppose?"

Levi's eyes narrowed, but then he chuckled. "Not suppose. I KNOW yours is bigger. Quite a bit bigger."

"I reckon that would make me number one and you number two, don't you think?" Josh's tone was jovial but mingled with raw insecurity. They had always shared an unspoken rivalry but only now was Levi realising just how much Josh craved to be the winner.

Just tell him what he wants to hear. "Yes, Josh. Your number one."

"Thanks, cum bucket. It's good to finally hear you admit it."

Years of unsaid competitiveness had finally been settled with a clear winner between the pair, and all it had taken was comparing the size of their dicks.

"You wanna see mine now?" Josh flashed him a provocative leer.

Levi nodded eagerly—far too eagerly—as the flutters in his chest became a hurricane.

Josh slipped his phone down to the wispy hairs of his treasure trail, slowly slipping one of his tanned hands into the waistline of his baggy boxers. "Fuck. Dad's back. Gotta go." And the call abruptly ended.

Levi nearly screamed in frustration. He cursed under his breath and angrily put his cock away. *Stupid fucking Dwight.* The man had the worst timing imaginable. Levi took a deep breath to calm down and reminded himself that he would have access to the real thing in just one more week.

He's gonna let me do heaps with him.

It certainly seemed like it. Josh appeared to have an eagerness to explore a side of himself that he probably didn't even know existed. But Levi could clearly see that side of Josh existed, a kinky trait Josh shared with his father, and Levi would make damn sure it worked in his favour before rubbing Dwight's nose in it.

CHAPTER 7

Fidel's was noisy and crowded, its tables filled with sleek, well-dressed patrons. People didn't come here just for the food—which was decidedly average—but to enjoy the views offered from the outdoor tables of the rooftop restaurant. The pretentious establishment sat atop one of the tallest buildings in Fitzroy, gifting views over the city and far up the coast. To guarantee yourself a table at Fidel's usually required booking weeks in advance—unless you were Peach Halcomb. Then all you had to do was turn up and say "Table for two."

That's exactly what Peach had done when her and Levi had rocked up to the counter an hour earlier. The flustered maître d' hadn't argued, simply led them to their own private booth before probably making an awkward phone call to apologise to some other customer that their table had been double-booked.

Levi had let Peach do most of the talking during their meal. He just sat there nodding along while his brain conjured up images of the kinky stuff he and Josh could get up to when Josh returned home from Bali. He was so lost in the fantasy that he only snapped out of it when Peach clicked her fingers and said, "Hello? Earth to Levi?"

"Sorry. What?"

"I said: Did you want me to invite Jessica out?"

Levi frowned. "Why would we invite Jessica out?"

Peach glared at him like he was an idiot. "So I can try and get her and Wade to hook up. Wade's band is playing at the Beaten Path tonight so it would be the ideal opportunity to take her out and get her so loaded she makes some bad decisions."

Fuck. He'd totally forgotten all about their plan to set Jessica up as a Benson Banger. "I don't think we need to do that now."

"Why not?" Peach choked out, incredulity written all over her face. "You do remember that she called me to try and throw you under the bus, right?"

"I just don't think it's worth it."

"She deserves to be taught a lesson though."

"I know but her and Josh have split up so I don't really need to worry about what she might say anymore."

"Josh and Jessica have split up?"

Levi nodded. "Josh called me earlier and told me."

"Just because she isn't dating Josh anymore doesn't mean she won't try going around telling everyone about how she saw you kissing his dad's feet. If anything it might make her even more determined to start spreading rumours."

Levi winced. When it was said out loud it sounded worse than what it actually was, he thought. Kissing Dwight's feet had made him feel like some sort of slave but there had been an erotic element to the whole degradation that had made it sort of hot.

"If she does say anything then I will just deny it," Levi said. "It's so fucking crazy that I don't think anyone will believe her anyway."

That really was how Levi felt about the situation. He'd been horrified when he first found out about Jessica witnessing his moment of footsy shame but now he just viewed her knowledge as a minor inconvenience. Who would believe such a crazy story? No one who mattered at least. Levi had fucked too many girls in the Flyer crowd for his sexuality to be called into question. Now that he was on the verge of having access to Josh in ways he'd only dreamed of, Levi was able to be honest with himself about why he had wanted to tarnish Jessica's reputation in the first place. So he could get her out of the way and score Josh for himself.

"It's your call, poppet, but just know that my offer is still there if you change your mind." Peach sounded composed but Levi could tell that beneath his pink-haired friend's calm demeanour was an itch to be allowed to destroy Jessica's reputation.

"Why do I get the impression you don't agree with me about letting this go?"

"It's not that I dislike Jessica but she did come to me with gossip about you and I know why she did that. She wanted me to use it against you."

"Just as well I know you would never do that to me."

"But Jessica didn't know that." Peach stabbed a fork at her garden salad. "I'm not sure what it is but something about her seems untrustworthy."

"You don't trust anyone though," Levi teased.

"That's not true. I trust you." Peach's voice matched the seriousness of the look on her face. She really meant that. They had each other's backs no matter what.

"Right back at ya, Peachy."

They shared a tender gaze, nod and smile.

"So where do you want to go after here?" Peach asked, casting a quick glance around the restaurant.

"What's the options?"

"We have Sadie Cunningham's."

Levi rolled his eyes. "Is there ever a weekend Sadie doesn't have a party?"

Peach chuckled. "So true. But to give Sadie credit, if she wasn't so desperate to be the perfect hostess then the Flyer's social calendar would only be half-full."

"What else is on?" Levi asked.

"We can go watch Wade's band play. I know it's not ideal that they are playing at the Beaten Path"—Peach pulled a revolted face—"but it might be fun to go watch Fitzroy's basic bitches and grunting rednecks in their natural habitat."

Levi smiled. "So we can make fun of them, you mean?"

"That should go without saying." Peach grinned. "Otherwise I think our only option is Jamie Dodds. He's having drinks at his apartment tonight."

"That's a hard pass from me."

"What's wrong with Jamie's party?"

"Because when Jamie gets drunk he starts flirting with me and gets all handsy... sometimes right in front of his boyfriend. He's almost as bad as Wade."

"Oh, come on, poppet, I thought you liked other boys getting handsy with you."

"Just because I *occasionally* explore male options, they still have to at least be somewhat attractive. Jamie looks like a ginger-haired sasquatch."

Peach giggled. "That's just mean."

"Yeah, but it's accurate. The guy's just lucky he has money or he'd never score."

"So what is it?" Peach asked. "Sadie's or the Beaten Path? Or do we just go down to the harbourfront and see what's happening at the bars there?"

Levi quickly weighed up the options. "I suppose it's been a while since we've done the Beaten Path. We can take bets on what dumb fuck in the club winds up a Benson Banger before the night is over."

"Sounds good to me," Peach agreed. "Did you want another drink before we leave?"

"I would but as you know I'm a peasant at the moment. Sorry."

"Don't be stupid. It's my treat."

"You're already paying for dinner—and my last two drinks—I can't bleed your generosity dry."

"Please let me pay for one more. It's been so long since I have had a poor friend, I've forgotten how good it feels to pity someone."

Levi laughed. "Okay then. I will have one more if you promise to hold it against me like the rich bitch you are."

"You can count on that." Peach gave her pink hair a snooty flick. "What would you like to drink? Same as before?"

Before Levi could respond, his phone blared to life in his pocket. When he pulled it out of his pocket and saw that it was another video call from Josh his face erupted with a smile. "It's Josh," he told Peach before swiping to answer the call.

"Hi, Josh. Me and Peach are—" Like an anchor dropping to the ocean floor, Levi's heart sank to his toes when he realised it wasn't Josh who had called him.

"Hello, Soggy." Dwight's dark, sexy eyes narrowed to nasty little slits.

"What are you doing using Josh's phone?"

"Never mind that. You and me need to have ourselves a little chat about what a busy little boy you've been."

"What do you mean?"

Dwight didn't fuck about, he got straight to the point. "My house got burned down last weekend. I was wondering if you knew anything about that?"

"I-I don't know anything about it," Levi stammered.

"Are you sure? Because I have a sneaky fucking suspicion your faggot arse knows more than it's letting on."

Peach twisted around theatrically to give Levi a brows-raised, silent, *"What the fuck?"*

Rather than let Dwight play the role of victim, Levi flung back an accusation of his own. "I don't know anything about your house burning down but I can tell you that some fuckwit made a purchase for a holiday to Bali on my credit card without asking."

Dwight chuckled darkly. "Oh, so you saw that then?"

"I did and I'm not impressed."

Dwight's smarmy grin vanished and his look of fury returned. "And I'm not too fucking impressed about not having anywhere to fucking live anymore you little cunt."

"Whoever burned your house down did you a favour, Dwight. Like you, it was a piece of shit."

Peach covered her mouth and farted a giggle into her hand.

Dwight's brows knitted together and he leaned closer to the camera. "You got someone with you, Soggy?"

"That's none of your business."

Dwight raised his voice. "Do they know you're a messy little faggot who has a thing for daddy dick?" His eyes glowed with malice. "Do they know how you let men just pump loads of cum up ya loose hole?"

Levi was past caring what Peach heard. "And does your son know you like fucking little school boys?"

"You wanna be careful what accusations you're throwing out there, Soggy. That shit could get you done for slander."

"It's not slander if it's true," Levi spat back. "You do fuck school boys… Kaleb Ladbrook for example."

"Who?" Dwight frowned.

"Don't pretend you don't know who that is, Dwight."

"I ain't got the foggiest clue what you're on about, Soggy."

"Kaleb is your friend Blondie." Levi smiled like he'd just won a game of cards. "You know, the boy who has your initials tattooed on his back."

Dwight's jaw ticked but he quickly hid his shock with a cocky laugh. "Is that his name, is it?"

Levi smiled wickedly. "It sure is."

"I hate to burst your Sherlock Holmes bubble, Soggy, but I don't give two shits what he's called. I just fuck him." Dwight returned a wicked smile of his own. "Sort of how I fucked you, cum bucket."

"Fuck you!"

"How many times do we have to go over this, Soggy. I don't get fucked; you do."

"Considering your povo arse has nowhere to live you might want to reconsider that statement because being homeless tells me you are more than a little fucked."

"Arson is a serious offence," Dwight growled.

"A bit like theft," Levi replied. "Now I don't know anything about how your house burned down, and I doubt you can prove that I do, but I can prove that you're the one who used my credit card and considering you already have quite the history of criminal charges I think I know who a judge is more likely to believe."

"Think carefully about how you play this, Soggy. If you mess with the big boys then the big boys will mess with you too."

"The only big boy messing with me will be your son. And as we know, he's much bigger than you, old man."

"Joshy ain't a faggot like you."

"Then why did he call me earlier and show me his cock? Maybe because he wants me to suck it when he comes home from his holiday. And we both know it isn't going to stop there if he takes after his homo father."

Dwight's eyes narrowed, and ruthlessness strewed across his handsome face. "You little fucking pri—"

Levi ended the call and put his phone back in his pocket, satisfied. When he looked across the table, he saw Peach staring at him with a horrified expression.

"Holy fuck," she gasped.

"I know, that was pretty intense."

"Holy fuck," she whispered again. And then again. "Holy fuck."

Levi inhaled deeply, intent on remaining calm. "I am going to ask if you can please pretend like you didn't hear any of that. Pretend like that call never happened."

"Of course, poppet. My lips are sealed."

"I hope so because you just heard a whole bunch of stuff no one is supposed to know."

"If it makes you feel better, I have done much worse than what it is he's accusing you of."

"What have you done that is worse than burning down someone's house?"

"Correction: you have not burned a house down. You are only being accused of it." She reached over and gave his arm a reassuring rub. "You were with me last weekend, remember? So there is no way you had a chance to go near his home."

Levi smiled. "Thanks, Peach." He doubted Dwight would go to the police but it was a relief to know Peach would offer an alibi if he needed. "And I'm sorry you had to sit through that."

"Don't be sorry. You know I love the dramarama. It was like being in the audience of a Jeremy Kyle show."

"I bet."

"I honestly have so many questions." She saw the stern look Levi gave her. "But I won't ask any."

"Thanks. I'd rather not get into it."

"But," she said, chewing on her lip. "Can I ask just one question?" She looked at Levi imploringly. "Pretty please?"

Leaning back in his seat, Levi exhaled loudly. "Okay, just one question." He was expecting a question that would be so personal he'd have to cough up a piece of his soul. She'd heard so many outrageous things that there was an ocean of scandal for her to sift through.

"Why does he call you Soggy?"

"Out of everything you just heard, and there was plenty, all you wanna know is why Josh's father calls me Soggy?"

"It could be a sexy reason," she quipped.

"He's called me it since I was twelve so I hope it's not a sexy reason."

"Oh… awkward." Peach laughed a little. "I still want to know why he calls you it though."

Levi was about to just say *because I pissed the bed* but because Peach was being so good about everything she'd just heard, he decided to give her the option to hear the whole story. "Do you want the short story or the long story?"

"Tell me both."

"The short story is I wet the bed when I stayed at his house once as a kid. I guess because I made the sheets "soggy" he has called me soggy ever since.

Peach looked genuinely annoyed on Levi's behalf. "As if I didn't need any more reasons for thinking the man is an utter twat."

"I think he was so mad about it because I was twelve when it happened… a bit too old to be doing that sort of thing."

"That still makes him a dick." She shook her head. "I honestly feel sorry for Josh having a father like that. If it was me, I'd never own up to such a piece of shit being part of my family."

Levi smiled. "Agreed."

"So tell me, poppet." She leaned forward; her eyes lit with curiosity. "What's the long story?"

Levi took a breath to settle his nerves that were frayed from just thinking about it. "The long story is what caused me to wet the bed that night."

CHAPTER 8

"And what made you wet the bed?" Peach asked.

"A recurring nightmare I used to have."

"Oh…" Peach looked almost disappointed, like she had expected more. But there was more. Much, much more.

"It was a dream I would have where I would be visited by something from my past." Levi shot Peach a half-smile like he always did when he thought of Lucky. Half-happy Lucky was gone, half-worried he might one day come back. "I didn't have the dream that often but when I did it was fucking terrifying."

"What do you mean by 'something from your past?'"

"I'm talking about an imaginary friend I had when I was a little kid. It's him I would dream about." *And everything else.*

"But wouldn't that be kind of sweet to get a visit from an imaginary friend?"

"Not this imaginary friend," Levi said flatly. "It started happening around the time I was eight years old and we had just moved into a new house in Brixton. We'd been living in an okay part of Brixton—if there is such a thing—but then Dad's best mate died in a car crash and he made us move to live next door to the guy's widow, Connie, so him and Mum could help her with raising her three kids."

"That's nice of him."

"You'd think so but it was less to do with helping her raise her kids and more so my dad and Connie could continue their affair."

"What man would be dumb enough to cheat on your mother. She is gorgeous."

It was a good point and one Levi had often wondered about. Even now Levi's mother was a beautiful and elegant creature but Connie Jacobs had always been sinew and bones, an overly skinny woman with a pack-a-day smoking habit to accompany the bottle of vodka she always kept nearby.

"I'm not sure what Dad saw in Connie but they had it off for years. They thought it was a secret but everyone knew what they were up to. Even Mum. Not that she cared. I think if anything she was relieved someone else was willing to sleep with him so she didn't have to." Levi laughed but Peach didn't appear to find it funny. "Anyway, we ended up moving in right next door. It was a fucking shitheap of a house and on one of the worst streets."

"Oh god. I dread to think."

"To begin with everything was pretty normal but after about six months I began hearing a voice coming from the closet in my bedroom. It was so quiet, just a whisper, and I couldn't make out the words that were being said but I definitely could hear someone. I can remember going to my closet and opening the door and looking for who was making the noise but there was no one there."

"Oh my fuckity." Peach giggled. "You are giving me goose bumps already."

"Just wait." Levi waggled his eyebrows. "It gets WAY creepier."

He continued with the story, telling Peach how the whispers soon grew to a clear voice, one that belonged to a male. It seemed to know Levi's name and told Levi that its name was Lucky. One day while Levi had been playing in his room with his G.I. Joes, the voice asked if he could play too. Being a lonely eight-year-old at the time, Levi had said yes on the spot, keen for a new friend. But the voice didn't come out to play, it remained hidden in the closet.

"Aren't you going to come out and play?" Levi had asked.

"When I'm ready, Levi. When I'm ready."

It was several weeks later when Levi would get the chance to see what his friend in the closet looked like. He'd been fast asleep in bed when it happened, waking up to the sound of shuffling feet and heavy breathing. When he rolled over and opened his eyes, he saw a naked boy standing beside his bed with a deranged smile on his face.

"He was naked?" Peach asked, like she couldn't believe it.

Levi nodded. "Lucky never wore any clothes, but his body was covered in stickers. They were everywhere. His chest, his arms, his legs… even some on his cock." Levi smirked. "Pretty fucked up, right?"

"It is, but then all the best people are fucked up." She blew him a kiss. "So what was Lucky like?"

"An absolute bastard." Levi laughed even though the memories were not funny. "I must be the only kid to have conjured up an imaginary friend who picks on them."

"What did he used to do?"

"All sorts." Levi chewed his bottom lip, wondering what parts of the story to share and what parts to leave out. To share everything would be too much. Far too much.

∞

After the first night Lucky introduced himself, he began appearing more often. He wasn't like Levi's friends at school. He didn't like to talk about cartoons or play games. He just liked to talk about rude stuff all the time, waltzing around Levi's bedroom with no clothes on, shaking his thingy around, spouting off tonnes of bad words. Rather than be scared of Lucky though, Levi was actually quite fascinated by the skinny boy with spiky blond hair who lived in his closet. He wasn't sure how old Lucky was but he looked a little bit older than Shay who lived next door.

While he wished Lucky would put some clothes on, Levi did like to look at all the stickers Lucky had plastered to his milky skin. Lucky was covered in them. They were all sorts of colours and shapes, glittering and shiny, the kind of stickers Levi wished his mum would buy him to put on his school books.

Nobody else could ever see Lucky for some reason, not even his parents. If either of them came into his room Lucky would waggle his bum at them or tug on his willy while he licked his lips. Levi found this hilarious and would fall into a fit of giggles, and if his parents asked what he was laughing at, Lucky would raise a finger to his lips to let Levi know not to say anything. So he didn't.

To begin with it was kind of fun having a secret friend to share his bedroom with but it soon became a problem when Lucky began telling him spooky stories at night. Lucky would lean over the bed, his rancid breath fanning Levi's face, and tell him about the "bad things" living in the garden.

"There's lots of them too. And they hate your family," Lucky would say. "And they especially hate you."

"But I haven't done anything to them."

"They still hate you. And one night they are gonna come up out of the ground and get you, ya little maggot." Lucky would laugh hysterically before going into gross details. "They will come inside the house and cut your mummy up into pieces, eat her tits and pussy for dinner then they'll come and get you and chop your little dicky off and have it for dessert."

"My dad will save us," Levi would say. "He's not scared of anyfink."

"Your daddy is the one who put the monsters there you dumb little cunt."

"No he didn't, Lucky. You're lying."

83

"One day you'll see that your daddy is also a monster. A monster who will want to do to you what he did to all of us."

"Wh-What did he do to youse?"

Lucky leaned right down and whispered in Levi's ears. What he said were warped things, twisted things, things Levi's young mind didn't fully understand but instinctively he knew they were wrong.

"Eww, Lucky. That's gross. Dad would never do those things to me."

Levi's shocked response only served to set Lucky off in one of his hysterical bouts of laughter. "He'll stick his diddle right in there. Trust me. Not until you're a bit older maybe, but he will do it one day. He'll do all those things." Lucky studied him for a moment before a slow grin tugged at his lips. "I can see how you will turn out. You're gonna be a pretty boy. A very, very pretty boy. And your daddy loves to fuck pretty boys."

"Stop saying stuff like that."

"And do you wanna know what else?" Levi didn't want to know what else but Lucky told him anyway. "You will let him do everything he wants to you because you're just a dirty little bitch like that Connie slut next door."

"Why are you so mean to me? We're supposed to be friends."

"I'm not your friend you dumb little pig."

That made Levi cry. He hoped Lucky would apologise for being mean to him but instead Lucky just laughed some more before slithering off to the closet like his job was done for the evening.

This continued for months, Lucky appearing at night beside Levi's bed like some bad bedtime story. Levi would usually hear him before he saw him; the sloppy thuds of Lucky's bare feet approaching the side of his bed followed by Lucky's husky snarls eager to pollute Levi's young ears with macabre and disgusting tales. Over time

Lucky began to do more than just tell stories. He began to try and touch Levi.

"What are you doing?" Levi asked when he saw Lucky reach out to try and touch him. Lucky had never done that before and Levi didn't like it. He especially didn't like where Lucky's hand appeared to be aiming for.

"Nothing. I just wanna have some fun."

"No." Levi wrapped the blanket around him tighter. "Why are you being so weird."

"Look, kid, you're not exactly my type but you're the only one here I can have fun with."

Levi didn't know exactly what Lucky meant by "fun" but judging by the strange look on his face it didn't look like the kind of fun Levi would enjoy. "I don't want to have fun with you."

"I didn't want to have fun with your daddy either but I didn't get a choice." Lucky swatted his hand down on the bed where Levi's private parts lay but his hand sank through the blankets without making contact. All it did was send tickly shivers coursing through Levi's body.

Lucky tried touching him again, but again all his hand did was sink through the blanket without making contact. He then closed his eyes, concentrating really hard like he was summoning the strength he needed to break through whatever invisible wall was holding him back, but no matter how hard he appeared to try, nothing he did seemed to work. He got so angry he began kicking the bed, but that too failed to make a physical impact.

Levi quickly went from feeling wary to finding Lucky's tantrum quite funny. He giggled. "Lucky, you're so silly."

"You won't be laughing when I work out what's stopping me." Lucky's eyes glowed nastily. "It took me a while to work out how to show myself to you and I managed that, didn't I?"

"Goodnight, Lucky," Levi replied smugly. He went to sleep that night with a smile on his face and feeling like he was playing a game of tag he could never lose.

But one night he did lose…

It was a night like any other when Lucky broke through the invisible wall. Levi had been in bed trying to sleep while Lucky stood in his usual spot beside the bed telling him dirty stories. Lucky had been describing vividly all the things he'd like to do to Levi's mother. While it wasn't nice to hear such lurid things about his own mother, it was a relief not to hear Lucky say what he would do to Levi if he could—which Lucky had been going into great detail for weeks.

"Then I'd spread her legs open, get down on my knees, and lick her pussy out. Big fat licks too. A real decent cunt munch. Mmm. I bet your mother has a real tasty pussy."

Levi had already learned by now Lucky wasn't talking about Mr Jingles, the family cat. Lucky had taken great delight in educating Levi in the different words grownups used for different body parts.

"Do you think she shaves it?" Lucky asked. "A few whiskers don't bother me but I don't want to make out with a sasquatch. Nothing worse than getting pubes stuck between ya teeth."

"Go to bed, Lucky. It's late."

"Some of us don't have a bed to go to, bitch."

"Go to the closet then."

It was a few seconds before Lucky spoke again. "I used to have a really cool bedroom. You would have really liked it. It was a coloured box that hung from the ceiling. Reds, blues and yellows. Sort of like a giant Rubik's Cube."

That did sound really neat but Levi didn't want to ask Lucky about it just in case the conversation somehow went back to dirty stuff—like it usually did.

"You would like where I used to live too. It was a castle."

"Go away, Lucky. I'm trying to sleep."

"Don't you want to hear about my castle, Levi? It had lots of slides. Big curly, yellow ones. There were ball pits too. And toys." Lucky sniggered. "Lots and lots of toys and lots and lots of boys who like to play with each other."

"Just tell me tomorrow. I'm tired." Levi rolled over and buried his face under the blanket, waiting for his irritating imaginary friend to disappear. Even though he couldn't see Lucky from under the blanket, he could hear his vile breath hovering above the covers. Then he felt him. Felt Lucky's hand rubbing his back through the blanket.

"You can feel me can't you, Levi?" Lucky said, his voice an ungodly whisper. "I've been practising just for you, getting myself nice and strong. We can have some real good fun together now. Just you and me. I can show you the sort of things your daddy likes to do."

Levi was terrified but he tried to block Lucky's prodding out. "Leave me alone Lucky. Please."

But Lucky didn't leave him alone, his hand snaked its way down Levi's blanketed body and slipped under the covers, his icy fingers gripping Levi's foot.

The touch of Lucky's hand was so cold it actually burned. And it didn't just burn Levi's skin. It burned perverted pictures into his brain—ghastly images—that felt like they could echo in his mind forever. He screamed for his life and jumped out of bed, racing to the lounge where his parents were up late watching television.

"Darling. What's the matter?" His mother asked, genuinely concerned.

His father's response was less caring. "What the fucks got you acting like a Nancy?"

As best he could, through sobbing breaths, Levi explained to them for the first time how he had a boy living in his closet and that he had just touched his foot and burned him.

His mum—no doubt thinking it was just a case of a child's overactive imagination—suggested he ask his "friend" to go find someone else to play with so Levi could get some sleep.

Levi's father scowled at him. "What the fuck is wrong with you, boy? You're too old for this sort of nonsense."

"He's only a child, Barry," Levi's mother said.

"No, Jenny. The boy has to learn to grow the fuck up and stop living in a fucking fantasy land."

"But Lucky's real, Dad," Levi pleaded. "He's real and he's not nice."

His father shot upright in his chair. "What did you say his name is?"

"Lucky."

That was the wrong thing to say. His father erupted like Krakatoa. He leapt from his chair and dragged Levi back to his bedroom. He then removed his belt and ripped Levi's pyjama pants right off, whipping Levi's bare butt until it bled. His mother ran into the room and begged him to stop hurting Levi—earning herself a turn being whipped with the belt. Once mother and son had both finished getting their beatings, Levi's father locked Levi in his room and Levi banged at the door, pleading to be let out.

Lucky soon emerged from the closet, laughing and smirking. "You really do cry like a little bitch, you know that?" He stepped closer, studying Levi's bleeding backside, a crude smile on his face. "Did you want me to kiss it better for you?"

"Go away! Go Away! Go away!" Levi screamed, still pounding on the door to be let out.

"Your daddy made me bleed too," Lucky said, his menacing breath fanning Levi's stinging butt cheeks. "Just not in quite the same way."

Levi's heart nearly jumped out his throat as he waited for Lucky to do bad things to him. The kind of things that were probably the reasons his Mum and teachers at school said why kids should never talk to strangers. Fresh tears streamed down his cheeks when he felt Lucky stand up again and inch closer and closer until their bodies were as close to each other as humanly possible without becoming flesh-on-flesh. He braced himself for the worst.

Lucky made slippery slithery slurps with his tongue, like a man-eating lizard. With his poisonous breath right in Levi's ear, he lowered his voice to an evil, croaky tone and whispered… "Boo."

Levi cried out like he'd been shot and piss started to dribble down the inside of his thigh, pooling around his feet. As he stood there, gasping for breath and standing in his own urine, he realised Lucky hadn't even touched him. Not even a hair on his head. Levi slowly turned around and saw Lucky swaggering his way back to the closet. Confusion spiked through his body. "That's it?" he muttered. That was probably a stupid thing to say to someone who'd spent weeks threatening to rape him but Lucky's actions—or lack of them—made no sense.

"Yes, Levi. That's it." Lucky winked. "I'm not like your daddy. I don't get my kicks from little boys."

In hindsight that was perhaps the most chilling thing about Lucky; he knew a lot more about Barry Buttwell than anybody else did at that time.

CHAPTER 9

Peach gave him a rueful lip twitch. "Lucky sounds absolutely vile. What do you think made you dream someone like that up?"

My father. "I probably watched a scary movie I shouldn't have."

"Remind me to never watch whatever movie that was," Peach said. "When did you stop seeing him?"

"Not until I was ten years old, after I told the boy next door about him."

∞

The naked, sticker-covered terror didn't appear every night but he would make his presence known at least once a week, showing up and trying his best to torment Levi in some way or another. He never tried touching Levi sexually—Thank God—but Lucky still liked to slip his hands under the bedclothes and grab his feet to frighten him. Levi would yelp every time, not so much from the shock, but because of the depraved visions Lucky's coldness evoked. The images were like a window to hell.

The other thing Lucky took great delight in was kicking and shaking Levi's bed. He'd make sure it banged and rocked loud enough to wake Levi's parents up. That's how Lucky got his jollies. He'd stand and watch on as

Levi's father burst into the room and gave Levi a thrashing for not behaving himself and being asleep like he should.

Levi sat his tender butt down on the bed. Man, it stung. His father had just come in and given him another walloping for all the noise of the bed banging against the wall.

Lucky lay on the floor with his hands behind his head, laughing to himself. "This never gets old. I love seeing him lay into you. I just wish you'd cry more like you used to."

"Why do you like getting me into trouble so much? You know Dad whips me for it."

"You just answered your own question, dumb arse." Lucky shot him a shit-eating grin. "I can't hurt your daddy but I can get him to hurt you and that's as good as the same thing."

"That doesn't even make sense though."

"It makes perfect sense. You're his son and you have to pay for his sins."

"That still doesn't make any sense," Levi snapped.

Lucky sat up and hugged his arms around his knees. "One day everything I have told you will make sense. That's when you'll wish it didn't."

Over time, Levi began to hear two more voices coming from inside his closet. One spoke in sobs while the other was deep and gravelly—both were too low to be heard clearly even though their tones conveyed urgency. Eventually the owners of these new voices managed to find their way out of the closet and began parading around Levi's bedroom at night.

It turned out that the one who had been sobbing was a tall boy with freckles and reddish-brown hair. He seemed really timid and shy, and frightened all the time. The owner of the deep and gravelly voice was a muscular man whose arms and back were covered in tattoos. Although he didn't sob like the tall boy, he too wandered about uneasily as if there was something to be frightened of.

Like lucky they too were naked, but unlike Lucky they weren't covered in pretty stickers, nor did they taunt Levi or prance about like sex-crazed maniacs. But the new guys did do something a little weird; they would kiss each other. Full on tongue and everything. They didn't do it all the time, just sometimes, but each time they kissed was pretty creepy because neither of them looked like they were enjoying it. They would groan and grimace, reluctantly opening their mouth for the other to stick his tongue in and plunder. If Levi didn't know any better, he would swear there were invisible hands behind them pushing their lips together.

Lucky found his new closetmates kissing hilarious. *"Here we go. The homos are back at it again."* He'd laugh nastily at them and then rush over and tease them, asking if they'd like to kiss his cock instead. Levi could see they didn't like being teased but not once did they react with words or punches. In fact, they reacted to very little. They never spoke directly to Levi or Lucky, only ever to each other, which meant Levi never got a chance to learn their names so he just referred to them as Mr Muscles and Tall Boy.

Despite their blatant attempts at ignoring Lucky, they did occasionally acknowledge his presence—even if it was only through scowls and disgruntled looks—but never Levi's. He sometimes wondered if they even knew he existed. Did they know they were living in a ten-year-old boy's bedroom? One night he would discover that they did know he was there and that they weren't as meek and mild as Levi had assumed.

Lucky was in one of his foul moods again. He'd been calling Levi nasty names for the past fifteen minutes, telling him how much he hated him and how much he hated being trapped in his room. "If I had to be stuck somewhere why couldn't it be in some hot chick's bedroom? Not with two frigid homos and some stupid little twerp who doesn't even know what a blow job is."

Lucky was wrong. Levi did know what a blowjob was. It was Lucky who had told him.

"You're years away from being any use to me but even then you won't have the parts that I want." Lucky looked up at the ceiling and let out a tortured howl, stomping his foot on the floor. "You'd think I shouldn't be horny but I'm horny all the fucking time. Never mind blue balls. I have fucking ghost balls!" He yanked on his testicles, howling again. "And it's all your fault. And you want to know why?"

Levi rolled his eyes and recited the answer Lucky had told him a thousand times. "It's all my fault because what my dad did means the same thing as if I had done it."

"That's right. It's the same fucking thing. He is you. You are him." He jabbed a bony finger in Levi's direction. "You put me here!"

Levi didn't like it when Lucky talked like this; like he had once been a real person. Not because it made him feel sorry for the spiky-haired dickhead but because if Lucky had once been a real person then that meant Levi was sleeping in a room filled with ghosts. Stuff that. He much preferred the idea that Lucky and co were imaginary friends. Well, imaginary somethings.

While Lucky continued to rant and rave, telling Levi how much like his father he was, Mr muscles and tall boy sat against the far wall talking to each other in drowned whispers. They'd just finished one of their kissing sessions, which was part of what had set Lucky's bad mood off to begin with. The sex-mad critter had gone over and tried sticking his willy into their kiss. They had kept putting their hands up to stop him, not wanting Lucky's gross diddle anywhere near their faces. It was this rejection that had sparked Lucky's bad mood.

Levi winced when Lucky spun around and began kicking the shit out of his bed. Each thump of Lucky's foot sent the *headboard banging into the wall, making an echoing thud that would soon alert Levi's parents to the fact he was awake past his bedtime.*

"Fuck you. Fuck your dad. And fuck this house." Lucky was panting from how much effort he was putting into the kicks.

Levi braced himself for the inevitable beating he would soon get but suddenly the other two leapt to their feet and ran over, tackling Lucky to the ground. "Leave the kid alone," Mr Muscles said. "He ain't done nothing to you."

"Get off me," Lucky spluttered. "Get the fuck off of me."

"We've had enough of you," Tall Boy said, grabbing Lucky's feet while Mr muscles held Lucky's arms.

"Fuck youse. I was here first," Lucky screamed as they began carrying him towards the closet.

"And you'll be the first to leave," Mr Muscles replied.

Levi cheered Tall Boy and Mr Muscles on, willing them to get rid of Lucky for good. His hope to finally be free of Lucky was short-lived though. Just as they were about to hurl him into the closet, black smoke rose from the floorboards and started to swirl around the room. It rose up like a sinister shadow with tentacles, engulfing all three of them into its inky blackness. When the smoke cleared, only Lucky remained.

Levi didn't know why but he instinctively knew Lucky was to blame. "What did you to them? Where are they?"

"Settle down, pipsqueak. They'll be back. We always come back."

"Where did they go?"

Lucky pointed with his eyes to the closet. "It don't lead to Narnia but it is a lot bigger in there than you think."

"How much bigger?"

"Big enough for you to join us when your daddy finally has his way with you."

"Shut up, Lucky."

"He's already started thinking about it, you know." Lucky took a step forward that ate up the distance between them in an

instant. "He's wondering how much longer he has to wait until you're ripe for the fucking."

"Stop being disgusting."

"He's been thinking about your friends too. Wondering which of them will grow up to be his type. Will it be sporty Jackson? Bookworm Hemi? Or little snotty Scotty?"

"Dad's not like that."

Lucky ignored him and continued with his twisted spiel. "He really wants to play with Shay too. I can't blame him though. Even I would be down for fun with a dude like that."

"Shay's tough as and he will kick your arse if you do anything to him."

"No one can kick my arse!" There was real venom in Lucky's voice, and it was clear he didn't appreciate the threat. He took a breath and calmed down a little. "Besides, it's not me Shay has to worry about. But don't worry, your daddy is trying really hard not to give into his urges with Shay. He doesn't want to shit in his own nest too much just in case that slut Connie finds out what he's been up to." Lucky laughed. "Little does he realise that she already knows."

"Knows what?"

"About the monsters in the garden."

"There's no such thing as monsters. You're just making it up."

Lucky shot him a crooked smile, idly scratching at one of the stickers on his chest. "Then what am I, Levi?" His smile became crestfallen and his voice fell to a lonely whisper. "What the fuck am I?"

A few weeks later Tall Boy and Mr Muscles returned like Lucky said they would. They never tried protecting Levi again though. They had learnt their lesson, and from that day on they kept to themselves and let Lucky kick the bed as much as he liked—and anything else he chose to do.

Levi grew used to the physical pain of his father's beatings but he never got used to Lucky's psychological abuse. The stories Lucky would tell him about his father just kept getting more depraved, and Lucky's ghostly touches that triggered movies in Levi's brain also remained twisted. Levi wondered if he was doomed to be picked on forever by a nasty boy who spouted loads of lies. That was until the day Shay caught him crying in his bedroom.

"What's wrong, Little Prince?" Shay asked as he entered Levi's bedroom. "Why you so sad?"

"I'm okay," Levi sniffled, too scared and embarrassed to tell him about Lucky—who was stood in the corner of the room watching them as he waved his diddle around.

"Obviously you're not fine or you wouldn't be crying." Shay sat down on the bed beside him and looped an arm over Levi's shoulders for a one arm hug. "Tell me what's wrong."

Levi shook his head, his lips trembling, eyes red and damp. "I can't say. You'll get mad."

"No I won't." Shay turned Levi's face towards him and used a hand to wipe away his tears. "You're the Little Prince. You could never make me mad."

"You really promise you won't get mad?"

"Cross my heart and hope to die, stick a needle in my eye." A concerned look fell across Shay's face as he looked in the direction of the lounge. "Is somebody hurting you?"

"Lucky is."

"Lucky?" Shay frowned. "Who's Lucky?"

Levi took an inward sigh, waiting to be laughed at. "My imaginary friend."

Shay didn't laugh. He just nodded. "Okay. Tell me more about Lucky."

"If you tell him about me then there will be consequences," Lucky said from across the room. "He will get hurt. And so will you. Even more than you already do."

Levi glanced over at Lucky, giving him a real fuck-you sneer. He then focused back on Shay's comforting face and proceeded to tell him everything about Lucky: what he looked like, his stinky breath, how he behaved and the scary things he had been saying.

When Levi was finished talking, Shay said, "Lucky is very unlucky because I know someone who can get rid of him."

"You do?"

"You leave it with me, LP. Lucky is gonna be goneburgers in no time. And until he is gone, I will stay every night in your room with you."

"Really?"

"Yeah, bro. We can top and tail and if Lucky shows his ugly mug..." Shay curled his fingers into a fist and punched the open palm of his other hand. "Then he's gonna get dealt to Brixton style."

Lucky snorted, coming closer. "I'd like to fucking see you try, cunt."

"He's angry with you," Levi whispered to Shay.

"Is he here right now?" Shay looked amused. "Where is he?"

Levi gulped. "He's standing right in front of you."

And Lucky was. He was stood, hunched over, baring his rotten teeth right in Shay's face. The stench made Levi wince but Shay didn't seem to smell a thing.

"If you can hear me, Lucky, I want you to know you can suck my big Maori balls." Shay sniggered, nudging Levi with his elbow. "I probably shouldn't say that. He'd probably enjoy it too much. He's gotta be a homo if he walks around naked with stickers all over him, aye?"

Levi dared to laugh, irking Lucky to the point he swiped his hand like a reaper's scythe to Levi's face, but it made no contact. Not even a ticklish shiver. Levi's heart soared with hope for the first time in a very long time. He knew he would be safe with Shay around.

"And if anyone else ever hurts you, not just imaginary friends, LP. Real people too. No matter who they are. You tell me, okay?" Shay paused, then lowered his voice. "Even your dad."

"Dad doesn't hurt me," Levi whispered, staring at the floor.

"We hear him, LP. Our homes are real close together, remember? And we've seen the bruises."

Levi blushed, embarrassed to find out people knew how many hidings he'd been getting. Most of the time his father hit him was because of Lucky's antics but not always. The man had a bad temper and a very short wick. "He only hits me because I'm so naughty."

"Kids are supposed to be naughty. What they're not supposed to be is black and blue. The next time he goes to hit you, I want you to run. Just fucking run."

"But that will just make him madder."

"So what? He's too chubby and slow to catch you. He'll just end up passing out and probably won't remember a thing."

"But where would I run to?"

"You run to me."

∞

"What did Shay do to try and stop Lucky bothering you?" Peach asked.

"He got his grandmother to come bless the house."

"Did it work?"

"Yep. After she blessed the place, I never saw Lucky in my bedroom again."

"So you think Lucky was a ghost?"

"I'm not sure. All I know is that it worked… sort of."

"Sort of?" Peach parroted.

"I never saw Lucky again but sometimes I would hear him in the closet."

"This is so fucking creepy," Peach said with a shiver to her voice.

"Not as creepy as the nightmares I started having."

"What happened in them?"

In many ways the dreams Levi had as a child felt like they had happened to someone else. A him he no longer was. They were just fuzzy memories now, but if he chose to, if he dared, then he could force himself to remember. Like a scab that never fully healed, the memory of those dreams could be picked open and ooze out.

For the sake of remembering so he could tell Peach the story, he picked the scab open. The memory of the nightmares came back with a roaring intensity, and once again Levi struggled with how much he should share.

∞

The nightmares had begun not long after Shay's grandmother had cleansed his bedroom, and they only ever happened when he was staying away from home, but even then it wasn't guaranteed he would have one. In total he only had the nightmare five times but it was five times too many.

The nightmare started the same each time. Levi would find himself in his bedroom back home. The room would appear more dreary than normal, its walls bathed in a gloomy blue. He wouldn't be panicked at first, just confused as to why he was there when he thought he was spending the night someplace else. The next thing that would happen would be the closet door opening up and Lucky stepping out to join him. After that point, each nightmare took its own path but it always ended the same way—witnessing evil. But none were more evil or more frightening than the last nightmare he had. The night he stayed at Dwight's house.

"Hello, Levi." Lucky stepped out of the closet, looking how he always had before being banished: buck arse naked and covered in

stickers. As he stepped towards the bed where Levi was sitting, he left puddles of blood in his wake, his feet oozing trails of red.

"You're bleeding!"

"I always bleed." Lucky grinned. "You'll be covered in blood too one day."

Levi ignored the comment. "Why are you here? You're supposed to be gone."

"That old bitch did quite a good job of getting rid of us but she didn't quite do it properly. But you already know that." Lucky paused to play with his cock for a moment. "You still sometimes hear me at night, don't you? Calling out for you."

"I'm too old to have imaginary friends, Lucky. It's time you just go away for good."

"Fuck you too." Lucky sniggered as he picked at his nose. "Speaking of which. Have you started fucking yet?"

"I'm only twelve, you dickhead."

"So..." Lucky glared at him. "Your friend Jackson already has."

"Jackson's two years older than me."

"And what?" Lucky glared back indignantly, picking his nose again. "Funnily enough, Jackson's getting laid right now."

"Good for him."

"Do you want me to show you?"

"No." Levi huffed, folding his arms. "Piss off."

"That's no way to talk to your dear old Lucky."

"Dear old lucky can kiss my arse."

"Thanks for the offer, kid, but rimming really isn't my thing."

"Rimming?"

"Rimming is something that happens when two people who love each other very much, and don't mind the taste of shit on their—"

"I don't want to know," Levi snapped. "You're such a fucking weirdo."

"Not as weird as you, ya little maggot."

"I'm not a weirdo."

"Maybe not yet. But you will be when Daddy's finished with you." Lucky let rip a creepy laugh. "He is gonna mess you up good. Yes indeedy. You will be one twisted little fucker one day."

"My dad's not gay, he doesn't try touching me, and I don't call him daddy. He's just dad. Plain old dad. He's definitely a prick but he's not a paedo."

"Somebody's turned a bit sour on his daddy since I last saw them," Lucky said, sounding amused.

Levi had gone off his father in a big way the past few months as he started to see how nasty and controlling the man was to him and his mother.

"As much as I hate him, I still don't hate him as much as I hate you." Levi flung back.

"Mmm. I love how feisty you're getting now that you're a little older." Lucky groped himself, licking his lips. "It's such a turn on."

"I forgot how much of a faggot you are," Levi replied snarkily.

"Says the boy who has started looking at Shay in funny ways."

"Whatever, dickhead." Levi decided he'd had enough of loopy Lucky. He climbed off the bed and walked to the bedroom door. When he turned the handle, opening it just a smidge, the putrid smell of rotting flesh hit his nostrils. He slammed the door shut immediately. The stench did more than make him want to vomit, it reminded him he was having the dream again. "Oh my god. I'm having the nightmare." He looked over to Lucky who smiled wickedly. "Why didn't you tell me it was the nightmare. You know I don't like it."

"That would just ruin the fun. I like to see how long it takes you to work it out for yourself."

Levi rushed back over to Lucky, standing behind him for protection. "You gotta help me, Lucky. Please."

101

"I love how this is the only time you ever wanna get close to me." Lucky turned around so they were face to face. "But sorry, kid. I can't do shit to help you. You know this."

The hideous smell was beginning to slip under the cracks in the door, wafting its way around the bedroom like an army of predators.

"Please, Lucky." Levi began tearing up. "Do something. Do anything. Just make it stop."

The closet door swung open and out stumbled Tall Boy and Mr Muscles. Levi knew what was about to happen next. He shook his head, his heart galloping in his chest. "Don't do it guys. Please don't do it." He edged away from them as they all stood together in a line. "Lucky... don't you dare. I know you can make them stop. I'm sorry for being rude to you. I promise to be nicer next time. I-I I'll let you tell me any dirty story you like. Just don't make that noise."

But it was too late. All three of them went rigid, their eyeballs rolling back until the windows to their souls were just ghostly grey ponds. In unison their mouths dropped open impossibly wide, their jaw bones snapping in painful cracking noises. He placed his hands to his ears to try and muffle the macabre sound that would soon follow.

RRRRRRRR RRRRR RRRRRRRR

Their mouths spewed out the ghastly screech that sounded like chainsaws being revved up. It was so loud, terrifyingly sinister.

RRRRR RRRR RRRRR RRRRRR RRRRR

Against his will, Levi's legs carried him out of the bedroom, and down the hallway towards the kitchen and out the backdoor into the backyard. The horrible noise of his imaginary friends' chainsaw symphony faded into the distance but he was now battling with the rotten stench attacking the air, and he knew his eyes would soon be corrupted with a horrible scene going on inside the garden shed. In the real world, Levi's backyard didn't have a garden shed but in the landscape of his nightmares it did.

He was like a passenger in his own body as he travelled towards the vine-covered wooden shed in the far corner of the *backyard. Levi's legs only stopped moving when he was stood on a barrel beneath the small window that looked into the tiny den of hell. "No, no, no, no, no," Levi cried out, screwing his eyelids shut. But just like every other time, his eyes were peeled back open by some dark force that insisted he witness the cruelty taking place inside.*

"Oh my God," was all Levi could utter in a breathless whisper when he saw what was happening inside. Every other time he'd been here, forced against his will to stare into the window, he had seen vile and unspeakable acts taking place, but this time was by far the worst. Usually it was some nameless young man being raped and tortured in hideous ways, which was mostly the case again, but the difference this time was it wasn't a nameless young man. It was Levi's friend Jackson.

Gagged and tied face down to a wooden board, Jackson was doing his best to wriggle free but his hands and feet were fastened to the board and he had no way to escape from the masked man robbing innocence from his young body.

"I told you Jackson was getting laid," said Lucky, suddenly appearing standing on the barrel beside Levi.

"You have to help me save him. Jackson's my friend."

"Sorry, kid." Lucky patted Levi's arm, his touch was sympathetic for a change, void of its usual burning ill-intent. "If it's any help, Jackson won't be in pain much longer. This guy likes to get things done pretty quickly."

Levi's helplessness was an agonizing knot in his throat. He cried and cried, trying to remind himself this wasn't real. It was all a dream. But that didn't make it any less horrendous as he was forced to endure the whole ordeal until Jackson's young life was ended with a brutal slice to his throat that nearly severed his head.

The man then went to a shelf right below the window Levi was staring through. He didn't appear to see Levi or Lucky perched on the other side of the dusty glass, just picked up a chainsaw from the bench and went back to Jackson's lifeless body to do what the men always did when they were done having their fun.

"Please don't make me watch anymore," Levi sobbed. "Not this part."

Lucky glanced around the garden, like he was looking for someone or something. He looked scared. Really scared. He turned to face Levi and wrapped him into a comforting hug.

∞

"And that's the part where I would always wake up and realise I'd wet the bed." Levi let out a humourless laugh. "Like I did the night at Dwight's house and got given that stupid fucking nickname. Soggy."

"If Josh's father knew the whole story, I would hope he'd see what an arsehole he is for doing that."

"I doubt it. Dwight's a grade A bastard."

"Who you've had sex with how many times?"

"Hey. I said you could only ask one question." Levi grinned, feebly raising three fingers.

"He must be pretty good to go back for thirds."

"No comment."

"That's the problem with men who are bastards," Peach said wistfully. "They have a tendency to be more than a tad irresistible."

Levi waggled his dark eyebrows. "I must be the biggest bastard of all then."

"That you are, poppet." Peach leaned back in her chair and wrapped her arms around herself, pretending to shiver. "But that story. My God. It really gave me the willies. And not the eight-inch kind I like."

Levi laughed. "Yeah, it's a pretty freaky story."

As they sat and enjoyed one more drink before leaving the restaurant, Levi's mind wandered to the scariest part of that particular dream. It had nothing to do with Lucky or the garden shed of horrors. It was what had happened three months later when Levi started his first year of high school—the summer Jackson Radcliffe was reported missing, never to be seen or heard from again.

CHAPTER 10

The Beaten Path was by far the largest nightclub in Fitzroy. It comprised of three levels, each with its own bar area and balcony where you could sit and overlook the dancefloor and stage on the ground floor. It was a total meat market and trashy as fuck with a sticky smell that clung to the air—a sour brew of cheap deodorant and body odour. It was the kind of place where you wished smoking inside bars was still legal.

The music was mostly cheesy eighties shit, but Levi enjoyed sitting on the top level and leaning against the rail to check out the talent. Sadly, the talent was few and far between at a place like this but occasionally he would see a girl worth hitting on. Even if he were out and proud, he doubted how much luck he'd have cracking onto a guy in a place like this.

"A bourbon for my lady," Peach said, startling Levi from his thoughts. She sat down with their drinks and handed him one.

"Don't call me a lady," Levi said, pretending to sound annoyed. "You know I'm too much of a slut for that."

Peach laughed. "Never a truer word said."

As they sat there talking, they caught interested stares from all over the bar. He liked to think it was because of how attractive they looked—which perhaps it partly was—but the attention stemmed mostly from who they were. The king and queen of the Fitzroy social scene. Even though the clubgoers here were highly unlikely to ever receive an invite to a Fitzroy Flyers event, they all would have come across Peach and Levi on social media. It was fame on a pathetic and local level, but it was still fame, and the pair of them drank it up.

"Don't you just love how they all stare," Peach commented.

"As long as that's all they do. I hate it when they come up and talk like they know us," Levi groaned. Shit like that annoyed him but to give credit to the social peasants, they rarely approached them on the rare nights he and Peach slummed it in this part of town. They might get the odd drunk gaggle of girls who would come over and say how much they love Peach's column, but for the most part people seemed to leave them in peace.

Peach gazed over the balcony at the sea of grinding bodies below. "Anybody sticking out to you yet?"

"Maybe her." Levi pointed down at a slim redhead dancing with a group of friends. "She looks alright."

"She is very pretty," Peach agreed. "Looks like a good girl though."

"Which is why it will be so fun to make her a bad girl."

"What about the guys? Any of them you like?"

Levi hushed her, glancing around self-consciously. "Keep your voice down."

"No one can hear me over the music, poppet. Relax." She simpered. "Now tell me. Which guy here would you like to get up close and person with?"

"I haven't been looking at any guys," he lied.

"Well, start looking. I am keen to see who your type is."

As if by magic, Levi was tapped on the shoulder and turned around to find himself staring at a guy who was very much his type. Brad Kenny.

Brad's blond hair looked freshly cut; clipped short on the sides and left longer on top. His cheeks showed a couple day's beard growth, which only enhanced his full rosy lips. "Hey, Levi. How are you?" Brad's handsome face lit up with a smile.

"I'm okay. How about—"

"Hello, Brad," Peach said, cutting Levi off. "How can we help you?"

"I was just coming to say hi."

"Hi," she said coldly, turning her back to him.

Brad remained where he was, staring awkwardly at Levi. "I, um, I was wondering if you'd finished the assignment for tech yet?" The stammered question was clearly an attempt at a conversation starter rather than a genuine interest in Levi's miserable study habits.

"Not yet," Levi replied.

"It's quite hard, aye?"

Before Levi could respond, Peach spun back around. "Are you seriously here to talk to Levi about school work or is there something else you're after?"

Brad bristled visibly. "I suppose I was hoping to ask you if I could buy a ticket for the Flyer Ball."

"Why would you want a ticket?" Peach asked icily.

"So I can go, obviously."

An incredulous laugh bubbled up Levi's throat before he could swallow it, and Brad's eyes widened. The dude was either stupid or incredibly desperate, surely he knew Benson Bangers weren't allowed to attend the annual ball.

A glimmer of frustration caught Brad's expression. "Why is that so funny?"

"Levi's laughing because all the tickets have sold out," Peach said. That was an outright lie but it was her way of giving Brad an out before the truth was rubbed in his face. He should have taken it. But he didn't.

"But I thought they hadn't started selling yet," Brad said.

Peach sighed. "If you know that then why are you asking me if you can buy a ticket?"

"I guess I wanted to check if it would be okay first because..." Brad's words abandoned him.

"Because you're a Benson Banger?" Peach's lips upturned very slightly, as though she enjoyed reminding Brad what he was.

"Yeah," Brad whispered.

Levi glanced from Brad to Peach then back to Brad. *This is fucking awkward.* The club may have been pulsing with eardrum busting music but the sudden tension between the pair was the only thing ringing in Levi's ears.

Peach took a few seconds to respond. "We have very few rules in our scene, Brad, but you broke the main rule. And there's a price to pay for that."

"Why do you have to be so rigid about this? It was a mistake and it wasn't like much even happened. All Wade did was kiss my neck before I pushed him away."

"That's not what Wade told me," Peach said.

"What did Wade tell you?"

Peach pursed her lips like she was tasting her words before sharing them. "He said he thinks you must have danced a lot that night because of how salty your dick tasted. He also said you sucked his too, not very well though, apparently you were a bit... toothy."

"He is a fucking liar!" Brad said heatedly. "I never put his dick in my mouth."

"But you do admit he sucked yours?" Peach's eyes glowed triumphantly.

Brad looked to Levi for support. Levi gave none. This wasn't his battle, not to mention it was a losing one. Brad switched his attention back to peach. "Even if he did suck me off—which he didn't—I don't understand what the big deal is about blacklisting…"

"Benson Bangers," Peach said.

"Blacklisting anyone."

Peach sighed like she was growing tired of the conversation. "I understand Crystal Thompson and a few others of Wade's used goods—including you—have tried arguing like this is some gross form of social apartheid, so I am going to break it down for you, darling. The Fitzroy Flyers, like many groups in society, has its own set of unwritten rules. For example, we don't make a habit of letting too many poor people into our scene, but I have never once heard you or Crystal complain about that. We're also a bit thin on the ground with the over thirties crowd—by choice. Did you ever complain about that and argue for us to let older people hang out with all of us? No, you haven't. But all of a sudden, you, Crystal and the others who have never cared about these sorts of rules suddenly think you deserve a free pass for a rule that excludes you? And might I add, this was one rule that you all had full control over not to break. None of you had to let Wade fuck you."

"He didn't fuck me, Peach." A resentful scowl thinned Brad's lips.

"I don't care if it was a kiss or if you and Wade tried re-enacting Two Girls One Cup," Peach's tone wavered towards anger. "Anyone who touches Wade gets blacklisted. Everybody knows that. So stop complaining and move on."

Brad gaped, taking a moment to gain composure. "Look, I don't mean to sound like I am asking for special treatment, but I'm just asking if you can make an exception

110

just this once. For me. As a friend? Please?" Brad ran a hand through his hair, his voice strained. "My sister will be eighteen soon and I know she'll start going to the flyer events and if she does I don't want her finding out about what happened." He quickly corrected himself. "About the Wade rumour. I'm not gay."

"No one said you were, darling," Peach said. "Bi maybe, but not gay."

"I'm not even bi!" Brad protested vehemently. He began a long spiel about just how straight he was and how it was crazy for anyone to think otherwise.

Levi was secretly enjoying the drama unfolding right before him because it allowed him to enjoy the sound of Brad's husky voice and watch his luscious lips. Even though he was clearly unhappy his mouth still moved in sexy ways. *I bet he sounds hot when he's having sex.* Levi almost wished Brad would lose his cool some more, start letting some f bombs fly, so he could hear him say dirty words.

"Brad, your sexuality isn't the issue here," Peach said. "You broke a rule and that is that."

"But it will never happen again. I really miss being a flyer. I'd do anything to be let back in." Desperation seeped into Brad's voice

"The term flyer is just a word," Peach said unsympathetically. "If you want to be a flyer then just call yourself a flyer. There's no law against that."

"It doesn't make it true though if I can't get into the parties and hang out with my friends."

Peach rolled her eyes. "Don't play the poor me card. It's not like you have no friends, otherwise you wouldn't be out tonight. I don't imagine you're here on your own. Now if you don't mind, me and Levi are trying to have a night out."

A very long and tense five seconds past before Brad spoke. "I'm sorry for bothering you both." He was trying to sound light, but it wasn't working. He couldn't keep the ice from his tone. "I'll let you both get back to your drinks." He turned to Levi and offered a parting smile. "I'll see you at tech on Monday."

Levi nodded and watched Brad's long, slim legs walk away.

"Can you believe him?" Peach blurted. "The audacity to come up and ask if he can be let back into the Flyers. He's dreaming."

Levi nodded. "He sure is. Sleeping with Wade is like a bad case of gonorrhoea. If his cock goes anywhere near you, your reputation starts burning."

Peach chuckled. "Nice analogy but it's not quite true. Gonorrhoea is curable. Their reputations aren't."

They both laughed.

After a sip on his drink, Levi's eyes strayed to the stairs where Brad was beginning to descend to the dancefloor. The lanky blond was definitely quite a sexy guy. If Peach wanted to know Levi's type when it came to guys then Brad would be a good example.

There was something about his husky looks and farm boy voice that stirred Levi's loins in a very needy way.

It was a shame someone so good-looking had been ostracised from the group. Straight, gay, whatever he was, Brad was poisoned goods now. There was no way Levi could ever hook-up with a Benson banger, not if he wanted to remain king of the scene.

What the fuck?

Levi's heart jumped when he saw who Brad was walking towards.

It can't be.

But it was.

You have got to be fucking kidding me.

In the middle of the dance floor, dancing, grinding and kissing, was Lucas and Sophie. Like a train running off

112

the tracks, his emptions jolted and crashed in a shuddering frenzy. There was lust, envy, fury, and a whole bunch of feelings he didn't have names for.

It had been four years since he and Sophie had split up and it was the first time he had ever seen her and Lucas partying in town. He just assumed their lame arses stayed at home with their dumb kid each weekend, probably too poor to do anything else. Yet here they were. With Brad.

"Whose caught your eye," Peach asked. Her eyes followed Levi's gaze. "Oh…"

"Since when did they become such bosom buddies with Brad?"

"Brad and Lucas were quite close back at school," Peach offered.

"Yeah but I didn't think they still hung out."

"It's probably a new thing since Brad got booted from the group. He's having to dredge up the trash from his past to find friends."

"Emphasis on trash," Levi muttered.

When Brad joined Sophie and Lucas, the happy couple let go of each other and allowed Brad to dance with them in a happy little circle. Judging by the fake-arse smile on Brad's face they wouldn't have had a clue he'd just humiliated himself with grovelling to be let back in with his old crew.

Levi tipped his drink back and downed what was left in three gulping swallows. Wiping his lips, he asked Peach if she could shout him one more drink.

"Of course, poppet." She rubbed his arm. "You can have as many drinks as you like."

"Thanks. I have a feeling I might need them if we stay here the rest of the night."

"Did you want us to leave?"

Levi shook his head. "Fuck that. I wouldn't give them the credit."

"Exactly. Who cares what they think. They are nobodies." She quickly finished her drink and toddled off to the bar to buy another round.

As he waited for Peach to return, he continued to watch Sophie and Lucas with venomous eyes, willing one of them to trip and fall on their face.

While he refused to let them rattle him to the point of running away like a coward, Levi did wish he'd spotted them in one of the bars down at the harbourside so he could have asked one of the bouncers to boot their arses out. Unfortunately his Flyer popularity didn't have the same sway in a place like the Beaten Path.

When he grew tired of trying to will them to trip over, he let his eyes wander between Brad's biceps and Sophie's jiggling tits. Both were pleasant to look at, Sophie's a little more so because he knew just what they felt and tasted like. The memories of the countless times they'd had sex brought on a resentful erection and he discreetly lowered a hand under the table and squeezed himself.

Then to his horror, Sophie looked up and spotted him. Their eyes only locked for a second before Levi glanced away but it was enough for her to tap Lucas on the shoulder and point up to the balcony where Levi was sitting.

In his peripheral vision he could see Lucas waving one of his large hands, his dumb face smiling and grinning. Sophie yanked Lucas's arm and he lowered his head so she could talk in his ear. Lucas then put his mouth to Brad's ear, which made Brad glance up to where Levi was sitting. Then, to Levi's horror, Sophie and Lucas began making their way for the stairs.

They were coming up.

CHAPTER 11

Levi looked towards the bar, scrambling for any sign of Peach. He was desperate for her to get back with their drinks so he didn't have to face Sophie and Lucas on his own. They'd left Brad downstairs, dancing on his own like a maniac.

Hurry up, Peach. Hurry the fuck up. He saw the back of Peach's head; she was only just now talking to the guy behind the bar to order the drinks. Lucas and Sophie were now on the third level and only seconds away from approaching his table. His stomach knotted. He was gonna have to endure this painful catch up all on his own.

"Hey, Candy," Lucas said in his deep, booming voice.

"Hi, Levi." Sophie gave a friendly smile. "It's been a while."

Levi froze in his seat, shaking more than a bit and desperate not to show it. "Yep. It has been that."

Lucas smirked, his six-four height towering over the table. His presence was commanding and hogged the air. "You out on the hunt looking for a new missus?" He wrapped a possessive arm around Sophie's back. "Too bad the best one is already taken."

Sophie stepped free of Lucas's arm and gave Levi her full attention. "Lucas told me about what happened last week at the cafe and we wanted to come and apologise." She nudged Lucas. "Didn't we?"

Levi's cheeks pinked. He didn't want an apology. He just wanted to be left alone. It was bad enough being punched by someone he hated but he felt it was way more humiliating having Sophie come up here and force Lucas to give him an apology. Her intentions were probably good but it was so damn emasculating. She may as well have asked Levi to flop his cock out on the table so she could chop it off.

Lucas cleared his throat, the smirk on his face promptly fading. "Uh. Yeah. Sorry about that."

"Lucas," Sophie said, like she was prodding him to do a better job of apologising.

"I'm really sorry, Candy. I shouldn't have done what I did—but then you shouldn't have said that nasty stuff about Mia."

"Lucas," Sophie scolded.

"Sorry," He muttered to Sophie before reattempting his apology. "I lost my cool, man. That was wrong of me and I shouldn't have knocked you out like that."

"You didn't knock me out," Levi snapped.

"Maybe not, but I still shouldn't have hit you." Lucas flashed him a nasty grin while Sophie wasn't looking. "It's not fair for a man of my size to take on such a weaker opponent."

Levi had heard enough. "Fuck off, Lucas."

"Hey, man. I'm trying to apologise here." The smug as fuck expression that flashed across Lucas's face said otherwise.

"You can shove your apology up your arse."

Sophie looked flustered. "Lucas really is sorry. We talked about it and we agreed that we don't want to teach Mia that violence is the way to solve problems."

Oh my god. Can these two be any more pathetic. Levi bit down on the groan threatening to slip out of his mouth.

"Sophie, if you're worried about me pressing charges then don't. I wouldn't waste my time or money on this arsehole."

Lucas chuckled.

"It's not that," Sophie said, although the look of relief on her face said otherwise. "But thank you for not doing that. We really don't want any trouble and Lucas is very sorry."

"Honestly, Candy, I am," Lucas said, stepping forward. "I made a mistake and a real man owns up to his mistakes." He extended his hand like a peace offering. "From me to you, I sincerely apologise."

Levi left Lucas's hand hanging. "Whatever."

Lucas took his hand back. "Well, you can't say I didn't try."

"What do we have here," came Peach's voice.

Levi took an internal sigh of relief when he saw his pink-haired friend reappear. She handed him his drink then sat down beside him, gazing fearlessly at Sophie and Lucas. "What an unexpected reunion. I don't think I have seen you two out in town before. Special occasion is it?"

"Brad invited us out," Lucas replied, like it was something to be proud of.

"Did he?" Peach pretended to be surprised. "I didn't know you would be friends with someone like Brad."

"Why wouldn't we?" Lucas frowned. "Brad's a cool sort."

"No, I just mean that I didn't realise you would be an LGBTQ ally."

"A what?" Lucas frowned.

"You know... Lesbian. Gay. Bisexual. Trans. Queer." Peach grinned facetiously. "I'm not sure if he's a G or a B or maybe a Q. But he's definitely got himself a letter."

"Brad's not a homo," Lucas said staunchly.

"Maybe you should ask Wade what he thinks. He's the one who slept with him."

Sophie gaped. "You mean Wade Benson?"

"Mm-hmm." Peach nodded. "They had a bit of a fling together a few months ago."

The word *Benson Banger* formed on Sophie's lips silently.

"What do you mean they had a fling?" Lucas asked.

"A fling. You know… sexual intercourse."

I love this chick. Peach had come to Levi's rescue like she always did. Not only had she broken up the awkwardness of an unwanted apology but she'd just dropped a little bomb of scandal on two unsuspecting idiots.

"You're wrong, Peach," Lucas said firmly. "Brad's not like that. He ain't a faggot." When Sophie shot her boofhead boyfriend a snotty look, he quickly added, "Not that there's anything wrong with being a faggot. Uh, I mean gay."

"I'm so pleased you feel that way," Peach said. "It would be hard for you otherwise to put up with what some people might be thinking."

"What are people thinking?" Lucas asked.

"Some people who know about Brad might think he's having a night out with his boyfriend and faghag."

Lucas blinked. "Huh?"

Sophie sighed and proceeded to translate for the moron. "What she's saying, babe, is that people might think you and Brad are together."

Lucas looked like he'd just swallowed shit. "Eww. Fuck off. Nope. None of that please."

"Peach is just teasing," Sophie said. "Aren't you Peach?"

"No. I'm being serious. Brad has a thing for dick and Lucas has one of those."

Levi sniggered.

"Fuck up, Candy. It's not funny."

"Settle down, darling," Levi replied in a camp voice. "You don't want to be all angry for when you get back downstairs to your *boyfriend*."

Lucas bit his bottom lip, shaking his head. "Not fucking funny."

"Babe, calm down. It's not a big deal," Sophie said.

Peach aimed her attention on Sophie. "I wanted to tell you how beautiful your daughter is. Lucas showed us the pictures. She really is lovely."

Sophie nodded politely. "Thank you."

"It's amazing how much she looks like her daddy," Peach said.

"Do you think so?" Lucas asked excitedly.

"Definitely." Peach nodded. "She's a deadringer for dad."

A tiny muscle twitched at Sophie's temple; her lips thinned. She grabbed Lucas by the arm and smiled. "It's been nice catching up but I guess we better get back to the dancefloor. I don't want to keep my boyfriend's boyfriend waiting."

Levi laughed—loudly. He'd forgotten how witty Sophie could be.

"Don't say shit like that, babe," Lucas muttered under his breath. "It's not funny."

Once they were gone, Peach looked very pleased with herself. "I thought that might help get rid of them."

"Yeah. It worked a treat." Levi chuckled. "Telling them about Brad and Wade was fucking genius."

"I wasn't talking about that."

"What were you talking about?"

"You really don't know?"

Levi frowned. "Know what?"

Peach studied his face, as if she were searching for a long-buried secret. "Never mind, poppet."

CHAPTER 12

Danny was perched on the couch in the games room, playing Xbox while he waited for Levi to get home. His body was gripped with hopeful expectation, running on an invisible fuel that had him up well past his usual bedtime. It was now 3 a.m. and he was beginning to wonder if Levi was coming home at all.

I should just give up and go to bed, he thought. But he couldn't give up. Not just yet. He wanted to cast his eyes on Levi's handsome face one more time before he went to sleep and dreamed about him. What they had done together last night was sacred and special and it had stirred his soul in ways he could not believe. There was no greater closeness two human beings could share with each other than their bodies merging into one.

Since waking up from his night of firsts, Danny had found himself wanting to be around Levi constantly, getting an emotional high just from being in his presence. He wanted to be near Levi so darn bad that he'd told his dad he no longer wanted to go away for his birthday, bailing on a trip he'd been planning for months. But it was worth staying home if it meant he got to stay near Levi.

Danny knew he wasn't gay. He liked girls. He liked girls a lot. But after what happened last night he was beginning to question if maybe he liked boys too? He certainly liked Levi. Of that he was certain. Levi had made him feel wanted in a way no one ever had before, seen him in a light no one else's eyes ever had, and Danny was incredibly grateful to Levi for both those things.

Before the magic of last night, he had always harboured conflicted feelings about his brother. On one hand he idolised him—Levi was the most popular guy in town and he could be a lot of fun and often made Danny laugh—but on the other hand Levi could be aloof and uncaring. But from now on he would only focus on Levi's positives.

He'd masturbated five times today while remembering how they'd made love. Just thinking about Levi's tongue inside his mouth left Danny weak at the knees. He didn't need to kiss anybody else to know that Levi was an expert kisser. His favourite thing to think about though was how Levi had given him a blowjob. Oh man, that had been something else. The other stuff had been less fun for him if Danny were being honest. Letting Levi fuck him had been the most challenging part of the evening but it was also the most rewarding because it was that act which had taken his virginity and made him a man. *That's right. I'm officially a man now. Not a boy. A man.*

Danny squished his legs together, resisting his desperate need to pee. He'd been like this all evening, doing his best to hold off urinating, so that when Levi got home he could surprise him by giving him the kind of sex he wanted. When Levi first told him that if they were to ever have sex again then he expected Danny to wet his pants, kiss Levi's feet, and be fucked rough, Danny had run off scared. That was some seriously weird stuff. But as the day had worn on, and he thought about it some more, he decided maybe it wasn't so bad. He loved Levi and he wanted to give Levi the things he wanted—especially if it meant he had the chance to have sex again.

Just as he was about to give into the need of his burning bladder, he heard the undeniable sound of the front door being yanked open. *He's home! He's finally home!* Danny forced himself to wait, not wanting to rush out and greet Levi like some big dumb dog with an extra-waggy tail. He waited for a few minutes and then crept his way upstairs towards Levi's bedroom.

I wonder if he will let me spend the night in bed with him? The thought was a wonderful one. As special as last night had been, Danny had been a disappointed to wake up and find himself alone on the lounge floor. This time he wanted to wake up beside the person who had made love to him.

He tapped quietly on Levi's bedroom door then pulled on the doorknob and slipped inside. The room was mostly dark except for a small glow from a bedside lamp. Levi was hunched over beside his bed, shirtless and in the process of tugging off his socks.

"Whatcha doing, buuudy." Levi's words were slurred, his face soft and droopy. He was definitely drunk but he still looked beautiful.

"I was waiting for you to get home," Danny replied. He stood awkwardly and rubbed his heels together, partly from nerves but also to try and stop himself from pissing his pants prematurely.

"Why?" Levi slipped out of his jeans, flicking them away with his foot to join his t-shirt strewn on the floor.

"I wanted to see if you—" Danny lost his words when Levi stripped out of his briefs and stood there fully naked. His eyes zoned in on his brother's penis that dangled in a flaccid state over his hairless balls.

"You wanted to what?" Levi grunted before half-sitting and half-falling onto his bed. He slowly pivoted his body and lay his head on the pillows before slipping his nakedness under the blanket.

"I stayed up so we can do those things you wanted."

"What things?"

"You know…"—Danny blushed—"watch me pee my pants before you have sex with me."

Levi grinned. "Can't get enough of me, aye?"

"I've drunk gallons of water to the point I'm bursting." Danny glanced around the messy room. "Where do you want me to do it? Should we go to your bathroom?"

"Nar, buddy. Just go to bed."

"But I thought this is what you wanted."

Levi rubbed his face and sighed. "I'm not having sex with you Danny."

"What? Why?"

"Because I am fucking knackered and probably have brewers droop."

"Brewers droop?"

"I'm too drunk to get hard."

"Oh…"

"I appreciate the effort, but I'm fucking shattered and need to get some sleep."

"So you don't want to watch me piss my pants?" Danny felt absurd saying such a thing aloud, he felt even more absurd when Levi laughed at him.

"Not tonight."

Danny turned on his heels and raced towards Levi's en-suite.

"Where you going?" Levi called out.

"I need to wee," Danny hollered from inside the en suite. He stood at the toilet and unzipped his fly, sighing loudly when his dick unleashed a heavy stream of piss. When he was finished, he shook his dick to rid himself of any dribbles and zipped his pants back up. With the pain of a full bladder gone, he marched back into Levi's bedroom with a scowl on his face and in a sulky voice said, "Am I really that ugly?"

"Huh?"

"I must be super ugly for you to keep turning me down."

Levi didn't laugh this time, instead he shared an ultra-serious stare. "You know that's not true."

"Then why have you said no both times I have asked for more."

"Because it's wrong, Danny."

"Then why wasn't it wrong when you fucked me last night." His voice warbled and he could feel tears brewing in his eyes.

Levi sat up in bed and hissed, "Keep your voice down, idiot."

"Sorry," Danny whispered.

"Come here," Levi said, patting the mattress.

Danny refused to budge, despite wanting to get closer.

"Come on, man. Don't be sulky." Levi patted the mattress again.

Danny gave in and stropped his way over to stand beside Levi's bed.

"You're not ugly. You know that." Levi reached out and gently stroked Danny's crotch. "If you were ugly then I wouldn't have sucked that snake in your pants, would I?"

Danny cracked a smile, his dick pulsing from the light touch of Levi's fingers. He got excited, hardening fast, as he expected Levi to unzip his pants and give him a blowjob. But it didn't happen. Levi just smiled and lay back down like he was about to sleep. "Are you not going to suck it?" Danny asked.

Levi shook his head. "I feel your pain, buddy. I know what it's like to want something so bad and not get it."

"If you know how I feel then why don't you just give it to me," Danny snapped, quickly regretting it. "I'm sorry. I shouldn't have said that."

"Oh, Danny boy. You're too fucking adorable." Levi chuckled softly. He cocked a drunken eyebrow. "You can touch me if you want though."

"I can touch you?"

"That's what I said."

Danny almost had whiplash from Levi's sudden change of heart. He wasn't sure what was happening here but it felt promising. A fast-growing lump in his throat made his voice go hoarse. "Where am I allowed to touch you?"

"Anywhere you like." Levi cast the blanket aside and revealed himself. "Knock yourself out."

All the air whooshed out of Danny's lungs as he stared down at his naked brother. He slowly dropped to his knees, gingerly raised a hand and stroked Levi's ankle. He flattened his hand, running his palm over the dark hairs of Levi's shins, slowly heading north towards infinitely more interesting territory. Neither of them spoke as his hand climbed higher and higher, gliding its way to Levi's inner thigh and eventually grabbing hold of Levi's warm scrotum. His balls were clammy, he'd definitely built up a sweat on his night out, but Danny didn't mind.

Danny released a shudder as he gently squeezed the sweaty skin of Levi's ballbag. He liked how they were shaved smooth, so silky to the touch. He released Levi's nuts and wrapped his fingers around Levi's soft prick. Danny felt his tummy do a somersault. He was touching the piece of Levi that had been inside him, the flesh that had been within his flesh, the part of Levi responsible for making him a man.

"Jump up and sit between my legs," Levi suggested, spreading his legs open. "It'll make it easier."

Danny dutifully climbed onto the mattress and sat in the V of Levi's open legs. The sight of his brother's nudity was even more stunning from this angle and Danny found himself completely overwhelmed by the desire to kiss Levi's naked body. He bowed his head and showered Levi's thigh with tiny kisses, peck after peck of silent praise. Then, with a quick inhale of courage, he began kissing the tip of Levi's penis.

Levi groaned and raised his legs so they were bent at the knee, very gently raising his hips like he was saying *don't kiss it, suck it.*

Danny licked the crown then scooped the entire length of Levi's sleeping dick inside his mouth and sucked. His tongue was immediately hit with the salty taste of dick sweat and his nostrils whacked by the smell of Levi's musky balls that permeated his senses.

"Fuck yeah," Levi panted, arching into the intimate embrace of Danny's mouth. "Suck me."

Danny groaned, his mouth full of cock. At first, Levi's dick didn't seem to react, but after about a minute of slippery slobbers, he felt Levi's cock twitch inside his mouth. Then it twitched again. And again. *This is amazing!* He loved knowing he was responsible for the hardening inside his mouth, that he was gifting Levi this kind of pleasure. He jostled Levi's balls in his palm, encouraging his brother's sluggish erection to grow to its full size.

Levi covered his face with his arms but the low moans he was emitting made it clear he was very much enjoying what Danny was doing to him. "My balls. Don't forget my balls."

Danny let Levi's cock slide out of his mouth and lowered his head to service Levi's scrotum with his tongue. He wrapped his hand around Levi's shaft and gently stroked it.

"Yeah. Fuck yeah," Levi moaned, his body jerking and shaking uncontrollably.

Danny inhaled both balls into his mouth, rolling them around his tongue, absorbing the full flavour of his brother's balls. His mouth was flooding with saliva, and he coughed a little, the reflex tugging at Levi's sac. He withdrew and tongued the excess liquid coating Levi's scrotum, his mouth blasted with the acrid taste of Levi's perspiration mixed with his own drool as he swallowed it. He softly licked the length of Levi's shaft from bottom to top and back down, taking a furtive moment to catch his breath.

Danny sat up straight and dropped a hand to his zipper, pulling it down and freeing his swollen erection. He wasn't sure what came over him but he was gripped with a need to let Levi know how much he craved him. He shuffled forward and rubbed the tip of his cock dangerously close to Levi's crack. He then decided to be a bit daring, placing a hand under Levi's left knee and raised it up.

As if reading his mind, Levi lifted both his legs, resting his ankles on Danny's shoulders. The offering up of his legs allowed Danny an unobstructed view inside Levi's arse crack and the tightly-sealed surface of his arsehole. Levi wasn't smooth down here like his balls were, but that didn't stop Danny's cock from pulsing in hunger at the sight of Levi's closed rim. With one hand still masturbating Levi's dick, he used his other hand to guide his erection to the crevice of Levi's butt crack.

"Whoaaaa," he moaned in a horny whisper as the damp heat of Levi's crack made contact with his dick. He rubbed his precum-leaking tip up and down Levi's crack, desperate to push it inside. He could feel the hairs around Levi's arsehole scraping the helmet of his cock, teasing him and beckoning him to push forward. Danny rocked forward slightly, trying to push the tip of his dick inside but he was met with blunt refusal from Levi's sealed-tight orifice. He tried again, seeking to cross a magical threshold, but again his weak push—disguised as an off-balance sway—was denied entry.

Danny glanced up and saw that Levi had moved his arms away from his face and was smirking at him.

"You wanna put that thing inside me so badly," Levi said, grinning. Danny froze. Guilt painted on his face. "It's okay. Every guy is the same," Levi said casually. "We all want to try and slip it in."

"I-I wasn't trying to slip it in," Danny lied.

"Yeah you were." Levi pulled his ankles away from Danny's shoulders and dropped his feet back on the mattress. "You might be one of the good guys but you're still a guy."

"I'm sorry. It won't happen again."

Levi ran a hand through his hair, a sexy smile playing with his mouth. "It's okay. I don't mind."

"Are you saying... I can be the man?"

"The correct term is *top*. And that depends."

"On what?" Danny asked.

"On whether or not you can fuck me like a boss."

"What's that mean?"

"It means you have to make me feel submissive. Make me your bitch. Fuck me like I'm a piece of meat."

Danny had a rough idea of what Levi was asking for. He'd certainly watched some nasty porn before but not that much. He preferred videos where the sex was sensual and affectionate. "You mean stuff like spanking you?"

"Yep. And other stuff."

"Like what?"

"Talk dirty to me. Call me names. Tell me I'm a faggot. Whack your cock in my face... fuck, you can even spit in my face if you want."

129

"But I don't want to be mean to you." Danny said. "I love you."

"It doesn't matter if you love me, you just have to fuck me like you're the boss."

"Can we kiss while I do it?"

Levi shook his head. "Nope. Just fuck me. Fuck me and use me."

"I-I don't know if I can do that."

"Yeah you can. Just think of the prize."

Danny frowned. "What's the prize?"

"If you do it good enough then you earn the right to fuck me whenever you want. I won't be allowed to say no. I will have to do whatever master Danny says." Levi smirked. "Even kiss you."

"That does sound good."

"Of course it sounds good. We both know you want to put your dick inside me. And now's your chance." Levi sat up and reached down to touch Danny's cock, thumbing a pearly wad of precum from the oozing tip before putting his thumb in his mouth and licking it clean. "Remember, if you can fuck me like a real man, and fill my arse with lots of cum, then I am obliged to be your bitch as often as you like. That's the rules."

Danny wasn't sure what rule book Levi was referring to but it wasn't one he'd ever read. "When you say often as I like, does that really mean as often as I like?"

Levi nodded. "It sure does. If you fuck me, and cum in me, and own me, then you get access to my arse whenever you want it. You just gotta click your fingers and say 'bitch, bend over.'"

Danny wanted to laugh at Levi's drunken rambling but he was too blown away to do either. He lowered his voice to sound more confident than he actually was. "So you wanna be spanked and spit on and called bad names."

130

"I do. But first you need to make me do something humiliating to make me feel submissive. Something you can make fun of me for in the future."

"Like what?"

"This might sound a little weird but the only other time I went submissive for a guy was because he made me do something really shameful."

"What did he make you do?"

"He made me sniff someone else's dirty underwear." Levi waggled his eyebrows. "Gross, aye?"

"It is a bit."

"You wanna see me do something gross, right? And get me feeling hella submissive?"

"I guess so."

"Then you best go find me some guy's dirty undies to sniff."

"I can give you mine to sniff," Danny suggested.

"No. They have to be someone else's."

"But I don't have any other guy's underwear."

"Surely you can find a pair men's underwear from somewhere. It doesn't matter whose they are, just as long as its not yours or mine."

Danny scratched his head, struggling to comprehend what was going on as a taut silence hung in the air.

Levi's hazel eyes clouded and he looked down at his lap, his face twisting. "Forget all about it. I'm just drunk." He let out a humourless laugh. "Let's just call it a night and go to bed."

"No, no," Danny pleaded, clutching Levi's arm before he could lay back down. "I know where I can get a pair."

"You do?"

"I do but I just..." Danny winced.

"You just?"

131

"The only dirty undies I can get right now are dad's, and I doubt very much you want to sniff those."

Levi's brown brows furrowed as he looked at Danny inquisitively. "If they are the only ones you can get, then they'll just have to do."

CHAPTER 13

Each nimble step Danny took down the hallway felt like a step in the direction of sin. He couldn't believe he was agreeing to this, but he knew if he didn't come up with the goods then he would miss his chance to have sex for just the second time in his life. So while his stomach twisted like it was flooded with slime, his stubborn erection pointed straight ahead to the location of what would get him laid—his father's dirty underwear.

I can't believe Levi is willing to do this. I suppose he is drunk though… and drunk people do tend to do silly things.

But this wasn't just silly, Danny thought, it was downright gross. Levi was asking to sniff his own stepfather's underwear. It was so messed up and wrong, but still Danny kept sneaking down the hallway like a perverted prowler.

Once he was outside his dad and stepmother's bedroom, he poked his head inside to check if they were asleep. His father certainly was, the man's gargling snores testimony to the deep slumber he was in. It was dark so it was hard to see but once his eyes had adjusted to the shadows, Danny could see that his stepmother was curled up on her side and also fast asleep.

He dropped to his hands and knees, wriggling across the carpet like a sniper in the jungle. Despite the loud snores coming from his father's nostrils, the loudest noise Danny could hear was the *thud thud thud* of his own heart. When he reached the entrance to their en suite, Danny nearly shat himself when his father suddenly coughed and spluttered on his own snore and began to roll over in bed. Danny held his breath and closed his eyes, praying for the power of invisibility. After about twenty seconds he heard his father's snores revert back to their normal deep sound.

Phew. Thank goodness.

Rounding the corner of the en-suite, Danny raised himself up and knee-walked over the tiled floor towards the laundry basket. He fetched his phone out of his pocket, using the light from the screen to hunt for what it was Levi required to feel submissive. He put his hand inside the basket, fossicking through t-shirts, blouses and dirty socks until finally, right at the bottom he found a pair of his father's underwear—y-fronts covered in the Union Jack symbol. He cringed as he delicately plucked them from the basket, trying his best not to handle them too much.

He made his exit the same way he'd come into the bedroom, snaking his way over the floor on his belly. Once he'd made it to the safety of the hallway, he rushed back to Levi's bedroom where Levi was sat on the edge of the bed waiting for him.

"Did you find some?" Levi asked, a hint of filthy excitement in his voice.

Danny held the very-worn briefs up for Levi to see.

Levi smiled faintly. "Well done. Come put them down on the bed."

Danny dropped the sinful undies onto the mattress, glad to no longer be touching them. He gazed into Levi's seductive eyes. "What happens now?"

"Now I reward you." Levi's hands shot forward and he undid the buttons on Danny's pants.

Danny felt like he'd been unshackled when Levi pulled his pants and boxers down to his knees. His cock didn't even make one complete bounce before Levi's lips were wrapped around it. He erupted with a shaky groan, taking a moment to steady himself from the immense pleasure his dick was experiencing.

Levi grabbed hold of Danny's buttocks, his fingers massaging and prodding his taut arse cheeks while his throat spasmed around Danny's length. He pulled his mouth free. "Look at your balls," Levi marvelled, cupping them gently in his left hand. "They're almost the size of eggs!" He dipped his head and gave them a firm lick. "They're so much bigger than my little bitch nuts."

Danny snicker-snorted. "I shouldn't laugh."

"Yeah, you should." Levi tugged on his own nuts to emphasise his point. "They are laughable compared to your manly low-hangers."

"Isn't the size of a guy's penis more important? And I think yours is bigger than mine." *Think* was the wrong word. Danny knew Levi's was bigger. With his head tilted down, he had a bird's eye view of both their erect cocks and Levi had a good inch on him.

"The size of your dick doesn't count. It's how you use it." Levi gazed up with a slutty look on his face. "And you're about to use it on me any way you fucking want, master Danny."

Being called master Danny was weird but he played along. "That's right…"—*what the fuck do I say?*—"bitch nuts?" The insult came out more like a question but his brother appeared to like what he'd called him.

Levi flung him another slutty little glance. "You are such a fucking stud." He poked his tongue out and dug it in the groove of Danny's piss slit, digging out a sticky trail of precum.

Danny's eyes began to flicker. "You're so-so-so good at that."

"Fuck my face, master Danny. Fuck it like a pussy."

He gripped the sides of Levi's head and slowly rocked his hips back and forward, fucking Levi's mouth in a slow but firm pace. This hook-up was so different to what they'd shared last night but Danny wasn't about to ask for it to stop. He shoved aside his wishes for kisses and cuddles and allowed himself to descend to the depraved levels Levi wanted them to reside in.

Now and then Levi would pull his mouth free from Danny's cock and voice a suggestion. *Call me a faggot. Make fun of my small balls. Tell me how much better you are than me. Spit in my face.* Each time Danny would oblige, getting more and more sadistic with someone he would rather shower with affection. He just kept remembering what Levi had said; if he could fuck like a boss then Levi would let him fuck him anytime he wanted and however he wanted, which of course for Danny would mean sensually and with lots of kisses.

"You're such a pathetic faggot," Danny panted, fucking Levi's face.

"Yes, master Danny," Levi's dick-filled lips slobbered back. "I'm really pathetic."

With a ragged groan, Danny pulled his cock out of Levi's mouth and slapped him with it, leaving a wet smear across his cheek. "Open your mouth. Wide."

Levi did as he was told, probably expecting Danny to slip his cock back inside but instead Danny leaned down and spat right in his mouth. "Swallow it. Swallow my spit."

Levi hesitated but did as he was told, swallowing Danny's spit, then opened his mouth for more. Danny fired another spit bomb in Levi's mouth, and then another, and another. Each time Levi dutifully closed his mouth and gulped it down.

Danny felt guilty about what he was doing but he had to admit the power he was being given had a certain thrill attached to it. He wondered what else he could make his brother do in his drunk and submissive state.

Levi pointed towards the dirty undies lying on the bed. "Can I please sniff these now, master Danny? I want to show you how pathetic I really am."

Danny masked his disgust with a nod. He watched in horror as Levi picked up the underwear and buried his face in them and began to sniff. It was a deep inhale, the kind of breath that meant Levi wasn't just smelling them with his nose but trying to taste them with his mouth. "You're really messed up," Danny muttered—and he meant it.

Levi didn't respond, he just kept rubbing his face in the undergarment that had at some point been wrapped around Danny's father's private parts. He could just tell by looking at them that they must have stunk to high heaven, but that didn't stop Levi from consuming the scent like a greedy pig.

"What do they smell like?" Danny asked hesitantly.

"They smell like sex," Levi replied. He took another deep inhale. "And Dwight."

"Dwight?" Danny questioned. Levi didn't respond though, too lost in his drunken undie sniffing.

Suddenly, Levi sprung to his feet and turned around, folding himself over the edge of the bed and spread his cheeks. "Fuck me, Danny. Fuck me as hard as you like. Give me your load."

Danny swallowed a lump of nerves lodged in his throat. The time had come. He was about to experience the other side of sex. He grazed a finger down Levi's hairy channel, prodding the rim of his arsehole. His dick throbbed with an intense want, desperate to cross the threshold of another first time.

"Do you have some lube?" Danny asked

"In the bottom drawer beside my bed."

Danny fetched the lube and squirted some into his hand, lathering his cock until it was wet and slippery. He then smeared a generous amount of lube into Levi's buttcrack, coating his anal ring. Danny hesitated for a moment, looked down at the beautiful, pink, puckered target, then moved forward, placed the head of his dick against Levi's arsehole, and pushed inward. He only managed to get the tip in and Levi groaned in pain.

"Do you want me to stop?" Danny asked in a panicky whisper.

"I'm fine," Levi hissed, even though he didn't sound fine. "Just fuck me. Fuck the shit out of me!"

Danny began stabbing his way inside Levi's arsehole, not stopping until his hairy balls were squished against the warmth of Levi's butt cheeks. The heat and tightness of Levi's strangling arsehole was on a completely different level to the sloppy heat of his mouth. He admired the way his dick was completely absorbed inside his brother's back passage. Then, for the first time in his life, Danny began to fuck. *I'm the man this time.*

Levi moaned and drooled into the mattress, his face pressed into the stinky briefs like they were some sort of pain relief. Danny tried to ignore the fact he was fucking the arse of someone who had their face pressed into a pair of his father's grotty gruts. It wasn't hard to shut out that thought though, Levi's tightness was immense and commanded his attention.

Danny's inexperience soon began to show as his sexual rhythm became one of shaky half-plunge thrusts, the friction of Levi's clasping anal lips bringing him dangerously close to a premature climax. He shut his eyes for a moment, thinking of stinky sneakers and splattered roadkill, to avoid losing his load too soon.

Once he was sure he was safe from losing his lollies, Danny wield his hand back and began paddling

Levi's left butt cheek with a fiery rain of brutal smacks—not because he wanted to but because he knew it was what Levi wanted.

In a strange way the dishing out of physical pain helped heighten his sexual stamina, forcing him to concentrate as much on the spanking as he was on the sight of his cock sliding in and out of Levi's anus.

"Your dick feels amazing," Levi praised him through gritted teeth.

"So does your sexy butthole," Danny panted, cringing a little at his choice of words. He began firing gooey wads of spit all over Levi's back, rubbing it in with his hand in between vicious spanks.

"Fuck, man. You really know how to make a guy feel like a cheap faggot."

Play the part. Play the part. Be mean. That's what he wants.

"That's because you ARE a cheap faggot."

Levi let out a high-pitched whine, like he was begging for more insults. In the gruffest voice Danny could muster, he supplied them.

"Everyone thinks you're so cool but here you are being your little brother's bitch," Danny went on. And so did Levi's arse. Up and down on Danny's dick. In and out. "Mind you, the only thing little here are these." He reached around and tugged on Levi's balls.

"You can be the big brother from now on," Levi said, his voice sounding more girl than boy. "You're the boss, Danny. You're the boss."

Hearing that was a relief, and Danny felt like he'd done enough to secure sex from Levi in the future. He stopped with the nasty insults, degrading spitting and violent spanking, focusing instead on enjoying having his dick inside such a beautiful—*and apparently a tad strange*—human being. The more he fucked, the more he found

Levi's internal friction begin to melt away like snow on a summer's day. He was still plenty tight but he was now loose enough for Danny to saw in and out with more ease.

Steady *ah, ah, ahhh* gasps fell from Levi's lips, accompanied by the sound of Danny's meaty balls slapping the flesh of Levi's arse cheeks.

It was all too much. And not nearly enough. Danny withdrew his dick nearly all the way out then slammed back in with all his might, forcing Levi to whimper.

Uh oh...

His testicles began tightening and a furious throbbing gripped his cock as he tipped past the point of no return. He tried to hold the orgasm back, clenching his toes and clenching his jaw but it was to no avail. His hips jerked forward as a breathy obscenity burst out of his lips when he started coming. His dick shook and shook and shook, ejaculating spurts of cum deep inside Levi's channel. Danny clutched Levi's hips to keep his balance, his cock still throbbing to the rhythm of its intense release.

Levi lifted his face and glanced over his shoulder. A devious glint shone in his eyes. "I can tell you needed that, buddy." He chuckled and slowly eased forward until Danny's dick plopped out of him. He straightened up and reached behind himself and unashamedly began fingering his white-filled hole. Wet, lurid noises filled the room from each rigorous plunge of his finger.

Danny lost his breath when he saw rivers of his own cum leaking from Levi's gaping hole. It looked sore and used, but most of all it looked like it now belonged to him.

"Fuck it feels weird," Levi said. "There's heaps of it. If I was a chick I'd definitely be pregnant after this." He laughed.

"I'm sorry," Danny said in a dejected tone.

Levi removed his finger and turned around. "What are you sorry for?"

"For not lasting longer."

"Don't stress about that," Levi replied. "There's always next time."

"You want to do it again?"

"If you want to."

"Yes please," Danny said far too eagerly.

Levi laughed. "You don't have to use your manners with me anymore, Danny. You just made me your bitch for life."

"I have?"

"Mm-hmm. You did good. Which means you're the boss from now on, buddy." Levi smirked at him and quietly added, "From now on whenever you feel horny you have full permission to fuck me."

"Wow... that's pretty cool."

"Yep. That's the perks of being the boss. You can fuck me whenever and however you like."

"But what if you don't want me to fuck you?"

"Then tough titties for me. I have to do what you say. That's how this arrangement works."

"So the next time I'm horny, I just say 'hey, Levi, let's have sex'?"

"Pretty much."

"But what if there's people around."

Levi chuckled. "Do you think you might get horny at the dinner table or something?"

"Maybe," Danny said honestly. "I get horny all the time."

"Then how about we have a magic word just in case that happens."

"A magic word?"

"A word that when you say it I will know it means you want to fuck me," Levi said, stroking Danny's deflating dick. "I'll let you choose it."

Danny spat out the first thing that came to mind. "Bongo drums," he said. "That's the word. Or words, rather."

"Bongo drums it is."

Danny leaned forward and surprised Levi by kissing him on the lips. He didn't give a toss that Levi's lips had just been buried in a material stained with his father's ball sweat, he needed to kiss the one and only person he'd ever shared this kind of love with.

Levi seemed taken aback by the kiss at first, but then he grabbed Danny's arms and slowly pulled him backwards onto the bed. Their lips did not break away from one another's and they rolled onto their sides and continued the kiss which turned into a long, needy plunder of lips and tongue.

Danny groaned into Levi's mouth, his hand stroking Levi's hair, adding affection to the passionate liplock. Levi let Danny's tongue dictate the rhythm to begin with but after a while he took over, dictating the speed and force of their tongues as he guided one of Danny's hands to his still-hard cock.

I totally forgot about you. Danny pumped his hand up and down Levi's shaft while they kissed, determined to help get him off. It only took about ten strokes and Levi filled Danny's mouth with a gasp as his dick fired white streaks of cum over Danny's wrist.

Danny groaned again and dropped his hand from Levi's hair down to his chest and began to play with one of his nipples.

Levi replied with a groan of his own, seeming like he enjoyed his nipple being tweaked and pulled. His erection surged forward, bobbing around and prodding Danny's deflated cock.

Levi slowly pulled his mouth away, a thread of saliva connecting their lips. "Thank you, Danny."

"You're welcome." Danny gave him a peck on the cheek.

Levi smiled back, appearing a little uneasy. "Is it okay if I go to sleep now?"

"Of course. It is super late." Danny stood up and let Levi adjust his body so he could slip under the covers. "Is it okay if I join you?"

"What do you mean?"

"Can I spend the night in here with you?"

Levi looked like he was about to say no but relented anyway. "I guess so. But just make sure you're out of here before Mum and Mark wake up."

"I can do that." Danny raced around to the other side of the bed and scooted in beside his brother, wrapping him into a kissy cuddle. He could feel how tense Levi was with the affection being given but Levi didn't tell him to let go or stop kissing. Danny clung to him like a lifejacket, enjoying the feel of their slick limbs tangled together beneath the crisp white sheet. Levi dozed off within minutes, his sleepy exhales warming Danny's neck.

Two hours later, when the sun began to creep through the gaps in the curtains, Danny gave his sleeping lover a tender kiss on the cheek and snuck back to his own room. As he lay in bed, his head fuzzy with wonderful feelings, he knew he and Levi weren't just brothers anymore. They were much, much more. He wasn't sure what he could to do to say thank you to Levi for all these wonderful feelings, but Danny knew he would have to do something to show Levi just how much he loved him.

CHAPTER 14

Levi awoke to bright sunlight streaming in through his bedroom window. A glorious day was in store. Too bad he didn't feel glorious. His head pounded like an alarm clock and his mouth was dryer than the Australian Outback. He hadn't felt this rancid in a long time. His liver had taken a hammering last night and for the most part the evening was a blur.

He remembered going with peach to the Beaten Path nightclub, Brad begging Peach for a ticket to the upcoming Flyer's Ball, being approached by Sophie and fuckface Lucas who coughed up a half-arsed apology, and then... drinking way too fucking much.

After that, he didn't remember a whole lot of anything. But somehow or another, he'd ended up back home in bed.

Did Peach pay for me to come home in a taxi? He figured that was a pretty safe bet. There was no way she would have let him drive home wasted. Although it had been the sensible thing to do, it bothered him knowing that now he'd have to try and scrape together enough money for a taxi to go back and collect his shitty vehicle.

Fuck my life.

Stifling a yawn, he threw back the covers and rolled his naked body out of bed, and ambled over to the window. As he stood there, admiring the scenic view of the leafy neighbourhood, he absentmindedly scratched his butt crack which felt oddly wet to the touch. He stroked his butt crack again, prodding his sloppy hole with a finger before bringing his finger around to inspect the slippy substance. "What the…?"

Swimming into fuzzy focus came Danny's face. His gleaming grin. His hairy legs. The smooth plain of his chest. And the throbbing pulse of his curved five-incher that had ejaculated hot pulsing semen inside Levi's body.

OH MY GOD!

Levi's stomach curled in a way that had nothing to do with his hangover. He clenched his butt cheeks, acutely aware that he was full with Danny's tremendous load. He ran to his en-suite and slammed the door behind him, leaning heavily against it, heart pounding in his chest as he gulped at the air like a fish out of water.

He had to calm down.

Had to get a grip.

Had to keep his shit together.

He stumbled over to the bathroom sink and gazed at the mirror. His reflection staring back at him was white as a ghost. He ran some water into the bowl and splashed it over his face. He gripped the bowl with both hands and rested against it head down.

He lifted his head and dragged a hand through his hair. "This is bad," he said. "Really fucking bad." He wasn't sure why this was worse than what they'd already done together but instinctively Levi knew that it was.

Despite the split-second flashes of Danny's naked body, Levi's head was still cloudy, and the events of the previous night were mostly shrouded in mysteries he was almost sure would never be fully revealed. But one thing he knew for sure—his relationship with Danny would never be the same again.

After a long shameful moment on the toilet, Levi ran the shower and scrubbed his body clean, hoping he could wash the memory of last night away. Once he was out of the shower and dried, he threw on a pair of sweatpants and padded his way—barefoot and shirtless—downstairs.

Levi's eyebrows flew up upon entering the kitchen when he spotted his stepfather sat at the kitchen table with Ameesh, their new neighbour. It wasn't the guest that made Levi take notice, it was the pathetic outfit Mark had on. A white shirt covered in multi-coloured dots accompanied with a silver-glittery bowtie. *Fucking chump*, Levi thought. He ignored them both—and his stepfather's outfit—and made his way to the fridge and pulled out a bottle of orange juice.

"Aren't you going to say hello?" Mark's voice attacked his ears.

"Hey." Levi released the tension from his shoulders and nodded. "Ameesh."

"Morning, Levi," Ameesh replied with a wry smile, his eyes zeroing in on Levi's bare chest and sagging sweatpants. "Hard night last night, was it?"

"Something like that," he mumbled in response before downing a mouthful of juice straight from the bottle.

"You will have to forgive Levi," Mark said. "He doesn't really do mornings. Even if the morning is only minutes away from the afternoon."

"No need to apologise," Ameesh said. "I remember being his age. Sundays were all about staying in bed to sleep away my hangover."

"With the amount of times he comes home legless I would have thought Levi would be immune to hangovers by now." Mark chuckled.

"I'm not hung over," Levi snapped. "Just thirsty." The ghastly rainbow dots and glittery bowtie got the better of Levi, so he asked, "Is there a reason why you look like you're dressed to lure children into the sewer?"

"Very funny," Mark groaned. "I am dressed like this because I am going with the Fitzroy men's choir to sing to the old people in the Greenmeadows rest home. I wasn't supposed to be joining them today but with Danny cancelling his trip it means I can now go along."

Levi smirked. "Are youse being used as the audio form of euthanasia?"

"I'll have you know that the old people love us going up there to perform. It brightens their day."

"It brightens their day because they get to laugh at you dressed up like a dipshit."

Ameesh covered his mouth to hide his chuckle. It didn't work, slips of giggles fell out.

Mark smiled at Ameesh. "Don't encourage him. He already makes fun of me enough."

Ameesh grinned "Sorry. I do love watching father son bickering."

"He's not my father," Levi said quickly.

"Levi's right," Mark said. "I can't take credit for the ill-mannered bottle-guzzling superstar over there."

Ameesh cleared his throat, sounding nervous. He turned the conversation back to the choir. "Does the choir perform anywhere else? Or just for the elderly."

"We're quite often asked to go sing in church, and sometimes we have performed at the bowl as a supporting act for travelling musicians."

"That sounds fun," Ameesh said, his tone not really meaning it.

Mark sniffed an opportunity and pounced. "Would you like to join? We are always looking for new members."

Levi tried not to laugh at how Ameesh began squirming in his seat. "Uh, thank you for the offer, Mark, but singing isn't really my thing."

"It doesn't have to be your thing. We can all help teach you."

"Honestly, I'm a terrible singer."

"I thought your people were into singing and dancing though," Mark said.

Ameesh mustered a polite tone and replied, "Just because I am Indian doesn't mean I am out on the weekends auditioning for Bollywood film roles."

Levi groaned extravagantly. "Sorry about Mark. He can't help being a dickhead."

"It was just a joke," Mark snapped back. "And just so you both know, I wasn't actually talking about being Indian, I meant because you're a homosexual." The way Mark had emphasised "homosexual"—shit, just the fact he'd chosen it over the word gay—reeked of awkwardness.

The comment was so fucking cringe that Levi couldn't help but smile.

"Unfortunately, Mark, I don't come with the type of fabulosity as the gay men you might be thinking of," Ameesh said, his gruff voice not giving a hint of femininity. "But I can vouch for Martin being quite the Karaoke queen when he's had a few drinks. He might be keen to join. Emphasis on *might be*."

"I'll be sure to ask him when I get the chance to finally meet him," Mark said.

"Martin is still away attending a conference for work," Ameesh replied. "He's always off at the darn things, but when he gets back I promise to bring him over so you and Jenny can meet him."

"That will be great. Perhaps we could all have dinner. He might be more inclined to say yes to joining the choir if he's had a nice meal."

"You can only but try," Ameesh said. "Why are you so desperate for new choir members anyway?"

"Because it's lame and no one will join," Levi piped up.

"That's not the reason," Mark said, rolling his eyes. "It's because they keep dying."

Levi sniggered. "I told you it was audio euthanasia."

"No, smarty pants. They keep dying from old age. I am probably the youngest one in the group. Well, other than, Danny, of course, but he only sings with us sometimes."

"Where is Danny?" Levi asked cautiously, worried that if saying the boy's name too loud would suddenly make him appear.

"Your mum dropped him off in town this morning on her way to The Community."

"The Community?" Ameesh raised a questioning eyebrow. "Is that the hippy commune?"

Mark leaned back in his chair, hands over his tummy. "It's not a hippy commune. It's…" He paused, looking like he was trying to find a better way to describe his wife's spiritual sanctuary. He soon gave up. "Yeah, it's pretty much a hippy commune."

They all laughed.

It was one of the few things Mark and Levi agreed on. The Community was just a bullshit money making scheme run by its leader Johan Niemand who lured in wealthy housewives to donate ridiculous amounts of money to its coffers each month.

"While you are here," Mark said to Levi. "I wanted to say thank you."

Levi frowned. Those weren't words he was used to hearing from his stepfather. "What for?"

"For what you did for Danny on his birthday. I have never seen him look so happy."

"What did you do?" Ameesh asked, genuinely curious.

Got him drunk and then fucked the virginity out of him before sharing the story online with all my blog followers.

"Levi gave Danny a makeover. Danny looks amazing. I definitely approve."

Levi was surprised to hear Mark say this. "Really? I thought you liked him looking like a 40-year-old accountant?"

"What I prefer is for my son to be happy, and what you did for him has made him the happiest I have probably ever seen him. So thank you." A proud smile pulled at Mark's lips. "Mind you, as good as it is to see him so happy it means I have to worry now about him and girls. He's already come home with hickeys all over his neck, telling me all about how much more attention he's getting."

Ameesh chuckled. "Sounds like it must have been quite the makeover."

Mark nodded. "It really was. It's only been two days but he is already strutting around the house like he's a big stud."

Levi wasn't sure what was more pathetic; the idea of Danny strutting around like some sort of stud or Mark thinking his son could classify as one.

The sound of a phone blaring erupted from Ameesh's pocket and he pulled it out and looked at the screen. "Sorry. I have to take this. It's work." He stood up and answered the call, wandering towards the open door leading outside to the garden patio. Either he was being polite or he just didn't want them to hear the conversation.

With Ameesh out of the room, Levi seized the opportunity to try and cash in the good deed he'd done for Danny. "Hey, Mark."

"Yes?"

"I was wondering if it would be okay to have my credit card back."

Mark's face softened. For just a single moment, he looked at Levi with a small, affectionate smile, and then it vanished and was replaced with his typical sardonic eyebrow arch. "Have you found a job to pay off the fifteen grand you owe me?"

"No, but I was thinking you might want to give it to me as a reward for how nice I was to Danny."

Mark just laughed in response.

"Come on, you just said how I made Danny the happiest you've ever seen him. Surely that gives me some credit for some credit."

"How about trying to do good things because it is the right thing to do rather than cash in on it. As I have said I am grateful to you for the smile you have put on Danny's face but that smile does not negate the fact you have yet to learn how to handle money properly."

"Why are you being such a fucking dick," Levi whined. "Can't you be happy knowing you got rid of my car and left me with a shitheap. Isn't that punishment enough?"

"Swearing at me is not going to help your cause, Levi."

"Then what the hell is?"

"By being a man and learning to take care of yourself." Before Levi could respond, Mark spouted one of his favourite lines, "Responsibility breeds character and self-sufficiency breeds confidence. That is why I am not giving you back the credit card."

"I already have character and confidence."

"I would argue your character and confidence are not the kind I am talking about."

"Fucking hell," Levi muttered.

"Let's not argue," Mark said. "Instead, why don't you tell me all about this girl of Danny's."

"What girl?"

"The one who left his neck like he's been attacked by a vampire."

"Oh…" Levi stammered. "I, uh, I don't know her."

"Really? But Danny said you were the one who introduced him to her."

Danny you fucking moron.

Levi's mind scrambled for something to say while his stepfather stared at him waiting for an answer. He had a complete brain fart and blurted, "I think Danny fucked her." He winced even as he said it, but he couldn't take it back once it was out.

The random response worked though, saving him from giving details about the fictitious girl Danny had told his father about. Mark's face lost its hopeful glow and became replaced with a scowl. "That is not the way to talk about your brother and his… female friend." Mark's scowl slowly faded and became replaced with a cocky that's-my-boy look. "Mind you, I guess it was bound to happen sooner or later." He chuckled. "Us Candy men are quite irresistible."

Levi rolled his eyes. "No youse ain't."

"I'm including you in that."

"Are you?"

"Of course. You're a Candy, aren't you?"

Levi gaped as if stunned by the genuineness. "Since I am part of the family then I definitely should get the credit card back."

"You being part of the family has never been a question, you being sensible with money is."

Ameesh walked back inside, slipping his phone into his pants pocket. He didn't appear as happy as before he'd taken the call.

"Everything okay?" Mark asked.

"Not really." Ameesh sat back down at the table. "A victim in a case I have been working on has just passed away."

"Oh..." Mark said. "That's no good."

Ameesh ran a hand through his hair, sighing. "Phone calls like that are not a fun part of my job."

Mark nodded sympathetically. "Forgive me for being nosey but can I ask what's happened?"

"I'm not sure if you have read about it or not but over the past couple of months we have had a spate of robberies where a vehicle has been used to smash into local dairies and steal cigarettes."

"Yes. I've seen it covered a few times in the local paper. I haven't seen anything about it though for a week or more."

"Well, the dairy owner who was injured in one of the robberies just had his life support switched off."

"That's terrible," Mark said.

"Yes, it's very sad. He was only twenty-eight and has left behind a wife and three young children."

"I do hope the people responsible are caught and given what for," Mark said.

Levi leaned against the bench, listening to his stepfather and Ameesh discuss the need for tougher prison sentences for criminals. He didn't care much for the conversation but he felt safe in their presence, worried that if he went back to his bedroom he ran the risk of being cornered by Danny who could arrive home from town at any moment.

What am I going to do about that?

He was still unable to recall everything about last night but he knew enough to know he had a big problem on his hands. Danny had been pushing for a round two before Levi had given it to him, now that Danny had had another taste there was a risk of the boy thinking this would be a regular thing.

That ain't fucking happening.

Even if he did want Danny as a regular—which he most certainly did not—there was no way stepbrothers could be each other's fuck buddy. Especially when they lived under the same roof several days a week. That ran a huge risk of being caught, and Levi had no wish to be outed as being gay or bi or whatever the fuck he was, let alone the kind of person who fucked his school kid brother.

I should go stay at Josh's place for the next few days. That seemed the best plan. He could hide out there until Josh returned home from his holiday, spending each night laid out in Josh's bed sniffing Josh's briefs. The thought was intoxicating but it also triggered a small niggle in the back of Levi's mind like he was forgetting something. Then it hit him. Hit him hard.

Fuck. Fuck. fuck. FUUUUUCK!

Snippets of a particularly degrading scene flashed behind his eyes, forcing him to recall more of his submissive encounter with Danny's juvenile cock. *I sniffed Mark's underwear. I sniffed them while Danny fucked me!* Levi's stomach wobbled from the ghastly memory. He winced as he looked in his stepfather's direction, his eyes dropping to Mark's crotch, the home of a rich musky scent he shouldn't have been familiar with. *What the fuck is wrong with me?*

The grotesque knowledge of what he'd done made him furious and he wanted to blame Danny, or Mark, but neither of them were to blame for his fucked-up kink. It was on him. He was about to go get dressed and catch a taxi to get his car but then he overheard Mark say something that made the hairs on the back of his neck stand up.

"The crime rate out there is part of the reason we have chosen Wairua Valley to build—"

"What was that?" Levi cut in. "Did you say Wairua Valley?"

Mark nodded.

"What's being built at Wairua Valley?" Levi asked.

"It's where the council plans on building a new subdivision."

Levi's stomach dropped to his toes. Wairua Valley loosely translated to Spirit Valley, a scenic reserve and site of an old Maori Pa where the valley ran from forested foothills down to the coast. It was just south of Brixton and one of the few nice areas in close proximity to the shitty suburb. To most people it was just a lovely spot for a picnic but to Levi it was a gateway to the dead.

"The council can't put a subdivision there," Levi barked. "It's Maori land."

"Not the part I own."

"What? You own Wairua Valley?"

Mark nodded like it was no big deal. "The coastal area of the valley has been in the Candy Family for generations." He returned his attention back to Ameesh. "I suggested to the council last year that we should look at it for the site of a new affordable housing area. It's the perfect place because it is close to Brixton and can be used as a way to try and import some better-quality residents into that area. It will be a good thing for families looking to buy their first home."

"But it can't go there," Levi bleated.

Mark frowned. "Why can't it go there?"

"Because it just can't."

"As the person who owns the land, I am telling you that it can."

"Just because your family own some of the valley doesn't make it any less sacred."

"Since when did you become so concerned with the rights of the local iwi?"

"Considering I belong to that local iwi then it does concern me."

Mark scoffed. "Levi, you would be lucky if you had enough Maori blood in you to fill a big toe so don't give me that tangata whenua nonsense."

"It isn't nonsense. It's sacred land." Levi had never given a shit about his Maori heritage but when it came to Wairua Valley he was willing to care a great deal.

"Are you Maori?" Ameesh asked.

"On my father's side."

"I suppose that explains your nice tan," Ameesh said. If Levi hadn't been so stressed then he might have enjoyed reading into the flirtatious way his neighbour's eyes looked him up and down when he made that comment.

"I think you will find the tan comes from Levi's long heritage of being jobless and sunbathing by the pool," Mark said snidely.

"You can't build on that land, Mark. It's wrong," Levi said.

Mark sighed like he was losing his patience. "If it makes you feel better, the council have a team of archaeologists going there next week to search the grounds to see if they find any historical artefacts."

"What?" Levi blurted. "They're going to go dig up the ground?"

"I'm not too sure what they plan on doing but I think they just want to make sure that the area marked for the subdivision it isn't part of the ancient burial ground."

"And the subdivision is planned to be built at the coastal end?" Levi asked.

Mark nodded.

Oh fuck…

It was Ameesh's turn to make an insensitive joke. "I'm no archaeologist but after being a detective here the past five years I believe the only bones they will find that close to Brixton will be the bones of gang members and drug addicts with bad debts."

Levi gulped in horror while both men laughed. *Yeah, and the bones of my father.*

CHAPTER 15

Two minutes later, Levi slipped away and raced upstairs to his bedroom. The first thing he did was hunt down Mark's underwear, which he found buried at the bottom of his bed beneath the sheets. Holding the sweaty material of Mark's briefs between the tips of his fingers, Levi grimaced the whole way to the master bedroom where he dropped them in the laundry basket of the en suite.

With that gross chore taken care of, he went back to his bedroom to get some more clothes on. He had to get out to The Community as quickly as possible to tell his mother about their Wairua Valley problem. Maybe she could talk to Mark and get him to put an abrupt stop to the subdivision. That seemed unlikely but it would be worth a shot.

He cast a reluctant gaze towards his wardrobe, knowing that behind the door was the one thing in this world that reminded him how strong he could be. The bloodstained white t-shirt. He didn't want to get rid of it, he really didn't, but if his father's body was found then he wouldn't have a choice.

Thanks a lot Shay. You fucking idiot!

Shay had told Levi and his mum that Wairua Valley was the perfect place to bury the body, that no one would ever find Barry Buttwell in a million years. It turned out Shay was a fucking moron and didn't know what he was talking about. Mind you, it wasn't Shay who was to blame for why it was such a bad idea if the body be found. That was on Levi who had failed to do as he was told that night. A night that was etched in his memory like letters carved into a tombstone.

Seven years earlier

The gravel road leading into Wairua Valley was potholed and windy, the hills on either side covered in clumps of shrubby bush and blackberry plants. The further the road went, the bumpier it became, shaking Levi's bladder and bringing on a desperate need to pee. There was no time for stopping though, not when there was a body in the back of the van that needed burying.

Levi sat on the front seat between his mother and Shay, tension clotting the air around them. It was about two in the morning but thanks to a full moon acting like a 100-watt bulb the valley was well lit, allowing Levi to see the bare hills on either side and the glimmer of moonlight on the ocean ahead.

"Are you sure this is the right idea?" Levi's mother asked Shay, despite the fact they had discussed the plan for over an hour before loading Levi's father's corpse into the back of Shay's van.

Shay let out a frustrated sigh. "It's a little late to be questioning that now don't you think?"

"Is it though?" Levi's mother replied.

"Considering I've cut his hands off and pulled his teeth out then yeah, I think it might be a little fucking late, Jenny."

"There is no need to be angry with me. I was just wondering if there was another way. That's all." She folded her arms, huffing.

159

"I'm sorry for being angry but this is the only way," Shay said vehemently. "If we go to the police they are going to arrest one or all three of us, and I don't know about you but I'd rather not go to prison or see LP sent to juvenile detention."

"We could just tell them the truth," Levi's mother protested. "Surely they will believe us."

"Are you nuts? They aren't going to fucking believe us," Shay snapped, his hands pulling the staring wheel sharply to the right as the van manoeuvred a tight bend. The sharp turn sent Levi's dead father crashing into the wall of the van in the back, making a loud thudding clunk. "They will investigate us. All three of us. And you know they will find stuff out and paint a bad picture. Even if they do believe us, which they won't, do you really want the little prince growing up with the infamy of what his dad is?"

"Do we have to bring that up right now?" she said pointedly.

Levi sat between them as they continued arguing. He was hearing their panicked, heated words but at the same time he was so numb he didn't really register them. All he could do was look down at the front of the white t-shirt he had on which really wasn't all that white anymore. It was dark red all down the front, his father's blood having sprayed like a fountain when he'd sliced him with the knife he'd run and grabbed from the kitchen. He wasn't sad though. He was... he wasn't sure what he was but he knew he wasn't sad. Shay had said Levi had done the right thing, that he was brave and was a hero. Knowing that he had Shay's approval meant everything. If Shay said he'd done the right thing then Levi knew he must have.

Shay was shirtless, having ditched his singlet after it had become stained with blood. The rebel with a heart of gold was toned and muscular, especially his biceps which bulged with definition as he white-knuckled the steering wheel. Each time Levi found himself getting too stressed, he would cast a sly glimpse to his right and admire Shay's muscles, enjoying the warm feeling in his abdomen the sight gave him. He wasn't sure what the feeling was about but it was a good feeling and he had found himself liking the way Shay looked more and more the past year. The guy had the most beautiful blue eyes and Levi wished so much it wasn't so dark right now so he could see them properly.

Each time the van made a hard-right turn, Shay's arm would lift up and his armpit would release a faint whiff of body odour. Rather than be grossed out by the manly smell, Levi found it calming in a strange way. It was familiar and protective and it let him know he had nothing to worry about.

"This is so not how tonight was supposed to go," Levi's mother whispered. "You were only supposed to talk with him. Not kill him!"

"Why do you keep saying it like I'm the one who—" Shay didn't finish his sentence. He cast a guilty glance in Levi's direction before clearing his throat and adding, "If it wasn't for, LP, I wouldn't be alive. Somebody up there was definitely looking out for me."

"Let's just hope God's light keeps protecting us," Levi's mother replied.

"I guess now we know why the sick fuck insisted you spent weekends away from the house," Shay mumbled. "So he could—"

"Could we please not talk about that," Levi's mother hissed. "We have enough to deal with without having to talk about such unpleasant things."

"Sorry," Shay mumbled, changing gears to round another sharp bend.

Shay and Levi's mother had been horrified at the nightmare they had discovered inside the house. Levi wasn't. He'd sort of always known his dad did bad things while they were out of the house. For starters, Lucky—his old imaginary friend—had told Levi years earlier all about what his father liked to do, that Barry Buttwell liked to play funny games. The other reason why Levi knew was because over the past twelve month his father had started letting him see some of the stuff that went on while his mother was out of the house; weird games with strange men who appeared to hand over lots of money just to sit in their crumby lounge and drink beer while they played these weird games. That was how Levi had scored himself a television in his bedroom, a rare gift from his father on the provider that Levi never told anyone about what happened. And Levi honoured the agreement, not whispering a word of went on until last week when he'd confided in Shay about one particular game his dad had made him play that had left him sore in weird places.

"I am just grateful that you came home when you did, LP." Shay let one hand off the steering wheel and ruffled Levi's hair affectionately. "I owe you my life, bro."

Levi glowed with pride.

Levi's mum clasped her hands together and began to pray, soft murmurs of the lord's prayer falling from her lips.

The van started to descend a small hill and native bush began to frame both sides of their path and he could hear the ocean roaring in the distance. Tree limbs dangled inward like monster claws, grabbing for the road, leaving only shreds of moonlight peeking through. The van continued chugging along in the dark, 'till eventually they came to a large circular clearing signalling the end of the road.

Shay slammed the brakes on, bringing them to an abrupt stop and sending Levi's dead father hurtling into the back of their seats, jolting them like an earthquake.

Levi's mother screamed in fright.

"It's okay, Jenny," Shay said soothingly. "We're fine… we're fine" He turned the engine off then tapped Levi on the arm. "What about you, LP? Are you all good?"

Levi nodded.

They all climbed out of the van and Shay and Levi's mother went to the boot and grabbed out a shovel each.

"Me and your mum need to go find a spot where we can bury him," Shay said. "So I want you to wait here until we get back."

"Why can't I come with you two," Levi said, not at all wanting to be left alone with his father's dead body.

"We won't be long, LP," Shay replied. "Me and your mum need to go dig the hole and we need you to act as a look out just in case you see anyone coming."

Up until now he'd felt nothing but brave but the thought of being left alone with the man he'd murdered was threatening to unravel his nerves. Levi looked at his mother, his eyes begging for her to stay with him.

"You'll be fine, darling," she said. "We won't be far away."

Levi wanted to argue with them, demand he be allowed to help dig the hole, but he didn't want Shay to think he was scared. "Okay. I'll stay here and be the lookout."

"You're the man, LP," Shay replied with a smile. "We will dig as quickly as possible. And can you empty his pockets for me while we're gone?"

"Is that really necessary?" Levi's mother sighed angrily.

"Of course it's necessary," Shay said. "It has to be done and LP doesn't mind."

"How do you know if he minds or not?" Levi's mother glared at Shay. "Maybe you should stop barking out orders for just one damn second."

"Gee, I'm so sorry for trying to take control of a fucked-up situation," Shay snapped back. "You know I love you both but we need to get this shit done. Now!"

Levi found it strange to see his mother and Shay bickering like this. Shay usually called her Mrs Buttwell, spoken like a school boy addressing a teacher, but tonight he was letting the name Jenny slip through his lips as if he'd been calling her by her first name all his life. It was weird. But then Shay was right about it being a fucked-up situation, so perhaps they could be forgiven for not acting like themselves.

Levi's mother shook her head. "There's still no need to be such a bossy—"

"It's fine," Levi said, cutting his mother off. "I can do it. I'll empty his pockets."

"Are you sure, darling." She flashed him a look of concern. "You don't have to if you don't want to."

"I don't mind." Levi did mind but he minded more disappointing Shay.

"Cheers, bro." Shay smiled at him before glancing at Levi's mum. "Shall we?"

With a steely nod, Levi's mother followed Shay towards the trees, leaving Levi alone with the dark lump in the back of the van. He glanced around the moonlit valley, alertly surveying the surroundings, making sure no one was nearby. It was highly unlikely anyone would be outside wandering this far down the valley but he couldn't shake the feeling of being watched. But maybe that was God watching and judging him for what he'd done.

It took him almost five minutes to build up the courage to lean into the back of the van and rummage through his father's pockets. His hand trembled as his fingers wormed their way into his father's pants pocket, quickly fetching out his wallet and keys. As he pulled his hand away, his father's body made a farting noise.

"Holy fuck," Levi yelped, scurrying backwards. He stared wide-eyed at his father's body, expecting the man to get up and throttle him. But nothing happened. Not a thing. "It's okay. It's fine. It's just... just the body releasing gas," Levi reassured himself. They'd heard the same noise while carrying his father into the van and Shay had said then that was sometimes what happened.

Levi calmed himself down and reached forward again to check the other pocket. Just as his hand gripped what he assumed to be his father's cell phone, he let it go when he saw the lights of a car coming towards them. He pulled his empty hand out and raced towards the treeline. "Shay. Shay!" he called out. "Someone's coming. Quick."

Shay came busting out of the trees about twenty seconds later. "What?"

"A car. A car is coming." Levi pointed up the valley at the incoming lights.

"Fuck," Shay muttered. He threw his shovel on the ground and stormed towards the van and closed the boot. "Get in the front and duck down. Let me handle this."

Levi did as he was told, climbing into the front seat and hiding under the dashboard. It felt like a small eternity for the car to get to where the van was parked but in reality it was probably more like thirty seconds. His stomach dropped when he heard the car turn its engine off and someone get out.

"Shady fucking Shay," said a man's voice. "What the fuck are you doing out here?"

Shay laughed. "I could ask you the same question."

"Let me guess, you're out here for a root." said the mystery man.

Shay laughed again. "I was trying to until you turned up."

There was a pause before the man's voice replied. "Me and Beth were coming down here to do the same thing."

A woman burst out in a drunken giggle, "Shut up."

"Who you got in there?" the man asked. "Are they hot?"

"Of course," Shay replied.

"Do you think your girl would be keen to hook up with Beth while you and me watched."

Shay laughed while the woman snapped, "Don't be disgusting. I ain't a lezza."

"Go on baby," the man replied in a greasy voice. "I'd love to watch you do some licky licky."

Shay sniggered. "Sorry, bro, but my lady is only interested in licking one thing tonight."

The man laughed. "No worries, Shady Shay. Can't blame a man for trying. We'll let youse have this end of the valley. We'll go back the other way."

"Cheers, bro. I'll catch you up," Shay said before cheekily adding, "Happy rooting."

The car started up and slowly drove away and Shay came over and peered inside the van's passenger window. "You can come out now, LP."

Levi climbed out and looked up the valley, his eyes following the car's lights driving off in the other direction. "Who was that?"

"Just some clown I know," Shay replied before glancing into the back of the van. "Did you empty his pockets like I asked?"

Levi handed Shay his father's wallet and keys. "I got these but I—"

They both flinched when Levi's mother's shrill voice pierced the air. "What's the problem?" she called out.

Levi and Shay spun around and saw her standing on the treeline, a shovel in her hand.

"It's taken care of now," Shay called back.

"Good. Can we hurry up then and get this over with," she said, then stomped back into the forest.

Shay looked back at Levi. "Help me get him out the van."

"Shay I—"

"Let's save the chatting for later, LP," Shay said abruptly. "I don't mean to sound angry at you but we have work to do."

Levi nodded, choosing not to tell his idol that he'd not yet emptied his father's pockets. Besides, it wasn't that big of a deal was it? Not if they were going to remove the clothes before rolling him into the grave.

It took all their might to drag the heavy body out the back of his van and drag it across the ground and through the trees to where his mother was waiting beside the freshly dug grave in front of misshaped tree. Shay pointed the torch down at the body while the three of them gathered around staring at the empty shell that had once been a husband, father and friend. It wasn't a pretty sight. Levi's father was soaked in blood, his mouth was a mangled black mess and his hands were nothing more than bloodied stumps.

"Someone has to take his clothes off," Shay said as they stood around the body.

"Undo his belt and I'll pull his pants off," Levi's mother said to Shay.

"No way! I ain't putting my hand anywhere near that dirty cunt's penis."

"For goodness sake." Levi's mother knelt down and undid Levi's father's belt before tugging his pants halfway down his thighs.

Shay pointed the torch at the man's piss-stained underwear, sniggering. "That's too funny. The dirty fucker pissed himself."

Rather than be grossed out or find it funny, Levi was overcome with pride and confidence. Laying on the ground before him was a bully who had made his life hell for years, a man who had got a kick out of abusing him in dark and shameful ways, constantly telling Levi how pathetic and small he was. He wouldn't be doing that anymore. Not now Levi had reduced him to nothing more than urine-soaked flesh. So no, the sight of Barry Buttwell's piss-stained undies wasn't funny, it was empowering.

Shay sniggered again. "I guess he had to give himself temporary relief before he gets an eternity of whatever's waiting for him."

"What's that?" Levi's mother asked, getting to her feet just before she'd finished pulling the pants fully off.

They all spun around and saw in the distance another set of car headlights coming up the valley.

"For fuck sake," Shay grumbled. He looked around bewilderedly before spitting out, "Just roll him in the grave."

"But what about his clothes?" Levi asked, panicked.

"Fuck his clothes. We just need to get him buried." Shay used his foot to try and push the body into the hole.

"But—"

"No buts, just help me. Quickly!"

They all knelt down and pushed and pushed until Levi's father crumpled into the grave with a grim *thud*. Shay and Levi's mother began shovelling dirt on top of the body at a mad pace. Levi helped by scooping dirt in with his hands. The hole was only half-filled by the time the car had made it to the clearing. They all ducked down, hiding behind a tree, waiting to see what would happen. After two minutes the car just drove off.

"Phew," Shay sighed. "Let's keep filling it in."

They finished filling the hole in and tamped the dirt down with the shovels. Shay then went around gathering leaves which he scattered over the grave. "I think we're good," he said.

"Thank goodness for that," Levi's mother said. "Let's go."

"You two head back to the van. I've got one more thing I have to do," Shay said. He dropped the torch on the ground and widened his stance. His fingers fumbled with the belt of his jeans 'till the crisp sound of his zipper coming down pricked the quiet air.

"What the hell are you doing?" Levi's mother squawked.

"Paying my respects." Shay jutted his hips forward, and groaned lightly as he began splattering piss all over the grave.

"That is so immature," Levi's mother huffed, storming off.

Levi knew he should have followed his mum back to the van but he stayed where he was, overcome with a curiosity to take a closer look at what Shay was doing. He inched forward, trying to catch a glimpse of Shay's dick.

"You should take a leak too," Shay suggested, unaware of Levi's queer curiosity. "Ain't no better way to show a man who's the boss than pissing all over them." He laughed.

"I don't need to go," Levi whispered. He found himself holding his breath as he watched and listened to the strong stream of piss that gushed from Shay's dick and splashed onto the ground. It was too dark to make out much detail but Levi felt a squirm in his tummy that told him he would like to see Shay do this in the light of day.

When the heavy flow from the tip of Shay's cock slowed to a dribble, he shook off the remaining drops of piss and put his cock away. He zipped his pants up and patted Levi on the back. "Let's hit the road."

Levi nodded and turned to walk away. They were nearly out of the woods when Shay surprised him by swooping behind him and wrapping him into a hug, swaying their bodies gently in the wind.

"I'm so sorry you had to go through all this," Shay whispered in his ear. "I want you to know, bro, that I will always be there for you. Always."

"Thank you," Levi croaked, the hairs on his neck standing on end.

The hug was nothing but innocent, just Shay's way of letting Levi know he cared and was there for him. Levi cared for Shay too but as Shay's sticky-with-sweat chest pressed against his back Levi couldn't deny the presence of juvenile arousal rolling in his lower abdomen. It was the same storm of sexy adrenalin he'd gotten when Stacy Pomare had let him touch her breasts when they'd made out behind the bike sheds at school. It seemed odd that a boy could have the same effect on him but this wasn't just any boy. This was Shay. The coolest and bravest guy Levi had ever met. That probably meant it was alright, right? Yet Levi knew instinctively not to tell Shay about what was happening in his pants.

As the hug lingered, Levi swallowed hard, trying to ignore his swelling cock that began to strain against the rough fabric of his jeans. They were mere feet away from a man who was probably on his way to hell but in this tender moment Levi felt like he was in heaven, resting in the arms of a saviour.

CHAPTER 16

"I feel magnificent," Lucas said as he drove towards the hospital. He really was feeling magnificent and he couldn't stop himself from declaring it out loud on repeat. "I feel magnificent. Mag-fucking-nificent!" After a rough few years, and even rougher past few weeks, he was beginning to feel like his luck was changing.

Life had been pretty tough since dropping out of high school when him and Sophie found out she was pregnant. It got even tougher when he busted his knee and suffered a nasty concussion, ending what should have been a promising career in professional rugby. Still, it wasn't all bad. He was with the girl of his dreams and together they had created the most beautiful baby girl in the world. Asking for much more would have been greedy, Lucas always thought.

But after he was made redundant from his job at the chicken farm three months ago, that's when life had really got tough. It never bothered him how he'd never finished high school—he was smart enough to know that he'd never been smart enough for it to matter. He could even handle losing his dream of one day playing for the All Blacks. But losing his job and his ability to be a provider for his family, that was really fucking tough. It had crushed his soul and mocked his dignity, making him feel less of a man.

When Lucas was growing up his father—known as Shifty to his mates, and for good reason—had struggled to hold down a job and often turned to crime to supplement his income but the man never failed to provide for his wife and children. Even if his father was in jail—which he quite often was up until Lucas turned twelve—he'd always make sure before going inside that there was enough money set aside to take care of the family.

That was the kind of man Lucas had hoped to be for his own family. A provider. A man they could count on. Ideally he would have done it without resorting to crime but as his father had told him when Lucas went to him almost in tears after struggling to find a new job "beggars can't be choosers." It was that advice, and the fear of letting Sophie and Mia down, that had forced Lucas to accept Uncle Dwight's offer of employment.

"You can work for me 20 hours a week but only if you help me with a small side venture I've got planned," Uncle Dwight had said.

"What's the side venture?" Lucas had asked.

"The kind you can't tell anyone about it."

Lucas felt he didn't have any choice but to take Uncle Dwight up on his offer of helping him with his side venture. It was the only job he could find, and the 20 hours of lawnmowing on its own wasn't going to be enough to support his young family. Not with the shockingly high cost of rent and ever-increasing food prices.

Sophie had no idea about the other work he was doing for Uncle Dwight. She still didn't, and Lucas planned to keep it that way. She wouldn't tolerate a partner who committed crime and ran the risk of ending up in jail.

To begin with it had been going pretty well—until it didn't. And when it went bad, it went real fucking bad. But waking up today, Lucas really did feel like his luck had changed. *I am a good person and good things are coming my way.*

"I feel magnificent," he said again. It seemed silly but he owed the wave of positivity he was riding all to yesterday. A day that had been packed with drama and tremendous ups and downs.

It had started with an up: Brad visiting.

Then a down: Finding out about Uncle Dwight's house burning down.

Another up: Driving to Dwight's property and seeing that the police hadn't found anything they shouldn't have.

Another down: stressing the whole drive home and worrying if Brad would have left before he got back.

Up: coming home and finding Brad hadn't left while he was out and was still keen to go town with them.

Down: Sophie forcing him to apologise to fuckface Candy.

And another Down: being told by Peach that Brad was a poofter.

Up: Brad telling him that Peach was full of shit and just making it up because he'd rejected her when she'd asked him out for a date.

Then one last up: coming home and making love to Sophie before falling asleep with her wrapped in his arms. A man couldn't have a better up than that.

It was the combination of all these ups and downs that had made him realise that despite the downs the ups won every time. "I feel magnificent!" He yahooed it so loud out the Ute's window that people walking on the footpath heard him and gave him a funny look. He didn't care. He felt magnificent.

As he turned the Ute into the hospital carpark, he glanced across the road at the café where he'd decked the shit out of Levi a week earlier. He smiled, remembering how good it felt to punch the rich prick in his smug prettyboy face.

"He totally deserved it though." Lucas smiled to himself. "And it made me feel magnificent."

As he parked up, he reached over to the passenger's side and picked up one of two bunches of flowers that he'd picked from the side of the road. One was to give to Sophie when he got home and the other was for Sameer. Lucas wasn't sure how much a man would enjoy getting flowers but he figured Sameer's wife and family might appreciate the effort.

Lucas had been coming to the hospital nearly every day since the accident, dropping by to check on the man who'd been in the wrong place at the wrong time. Lucas was wracked with guilt about what he'd done and he had hoped that by visiting to check on Sameer that it might help alleviate some of his guilt.

Dwight had warned him to stay away from the hospital, that it was too risky, but Lucas hadn't listened. The ramraid had all happened so fast that neither of them had even realised there was a man crushed beneath the debris of the shop wall. Lucas had read about what they had done the next day in the newspaper but at the time the newspaper said the man only had a broken leg. That sucked for the poor guy but at the time Lucas just figured it wasn't a hugely bad deal, it was after all only a broken leg. He certainly hadn't felt guilty enough to stop from helping Dwight commit another ramraid five days later.

But that is when shit got bad. Got really, really bad. Neither Dwight or Lucas had seen that the day after the initial report about the ramraid leaving a shopkeeper with a broken leg was a follow-up article saying that the man's injuries were worse than previously thought and that he had slipped into a coma and was now fighting for his life.

Lucas had totally freaked out. Not only had he nearly killed a man, he had gone on and committed another crime days later while the man was in hospital on the edge of death. He knew how bad that looked. Like he and Dwight didn't care about what they had done. But they did care. Well, Lucas did at least. Dwight didn't appear quite so riddled with guilt about what had happened but then it wasn't Dwight who had been the one driving.

As a way to try and cope with his crippling guilt, Lucas began visiting the hospital with flowers each day, leaving them at the nurses' station with a card attached to say who they were for. During one of his flower deliveries, Lucas bumped into Asha Patel, Sameer's wife, who happened to be at the nurses' station when he was handing the flowers over. She was so lovely to him, thanking him profusely and saying how touched she was that so many people in the community were reaching out to the family. He wished he could have told her the truth why he was there but of course he couldn't. Instead, he came up with a cockamamie story about how he was a regular customer at the dairy her and her husband owned, telling her he had gotten to know her husband quite well during his many errands to pick up bottles of milk on his way home from work. Thankfully she hadn't questioned the story, if she had then she would have realised Lucas lived nowhere near their dairy. Instead she had just smiled and asked him if he would like to go with her and sit with Sameer for a while.

He should have politely declined but no, his guilt forced the words out of his mouth before he could stop them. "Are you sure? Would that be okay?"

"Of course," she had replied with a smile filled with warmth. "Sameer will want his friends to be with him."

Lucas had then followed her down the corridor of the long ward until they entered a private room where Sameer lay in bed pricked with tubes and hooked up to beeping machines that were keeping him alive. As shocking as it was to see Sameer so helpless and injured, the worst part of entering the room was discovering that Sameer was a father to three young children—two boys and a girl.

It had taken all of Lucas's strength not break out into tears. He managed to keep it together though and stayed for fifteen minutes, chatting with Asha and playing with the kids to try and put a smile on their faces. Asha seemed to appreciate his company too and had told him before he left to "Please feel free to visit again."

After that visit, Sameer's wife began letting him in to sit with Sameer each time he visited. Lucas always felt like crying when he saw the man he'd nearly killed but behind the brewing tears was the knowledge that he was doing a good thing, he was helping, he was earning forgiveness.

He was also being punished for his crime by being unable to cash in on it. Dwight had said they could make a healthy side income if they kept low and sold to the right people, but after Sameer had been hurt Dwight had put a stop to all plans on selling the cigarettes, insisting they would have to wait for a few months until the heat around the case died down. Lucas didn't complain, even though he and Sophie were desperate for money. It didn't feel right to profit from something so terrible. He just hoped that Sameer would get better soon—Asha said they were hopeful he would—so Dwight could begin selling the stock so some money could come in.

Lucas pushed through the hospitals front entrance and was greeted with a pocket of warmth and the scent found in hospitals everywhere. He pressed the button for the fifth floor and stepped inside, humming a happy tune to himself. In the lift next to him was a middle-aged woman giving him a shifty glance. He wasn't sure if he was weirding her out with his humming or his appearance. Lucas knew that some people could be intimidated by his height and strong build, like they worried he would turn into the incredible hulk and rip their head off or something. Not a chance. He was a softy at heart really. Unless it was Levi he was talking with, then Lucas was more than happy to play the role of thuggish brute.

When the lift opened up, Lucas stepped out and made his way into the ward, passing the nurses' station where he smiled and waved at Angela, one of the nurses he'd become friendly with over the past few weeks. "Hi, Angela," he replied chirpily, continuing on to Sameer's room.

Angela ran after him, tapping him on the arm. "Sorry, Lucas. I don't think now is a good time."

"Oh. Are they changing the sheets?" Lucas asked. "I don't mind waiting."

Angela's face softened and in a warm but serious tone she answered, "Sameer passed away this morning."

Lucas winced, feeling like he'd just been shot.

"I'm very sorry," Angela said.

Tears leaked out of Lucas's eyes. "Uh, okay." He wiped his tears dry and scurried away, feeling anything but magnificent.

CHAPTER 17

The Community was only about five minutes from Levi's house but he'd had to take an hour-long detour to get there. The first leg of the detour involved catching a taxi into town to pick his car up from Peach's place. He hadn't bothered going in to see her, just jumped in his car and quickly drove to Josh's house so he could give Phoebe her food before continuing on his emergency journey back out to The Community.

He zoomed along the motorway, well-above the speed limit, desperate to get to his mother and tell her about their Wairua Valley problem. Barry Buttwell was probably just a pile of bones draped in baggy clothes by now but Levi knew that inside those clothes was a cell phone with incriminating evidence. If anyone saw what was on that phone questions would be asked, investigations launched, and arrests could be made. Even if Levi and his mother could avoid prison by pleading self-defence—which after years of lying about his father's whereabouts a jury would probably find doubtful—Levi knew that a scandal like this would taint him for life. He wouldn't just be known as the guy who killed his father but, depending on what the authorities uncovered about Barry Buttwell, Levi would also be known as the son of a monster.

As the edge of the suburb begun to give way to lifestyle blocks and vineyards, Levi slowed down and turned into the ill-defined dirt driveway which led to The

Community's visitor centre. Johan Niemand had bought the land when it was just grassy paddocks and had over the years turned it into an oasis of native trees, luscious gardens and a place of spiritual learning. Along the way, Levi drove past three small cabins tucked amongst the greenery, each with a sign stating its purpose. *Yoga, psychic ability, healing arts.* None of them appeared to be in use so he continued driving until he was parked up outside the front of the visitors centre. Aside from his mother's car, the place looked deserted.

Designed to look like some sort of Japanese temple, the visitors centre contained a function room, library and small café. Potential new members would come here to find out more about The Community and how could they sign up for one of the wacky classes Johan held. It was pretty simple; you just had to sign a contract that locked you into paying a gross amount of money each week for the privilege of 'freeing your mind.'

Being a Sunday, the visitor's centre was closed, but he found the door to the function room wide open. He stepped inside and saw a sea of grey carpet and black chairs. At the front of the room was a stage with a large projection screen behind it. Judging by the way all the seats were scattered about, Levi assumed there must have been been a seminar held earlier in the day.

"Hello. Anybody here?" he called out but got no response.

He exited the room and walked back outside and went around to the rear of the building where there was a large concrete patio overlooking the vast backyard that ran down a gentle hill. The section was massive, easily four or five acres in size, and was a mishmash of forest and brightly-coloured flowerbeds. Running through the centre of the picturesque scene was a little creek that cascaded down the slight hill, worming its way through the patches of trees and flower gardens. Levi could see why his mother liked coming here so much.

He scanned the land below, hoping to spot his mother somewhere in the dream-like landscape. *Where the heck are you?* He was about to descend the stairs to go hunt for her below but just before he did, he spotted his mother walking out of a group of trees before crossing a little white bridge over the creek. *There you are.* Just seeing her calmed him down a lot. At least together they would be able to try and solve the Wairua Valley problem.

Levi tried not to laugh at how ill-suited his mother looked clopping through nature. Dressed in high heels and an elegant red pantsuit, she looked more like a saucy business woman than a housewife hippy.

A few seconds later The Community's owner, Johan Niemand, also appeared from the trees and joined Levi's mother on the small bridge. Even from a few hundred metres away, Levi recognised the man on account of his long grey hair tied up in a manbun. Like always, the con artist guru was shirtless, showing off his dark tan and smooth chest. The dude probably had the most ripped body you would find on a man so close to sixty, a life of yoga and a diet of seeds and foul-tasting smoothies did a body good apparently.

Levi went to wave to get his mother's attention but just as he went to raise his hand, Johan spun her around for a hug. Levi frowned, wondering what the hell the man was playing at. *It's just a hug,* he told himself. *Hippies do shit like that.* But the hippy hug lingered and lingered and lingered until eventually it became a steamy hippy kiss and Johan's weathered hands slipped up Levi's mother's blouse, greedily groping her breasts. Levi wanted to run down there and deck the pervy old prick for taking advantage of his mother but it appeared that his mother was a very willing participant. Her lips were kissing Johan back while her hands did some roaming of their own, dipping into the front of Johan's shorts and—*Oh gross. Don't pull it out!* His mother didn't obey his mental command. Instead, she dropped to her knees and placed Johan's manhood in her mouth.

Levi turned on his heels and ran away. His stomach was sick, the image of his mother sucking off some old fart was going to be ingrained in his memory forever. *Is she fucking mad?* She must have been. Levi couldn't think of any other explanation. His feet carried him all the way back to the carpark where he jumped inside his car and clutched the steering wheel, feeling dizzy. *No wonder she spends all her fucking time out here.*

"This is bad. This is so fucking bad."

What his mother was doing wasn't just cheating, it was risking their entire way of life. If Mark found out she was being unfaithful then the shit would hit the fan in a big way. *He would divorce her. He totally would.* Mark was all about loyalty and there would be no way in hell he would forgive her cheating on him, even if telling her to leave would break his heart. Levi knew he could forget about staying living at the house if his mum wasn't there. Mark would take great delight in kicking his unemployed arse out of his house. And it was Mark's house, no matter how at home Levi felt there.

Images of being forced to move back to Brixton and a life of poverty plagued his mind. Mark was ridiculously generous to Levi's mother but if they separated, she wouldn't get a cent. The prenup would see to that. There was no way Levi could go back to living in a rundown shithole after becoming accustomed to only the best in life. Gone would be the overseas holidays, the designer clothes, the shopping sprees, everything— including his social status.

Without money his position in the Fitzroy Flyers would be unattainable, it was a group for the wealthy and privileged. Josh and Peach would keep in touch—Peach only in private—but he wouldn't be invited to all the clubs and parties anymore. Fuck no. You couldn't be a Fitzroy Flyer if you were poor, people from Brixton were little better than a Benson Banger in the eyes of his wealthy friends.

His hands curled into fists and he punched the door of his car. "You stupid fucking bitch!" he screamed.

You need to calm down. Stressing about this won't help fix the other problem.

His inner voice was right. As bad as what his mother was doing right now, it wasn't as bad as being prosecuted for murder, and as much as he wanted nothing more than to drive away and pretend like he hadn't just seen Johan's slimy prick plop inside his mother's mouth, he had to speak with her so they could figure out what they were going to do about their problem.

Rather than risk walking back to the scene of oral crime, Levi opted to stay in his car and beep the horn. He pressed down on the horn, letting it corrupt the tranquillity with its ugly urgent noise. He just kept pressing it, holding it down for ten seconds each time until eventually, maybe two minutes later, Johan came running out to the front of the visitor's centre. He looked wild, like any man would if they're cock's mouth-bath was interrupted, but Levi didn't care, he just kept beeping until Johan made his way over to the car and talked to him through the driver's window.

"Levi," Johan said with a fake smile. "You sure are noisy."

"Is Mum around?" Levi replied in a bland tone, trying not to stare at the man's shorts which appeared mildly tented.

"Yes, she's just out back in the garden. We've just been planting some new flowers. Celosias. They are a beautiful flower. Very bright and vibrant." Johan's face and tone were void of guilt or apprehension, giving Levi the impression that the man wasn't just a liar but also a very good one. "You should come and have a look. I bet the garden has changed a lot since you were here last. I've installed a bridge, solar lights, even got some peacocks out there now." He chuckled. "They're almost as noisy as you."

"I really need to speak with Mum."

"Okay. I'll just go get her for you." Johan gazed at him with concern. "Is everything alright?"

"I can't say. It's a private family matter." Levi didn't even try to hide the derision in his voice.

"I understand."

Johan raced off and in less than a minute, Levi's mother appeared in the carpark. She too wore a smile but hers was not void of guilt or apprehension like Johan's had been. Levi motioned for her to sit inside the car so they could talk.

"Darling. Why are you here?" She asked edgily. "Is something wrong?"

"There's something we need to talk about."

Any normal person would have wanted to know immediately what the topic was about, but not someone who'd just been up to no good. "Why were you honking the horn?" she asked instead. "Why didn't you just come and find me?"

"I went inside but I couldn't see you anywhere."

"Did you go look in the back garden?" She studied his face carefully.

Levi shook his head. He didn't want her getting upset knowing he knew her secret. He needed her as calm as possible. He got straight to the point. "Mark's building a new subdivision in Wairua Valley."

"He's what?"

"Apparently his family own the land so he has been given permission from the council to turn it into a new neighbourhood."

"But that's iwi land. He can't just do that."

"A team of archaeologists are going in there next week to search for any historic artefacts and if they don't find anything then it gets the go ahead."

"Oh…" She looked behind her to make sure Johan wasn't near. "But that doesn't mean they will find anything. I don't think they will dig very deep. Will they?"

"I don't know but if it does get the go ahead—which we both know it will because Mark always gets his way—then I know for sure that the diggers they send in to clear it all for the new streets will find something."

She nodded, chewing her bottom lip. "I think it will be fine though."

"How can it be fine? They will find the body."

"I don't like to remind you of such grim details but Shay took care of the risk of them being able to identify the body."

Levi winced, forced into confessing the mistake he'd made seven years ago. "About that. I never finished emptying Dad's pockets. And I think he still had his cell phone in the pocket I didn't check."

Rather than be angry, his mother's face radiated sympathy. "Oh, darling. Why didn't you tell us that night?"

"I don't know. I was scared it would annoy Shay, and I didn't want him to think I was a coward for chickening out of doing it."

A sad little smile formed on her lips. "Darling, you were just a little boy."

"I was nearly fourteen, hardly little."

"That's still too young to be expected to be part of something as ghastly as what we had to do that night."

Levi didn't want to wallow in his mother's pity so he focused on the problem at hand. "So do you see why I am so worried about them finding the body? Can you imagine what they might find on that phone?"

"I dread to think about it."

"So what do we do?"

"There's only one thing we can do," she said, sounding stronger than Levi often gave her credit for. "We dig your father's body up ourselves."

CHAPTER 18

Anxiety boiled in Levi's gut the whole way home after talking with his mother. The plan was for her to call Mark and tell him she was staying overnight at The Community for an event—something she did do on occasion; which Levi now knew why—and Levi would tell Mark about 9 o'clock that he was going out to visit a friend. Levi would then drive back to The Community and collect his mother so they could go dig up his father's body and get hold of the cell phone.

Levi wasn't concerned about Mark questioning them about their whereabouts. The man was used to his wife spending nights at The Community and he would never question Levi about going out to socialise, but Levi did wonder what the heck his mother would use as an excuse to Johan for her random absence. He just hoped she didn't fuck it up.

His steps up to his bedroom were wobbly, still dizzy from the shock of seeing his mother sink to her knees in front of a man who wasn't her husband. He flopped onto his bed and groaned like he was in pain.

He didn't know how serious it was between his mother and Johan but either way his mother was playing a dangerous game. Mark was a fuckwit but he was a fuckwit with lots of money. Money they only had access to if his mother stayed married to the man. Levi knew it was bad enough what he'd done with Danny, risky in its own way, but what his mother was doing was considerably worse, he believed. Perhaps that was debatable, fucking your stepbrother was pretty bad, but at least Levi knew Danny would keep his mouth shut about what they were doing. Would Johan?

After a few minutes of being laid flopped on his back, feeling lost to a world made of nothing but problems, Levi was snapped back to reality when his phone dinged with a text message. It was from Josh.

Hey cum bucket! Have you been wanking non-stop thinking about massaging my dick with your mouth? LOL

A message like that from someone so sexy should have made Levi slip a hand in his pants and play with himself, or at least smile, but he did neither. He was too worried about his future to even reply to the text. He put his phone back in his pocket and made a mental note to respond to it later. He closed his eyes and started a hope that slowly became a prayer, begging God to help him and his mother tonight when they shifted the body, and asking God to give his mother enough sense to end her affair with Johan. *Please God. I don't want to go to prison and I definitely don't want to end up living back in Brixton.* Levi damn near shit himself when he thought he heard God talk back to him.

"Hi, Levi."

He sprung up like a jack-in-the-box, his heart pounding so hard in fright, he thought it might explode in his mouth. "Fucking hell!" He clutched his beating chest. "Could you stop sneaking up on me like that. You're gonna give me a fucking heart attack one of these days." He cast an angry glare at his stepbrother stood in the doorway.

Danny was still wearing the jeans Levi had bought him for his birthday but the trendy top to go with them had been replaced with a baggy red t-shirt, the bright colour accentuating his pale, slender arms. "Sorry." Danny smiled guiltily. "Maybe I should start wearing shoes inside so you can hear me walking around."

Levi glanced down at the boy's socked feet. "Either that or put a fucking bell around your neck."

Danny laughed. "You've told me that before."

"Then maybe you should take the hint."

"Sorry," Danny apologised again.

Levi wasn't in the mood to be bothered, especially by Danny. He lay back down on the bed and draped an arm over his face, willing Danny to disappear. The last thing he needed right now was Danny trying to navigate them towards more sex. Last night had been a huge mistake and he wasn't in the mood for Danny to remind him about it.

"I wanted to show you something," Danny said meekly.

"I'm kind of busy at the moment."

"But you're just laying down doing nothing."

"Yeah. I'm busy doing nothing," Levi growled.

"Please. It won't take long."

Levi moved his arm from his face and glanced sideways at his stepbrother. "What is it?"

"It's a surprise."

"I don't like surprises."

"I promise you'll like this one." Danny pleaded with his eyes. "Please?"

You better not be talking about your dick.

"Fine," Levi heaved out in a heated breath, getting to his feet. "But it better be quick."

Danny beamed with a smile. "Follow me."

Levi trudged after his stepbrother, wondering where the hell Danny was taking him. They went downstairs and then to the end of the hallway to a lift that took them down to the basement. Technically it was the second basement. One half of their huge home was built into a hill, allowing two floors below the main entrance of the house. One floor of the basement housed extra bedrooms, a bathroom, and a large locked lair that Mark referred to as his "man cave." The bottom floor though, where the lift was taking them, was an extra garage. It was rarely used and was more a showroom to house Mark's non-work vehicles.

"Why are we coming down here," Levi asked.

"Wait and see." Danny grinned.

When the lift doors opened, Levi stepped out and immediately saw his surprise.

"Ta da!" Danny said, throwing his arms out like a gameshow hostess. "It's your car."

Levi raced over and stroked the bonnet of his Porsche as if it were the face of a long-lost lover. "When did this get back?" He walked around the vehicle, smiling.

"I got it back earlier today."

"You got it back?"

Danny nodded.

"How?" Levi asked.

"I went and saw Uncle Bob this morning and asked him if I could have it back."

Uncle Bob wasn't really an uncle, just a close family friend who Mark had sold the car to as part of Levi's punishment for spending too much on his credit card.

"But didn't Bob buy it?"

"Yes, but I bought it back." Danny pointed to the passenger's seat. "There are change of ownership papers there for you to sign so it can be in your name. That way Dad can't sell it on again."

"How much did it cost you?"

"That's not important."

"Yes it is. I have no money to pay you back."

189

"You don't have to pay me back. It's a gift."

Levi stared at his stepbrother, genuinely touched by Danny's kind gesture. "Thank you, Danny. That's… that's really nice."

Danny blushed, toeing the floor with his foot. "You're welcome."

Before Mark had sold the speedy red car, Levi hadn't been that fussed about it, merely viewing the Porsche as just one small part of his image, but after a week of driving around the shitheap Mark had replaced it with, Levi realised just how much the car meant to him. He was so happy he could almost give Danny a hug. *Almost.* He decided against wrapping their limbs together, preferring instead to circle the vehicle as he smiled ecstatically, running his finger along the glossy red panels.

Danny's hand dipped into his pocket and pulled out the car's keys, jingling them. "Did you wanna take it for a drive?"

"Fuck yeah." Levi raced over and grabbed the keys from him. He jumped in the driver's seat, ready to turn on the ignition when he realised Danny was still standing in the same place watching him. "Are you coming?"

Danny blinked, appearing surprised to be asked to join. "Can I?"

"Come on. Let's take it for a spin."

"Okay. I'll just go put some shoes on."

Two minutes later, Danny appeared with a pair of black Converse sneakers on his feet and jumped in the passenger's seat. Levi wasted no time doing a 180 turn before driving them up to the security keypad to unlock the garage doors then drove up the curved driveway that snaked around the back and side of the house. Once they were out on the street, Levi took them for a joyride through their treelined neighbourhood, past the local shops and then out onto the motorway.

Danny, not one to keep his mouth shut, was surprisingly quiet to begin with. Rather than talk, he just sat there smiling like a giddy dork as the wind rushed through the windows, messing up his black hair. Levi had felt obliged to let his kid brother join him for the ride but he'd secretly been nervous about it, worried if Danny would mention what had happened last night but it soon became apparent Danny had no intention of mentioning it either.

"Fuck this feels good," Levi said, pushing his foot down on the accelerator, risking a speeding ticket.

"So you're happy to have it back?"

"I'm more than happy." Levi threw his stepbrother a smile of thanks. "I definitely owe you one, buddy."

Levi took the offramp into the city centre, did a few lap of honours of Fitzroy's busier streets before deciding to be generous and ask Danny where he might like to drive to.

"Can you show me where you used to live?"

Levi frowned. "Say what?"

"Brixton. I'm curious to see the house you grew up in."

"Why would you wanna see that?"

"I wanna know more about you."

"You already know plenty about me."

"I know but... I'm curious to know more." The smile on Danny's face made Levi feel uneasy but he nodded anyway and exited the city centre to take them out to Brixton.

As they entered Fitzroy's dirty secret, Danny began studying the neighbourhood like a bobblehead tourist. Every now and then little "Whoas" and "Gollys" fell from his naïve lips, no doubt shocked by the rundown shops and the poverty he was seeing. Levi wasn't sure but he thought it was a pretty safe bet to say that this was his sheltered stepbrother's first time venturing into Fitzroy's poorest neighbourhood.

"What are they doing?" Danny asked, pointing at two kids, no older than twelve or thirteen, sat on the pavement with plastic bags covering their nose and mouth.

"Sniffing glue."

"Why would they sniff glue?"

"To make them feel good I guess."

"That's just weird," Danny said.

"People do lots of weird stuff to make themselves feel good."

Levi turned off Brixton's main street and began taking them into the poisoned heart of Fitzroy's worst suburb. If Danny had thought Brixton's main street was bad then he was in for a treat as they drove past rows of state housing in disrepair, every flat surface tagged with graffiti, including the road they were driving on.

When he finally turned into his old street, he pulled to a stop outside his former home. The front door was wide open, loud rap music spilling out into the street. The semi-detached house looked just the same as when Levi had lived here; rusted roof, peeling white paint, and lawns in desperate need of a mow.

"That's it," Levi said.

"This is where you and Jenny lived?"

"Yep." Levi pointed to a window with a bit of flappy plastic taped over a smashed panel. "That was my bedroom." He suppressed the shiver threatening to run up his spine as his imagination played a cruel trick on him, flashing an image of Lucky's demented grin staring back at him out the window.

"This is so..." Danny struggled to finish his sentence.

"Shit?" Levi offered with a chuckle.

"I was going to say it's quaint."

"Just say shit, Danny. That's what it is."

"I wouldn't say that. That's just rude."

"It's not rude if it's the truth."

Danny kept staring at the rundown property. "I can't imagine what it must have been like growing up here. It must have been really tough." He turned to face Levi, sympathy radiating from his eyes.

"It wasn't that bad," Levi said nonchalantly. "There's far worse places in the world to live when you're poor."

"Even so, it can't have been easy."

Levi didn't like the sound of pity in Danny's voice. He didn't need pity and it wasn't warranted. At the time he lived here it was all he knew so he never thought about it as being tough. Sure, his father made life difficult—and Lucky had made it extremely fucked-up—but the house and suburb were just part of his world back then. Not now though. Levi knew that if he were to ever move back then he would struggle immensely. He was too accustomed to the finer things in life to ever fit back into this world.

"Where to now?" Levi asked. He shot a smile at his stepbrother and saw mischief stirring in his baby blues. It was obvious he wanted to ask him something, but was holding back.

"I'm happy to go wherever you want."

"How about we head back home?" Levi suggested. "We can do more sightseeing another day."

"If you want." Danny turned to him, his gaze becoming sharper. "Maybe when we get home we can play the bongo drums."

Bongo drums. Danny spoke the word so softly but it hit Levi so damn hard. It felt like a missing jigsaw piece had just fallen into place and he remembered another forgotten element to what had happened last night. *He's asking for sex.*

He wants to top me! Levi swallowed, his hand nervously changing gears as he turned the car around.

"You remember what that word means, right?" Danny asked him.

Levi's pulse rocketed but his voice was steady. "I think so."

"You told me last night that whenever I say the word you would let me have sex with you. You said we have an arrangement because of what we did." When Levi didn't respond, Danny continued. "You said when someone ejaculates inside a person—which I did to you— that means they get certain privileges."

It sounded absurd because that's what it was. Absurd, crazy bullshit spouted by a sadistic twit called Dwight. But Levi had recycled the garbage apparently, passing it on to Danny during their sexing. Danny's crotch brushed the edges of his vision and Levi found himself cringing on the inside that he'd allowed Danny to put his dick inside him.

What the fuck is wrong with me?

Levi nodded stiffly, his heart rate ran rampant.

"And did you mean that?" Danny asked. "That we have an agreement?"

The boy was giving him an out, an opportunity to weasel out of the erotic promises he'd made. It would be lunacy to honour such an agreement but all Levi could say was, "Let's talk about this at home."

CHAPTER 19

They drove the rest of the way home in awkward silence, neither of them willing to break the quiet. Levi was still battling with himself about what to do. The sensible option was to tell Danny that he'd been drunk and had said and did things he didn't mean, that it was best if they both forget about last night—and the night before that.

However, Levi could not deny that he felt a sense of duty to honour the arrangement, to give his stepbrother what he wanted. For starters, Danny had bought his car back for him, surely that entitled the boy to some privileges. But deeper than that was a sense of obligation that he'd allowed Danny some sort of ownership of him, that by allowing the geeky teen unshielded access inside his body he'd gifted Danny a lifetime of superiority.

Kaleb came in me too but I didn't do what he wanted. That was true but for whatever reason, Levi was more willing to allow Danny to dominate him. He wasn't sure why that was but he suspected it had something to do with whoever it was Danny kept reminding him of. It was someone from Levi's past, of that he was sure, but who the fuck was it?

When they arrived back home, Danny silently led the way upstairs. Every third step he would glance over his shoulder to make sure Levi was following after him.

At the top of the stairs, Levi suddenly realised where they were headed. *He's taking me to his bedroom.* For a split-second, he thought he could skive off into his own bedroom and lock the door to evade Danny's horny wishes, but he succumbed to an invisible force insisting he continue following his stepbrother.

Oh fuck… I'm gonna do it. I'm actually gonna go through with this.

If submission was a virus then Levi was infected. He didn't want to be his stepbrother's bitch—he really didn't—but he knew it was required of him. They had signed an agreement in sweat and semen, and Levi felt forced to honour it.

Danny shut his bedroom door quietly behind them and went and sat down on the end of his bed.

Levi stood nervously in the centre of the room, his hands fisted at his sides. The awkward silence lingered a while longer as they both averted one another's gaze.

Danny's bedroom was much tidier than Levi's. His queen-size bed was perfectly made and the walls were bare other than a large world map pinned above an immaculately organised desk that had pots of pens and text books on it. It felt more like a middle-aged man's office than a teenage boy's bedroom, Levi thought.

"What happens now?" Danny finally asked.

Levi could feel the heat in his cheeks as Danny's question lingered between them. *What happens now?* What did happen now? He didn't know. So that's exactly what he said. "I don't know." He stared down at his feet, feeling Danny's eyes watching him. "What do you want to happen?"

"Sex stuff?" It sounded more like a question than a response.

Levi raised his head, nodding. "Then I guess that's what we do… *sex stuff.*"

"So the arrangement is real then?"

"I'm standing here aren't I?" Levi's tone hovered between obedience and resentment. The obedience came from a dark place in his mind that seemed attracted to the idea of submitting to other men, despite how much the less dark parts of himself hated the idea of it. The resentment though, he knew where that came from. He was resentful because he was about to give up the goods—for a second time—to a lesser man. *If you can even call Danny a man.*

Despite what had happened between him and Dwight, Levi still believed himself to be an alpha male at heart. He may not have the physique of a gladiator or the cock of a porn star but he was handsome, rich and had the confidence of a winner. He was certainly the alpha male between him and Danny, but right now Levi felt very much inferior to his meek stepbrother.

"Do you remember much about last night?" Danny asked.

"Not really." Levi sighed inwardly. "I was pretty drunk."

"You must have been super-duper drunk to want to sniff Dad's undies. That was so weird." Danny sniggered.

Levi almost scolded his stepbrother but stopped himself.

"I can't believe you did that." Danny grimaced. "They must have smelled gross."

Rather than delve into an awkward explanation about why Mark's ball sweat was like an aphrodisiac that reminded him of the best sex of his life, Levi just played the drunk card again. "People do stupid things when they are drunk."

"I guess so." Danny studied him for a lingering moment with a maddening mix of heat and hesitancy stewing in his blue eyes.

The uncomfortable silence just made things worse so Levi blurted the obvious, "You're going to fuck me, right?"

Danny rubbed his mouth like he was trying to hide a grin, then nodded. "I'm not in a rush though. I wanna take my time. Maybe look at you for a little bit." He lowered his eyes to the zipper of Levi's pants and whispered, "While you're naked."

As the request sank in, Levi tongued his top lip. "As you wish." He reached for the hem of his t-shirt and slowly pulled it off and dropped it to the floor. Next, he kicked off his sneakers, removed his socks, and pulled his pants and briefs off, tossing them in a bundle haphazardly against the wall.

With his hands at his sides, Levi stood in the centre of Danny's room naked and exposed, feeling much more vulnerable than he liked or expected. Being naked didn't usually bother him, but for some reason being naked in front of a still fully-clothed Danny made him feel small and insignificant.

Danny ran his eyes up Levi's naked body—toes to face—and ended looking into Levi's hazel eyes. He licked his slightly pursed lips, his tongue barely visible as it slid from corner to corner. "Come stand closer," he whispered hoarsely.

Levi crossed the room in pitiful steps until he was standing at attention in front of his young master. It was only now that he was standing right in front of Danny that he realised the horny teen was just as nervous as he was.

"You are so beautiful," Danny said, his young voice laced with awe. "I wish I looked more like you." He gingerly raised a hand, motioning for Levi's dick. "Can I?"

"You don't have to ask for my permission," Levi said, his voice tight. "I'm yours to use how you want."

Danny grabbed hold and began to squeeze and pull Levi's manhood, dragging a light moan from Levi's lips. "You have such a nice penis."

Levi didn't respond, his dick was doing all the talking for him, quickly swelling to its full size between his stepbrother's frisky fingers.

"Wow, you really like me touching this thing." Danny wiggled Levi's engorged member back and forth like it was some kind of obscene rubber doll. "I never thought I would do something like this. Touch another boy in a sexual kind of way, but I actually quite like it. The touching, the kissing." He blushed. "And especially the fucking."

"Did you like it more when I fucked"—Levi's breath hitched as Danny thumbed his piss slit—"you... or when you fucked me?"

"I definitely prefer being the man." Danny glanced up and saw the displeased look on Levi's face. "Sorry. You know what I mean." He dropped his gaze back to Levi's privates and began fondling his balls, plumping them in the palm of his hand. Danny's face became locked in concentration as he studied Levi's testicles. "I know you think they're small but they aren't too bad."

"I think they're small?"

"Last night you told me you have bitch nuts."

"Oh god." Levi ran a hand through his hair, angry with his drunken self for being so messy. "I'm guessing I said lots of embarrassing stuff last night. And no, that's not an invite to remind me."

Danny chuckled. "You weren't embarrassing. You were sexy." He dipped his head and gave the head of Levi's dick a sticky little kiss. "You're always sexy."

The dick and ball fondling carried on for at least five more minutes until finally Danny pulled his hands away and gazed up at Levi and asked, "Can you suck me off now?"

"If that's what you want."

Danny replied by spreading his skinny legs apart and sliding his hips—and crotch—closer to the edge of the bed.

Yep. It's what he wants.

Levi lowered himself to the carpet, scooting his knees forward and rest his hands on Danny's thighs, rubbing the denim material of his jeans. Levi then undid the jeans button and pulled down the zipper. Danny sat up momentarily and Levi skimmed the heavy denim down so that they circled the boy's feet. With the jeans out of the way, Levi was greeted with a pair of cotton boxers. Loose, blue cotton boxers tented with a begging piece of a cock inside of them. The area around the tip was drenched with precum.

He rubbed his hands up and down the forest of dark hairs covering Danny's legs, the most manly part of his stepbrother's young body. He leaned forward and mouthed Danny's manhood through the fabric, inhaling the strong, masculine scent of a male who was gaging to be satisfied. The musk coming from Danny's cock was attacking his nose without mercy and Levi was not defending. This pure aroma of masculinity seemed to have entered his bloodstream and fill his entire body until his whole world shrunk to the length and girth of his stepbrother's dick. He didn't even care that it was still clothed, his mouth just engulfed the tool and started taking care of Danny's arousal. He slid his tongue in the buttoned front hole of Danny's boxers, tasting the boy's warm, salty organ.

"Oh God..." Danny whispered, in a much higher voice than usual. He gripped the bedsheets and bucked his hips to shove his cloth-covered dick deeper into Levi's mouth. The fabric of his underwear began getting wetter and wetter with Levi's saliva—and Danny's juices.

His dick is like a fucking water sprinkler.

Levi pulled his mouth away and grabbed the front hole of Danny's boxers and forcefully ripped the button off, sending it flying away and falling somewhere on the floor. He needed Danny's cock free to help satisfy his own delirium of desire. Danny's cock was now fully released, glistening with pleasure. It was not the thickest or the longest cock in the world but Levi was going to worship every inch of it.

Without hesitation, he opened his mouth wide and plunged down the length of Danny's shaft, all the way to the bottom. Danny leaned back on the bed, whimpering like a little bitch while his cock oozed ridiculous amounts of ball juice. Levi pursed his lips hard and added as much suction as he could, enjoying feeling Danny's dick pulse and twitch like crazy inside his mouth.

Levi kept a brisk pace on him, moving the boy's meat in and out of his throat expertly. It didn't seem possible, but Danny's dick got even stiffer. The boy grunted, whimpered, panted, becoming a symphony of dirty desire as Levi played his pipe.

Danny began lifting his hips up off the bed with each "oh yes" and "uhh" that escaped his mouth, matching each of Levi's downward slurps with an upward hump. There was an audible slurping sound now, and Levi thought he could even hear Danny's balls smacking against his chin each time he buried his face completely in his lap.

Levi reached into Danny's boxers, hauled his sweaty ballbag out, and began slobbering over the hairy, crinkled skin. The testicles were heavy in his mouth. They felt full. Ripe. He soaked Danny's nuts with his tongue, cleaning them thoroughly, until finally they spilled out from his lips, and he returned his attention to the underside of his cock, which he kissed from the base until he reached the drooling crown.

Danny reached out and ran his fingers through Levi's hair. The gesture was tender and warm. *Don't touch me like that.* This was just sex, it wasn't supposed to be romantic. So to keep Danny off-kilter, Levi deepthroated him again while also fondling his balls. He felt Danny thicken, his testicles raise and his breath bleed hot. The end was near. With one final plunge, Levi knew he would have Danny's sticky release in his mouth and he would be able to put his clothes back on and leave the room and pretend like none of this ever happened.

"Stop," Danny cried out, pushing Levi's mouth off of him. "I-I don't wanna cum like this."

Levi wiped leaking dribbles of precum from his lips and gazed up at Danny. "Just cum in my mouth, buddy. I really wanna taste you."

Danny shook his head. "No."

"Come on." Levi smirked and reached out to stroke Danny's drooling cock but Danny swatted his hand away.

"I said no, Levi."

Levi scooted backwards, surprised by the stern tone of Danny's voice. It was the first time he'd ever heard his stepbrother sound remotely authoritative. Their eyes connected and something in Danny's lust-filled gaze told Levi he'd lost something he could never get back. *Respect.* Sure, Danny would always be Danny—a thoughtful boy who was well-mannered and polite—but he would never look at Levi like he was his idol ever again.

Age and size meant nothing anymore, Levi would no longer be the big brother in this dynamic. He had gifted Danny the position of superiority between them and he knew there was no way he would ever get it back. From now on he was Danny's inferior, someone Danny would go to when he wanted his dick cleaned and his balls emptied. It angered Levi as much as it turned him on. The whole thing was a bundle of contradictions.

Danny replaced his frown with one of his goofy smiles. "I'm going to fuck you now," he said matter-of-factly. He stood up and proceeded to toe off his shoes and remove all his clothes, folding them neatly and placing them in a tidy pile on the floor.

Levi's arsehole twitched when he glanced down at his stepbrother's curved five inches, knowing it would soon be buried inside his body. Even though Danny had fucked him just last night, this time Levi would be stone cold sober and would not have the luxury of being able to forget.

Danny nudged him towards the bed with a giddy snicker. "Lay down on your stomach. I wanna try it that way."

Levi climbed onto the mattress and lay down as requested, burying his face into the pillow he would soon be biting. He slipped a hand under his stomach and adjusted his boner before resuming his position of lying flat on his stomach with his head turned to the side resting on his arms on the pillow. He heard the bed creak as Danny climbed up to sit between his legs. Levi spread them some more to make room for him. He shivered and shook when Danny began trailing fingertips up the back of his thighs. Danny then planted two little kisses on Levi's arse. One on each cheek.

"You look so sexy." Danny chuckled. "Even if you do have a hairy bum."

"I don't have a hairy bum," Levi muttered, somewhat offended.

"Then what do you call this," Danny said, swiping a finger down the centre of Levi's hair-lined crack. "It's pretty hairy."

"Just hurry up and fuck me already."

Danny chuckled again. "Someone's keen for me to be inside him."

"Yeah… let's go with that."

Danny was immune to the sarcasm and simply replied, "I can't wait to make love to you again."

Levi rolled his eyes as he braced himself for the impending invasion. He heard Danny make a sound like he was hawking a loogey and spitting it out. Then he felt Danny's hand swipe between his cheeks again, rubbing warm saliva up and down his anal trench and over his arsehole.

Apparently satisfied, Danny pulled his sticky fingers away and began shifting around. Levi felt Danny's knees pressing against the insides of his thighs as the boy once again plied his arse cheeks apart. He felt more of Danny's body and weight looming behind him and then something hard, wet and warm was pressing against his spit-coated hole. Levi squeezed his eyes as Danny pushed the head of his cock inside his anus with blunt force, burying himself two inches deep.

Oh my god. Danny's dick. Inside me. Fuck. Fucking hell. Levi bit into the pillow, tensing every muscle in his body. Humiliation scorched through him without remorse.

"Just relax," Danny whispered, like he was some sort of expert, "I promise not to hurt you."

The rim of Levi's anus clenched around Danny's young prick, swallowing it tightly. He could hear Danny's excited, horny breaths brush his ear as the boy's curved knob slowly sank deeper and deeper inside his arsehole until finally Danny's testicles pressed against Levi's skin.

Danny let out a triumphant sigh and draped his smooth chest over Levi's back, resting his head on Levi's shoulder and kissing him on the cheek. "I'm all in now." He stayed in place, rooted in Levi's arse, his breath guttering out.

Levi's sphincter yielded to Danny's manhood, submitting to the stretch. Danny wasn't exactly huge but Levi was still shocked at how easily his arsehole was embracing his stepbrother's cock. While he knew he was still plenty tight, it was safe to say that his days of virginal friction were behind him.

Danny hooked his feet over Levi's ankles, pinning him down and locking him in place. Their leg hair brushed together, a sensation teeming with virility. He then grabbed Levi's hands, lacing their fingers together. Levi didn't think they could be more connected if they tried, but of course Danny found a way.

"Kiss me," Danny whispered. "Turn your head and kiss me."

Levi didn't respond, kept his face buried in the pillow.

"Kiss me," Danny repeated. "Come on, baby."

Don't call me that!

Levi relented, hoping if Danny's mouth was busy then he would stop uttering anymore soppy shit. He turned his head and met Danny's lips for a slow, sticky kiss. In the midst of their steamy lip lock, Danny pulled his fleshy spike back halfway and began to fuck, ploughing Levi's clasping anal-lips with a somewhat jerky rhythm.

Levi wished he was the one doing the fucking, showing Danny how it was done properly, but Danny's arse was off-limits from now on. Levi wasn't worthy of the honour. He was nothing more than a fuck-hole and filthy cum dump. But rather than bury his face in shame, he embraced his position like his arsehole embraced Danny's raw dick.

Like cigarettes and alcohol, what they were doing was probably bad for his health, but Levi didn't give a fuck. Pinned beneath his wimpy stepbrother's body was the one place he could escape his problems, the one place he could forget everything plaguing his mind. At his lowest he was flying his highest. And Levi knew he couldn't get much lower than being Danny Candy's bitch.

He broke away from the kiss, and in a voice laced with submissive seduction, Levi began spouting off a string of desperate words. "Fuck me, Danny. My arse. Fuck it. Fuck it deep. You own me, Danny. My arse is all yours."

"I will, baby. Don't you worry. I'm gonna give you all my love."

"Yeah, man. Fill me up. Give me your load!" Levi let go of Danny's hands and reached behind, clutching Danny's thudding hips, demanding he go deep-deep-deep.

Danny, surprisingly, rose to the challenge. He increased the tempo of his pathetic thrusts and began ploughing Levi's arse with ferocious fuck-motions. He slipped a hand beneath Levi's stomach, and gripped his knob, seizing it tightly.

"Mmmmphh," Levi groaned every time Danny's cock impaled him balls-deep. The speed of Danny's mediocre meat going in and out was impressive. He would withdraw nearly all the way, leaving just the engorged head of his cock inside, then slam back inside 'till his hairy balls were squished against Levi's arse.

Levi expected his teen lover to lose his lollies super quick but it was Levi who crossed the finish line first. With his arse being rammed with fuck-meat and his cock squeezed tightly, Levi was torn in pleasure on both sides of his body—too much pleasure.

Levi's eyes closed as his mouth fell open in a wordless scream. His slick hole clamped around Danny's drilling flesh, and his cock began spewing cum between the sheets and his stomach. Levi hissed through his clenched teeth in agonized relief while spasms rocked his body.

With his balls emptied, Levi's submissive mindset faded and, like a cold, wet bedsheet, the seriousness of what had just happened settled over him. *I just let Danny fuck me. Again. And he's still fucking me.*

Hips still pumping, Danny whispered in Levi's ear, "I think somebody just ejaculated."

Levi nodded brokenly.

Danny unfurled his fingers from Levi's dick and pulled his arm free, wiping his cum-coated fingers clean on Levi's thigh. "Are you okay if I keep going?"

"Yep. But be quick," Levi grumbled. "It's starting to hurt."

"Okay," Danny said, and he reignited his rhythm.

Levi shook in shivers as Danny rammed his cock inside his splayed sphincter. It hurt more now that he had cum, but he had an obligation to let Danny finish so he lay there being sodomized, stewing in his rapidly-multiplying feelings of anger and shame. The amount of times the word "baby" fell from Danny's lips, Levi was beginning to think he was being barebacked by a young Justin Bieber.

"It's coming, baby. My love. My love is co-co-coooomiiing." Teeth suddenly scraped Levi's shoulder, and Danny sunk his fangs in, biting hard. His young body shook and shivered as his cock spasmed violently, squirting a huge load of cum inside Levi's arse. When his dick finally stopped twitching and shooting, Danny pulled out and flopped onto his back, panting like he'd just finished a marathon. "That was so amazing. Thank you."

Levi's arsehole was warm with Danny's load, and he could feel the ache where Danny's prick had been. He carefully rolled over onto his back and cast a glance down his naked body, inspecting the sticky whiteness of his own load coating his stomach. "I suppose I better go get cleaned up." He went to hoist himself up and leave but Danny grabbed his arm, pulling him back down.

"Wait," Danny said.

Levi turned his head. His eyes narrowed as they bore into Danny's gaze, and he hoped the coldness in them would kill whatever conversation Danny wanted to have.

"I wanted to give you something." Danny rolled off the bed and wandered over to his study desk, opened the top drawer and pulled out a white envelope. He wandered back to the bed and handed it over.

Levi eyed the envelope suspiciously, hoping like fuck it wasn't some mushy romance card.

"Open it," Danny urged.

Levi sighed and ripped into the envelope, surprised at what he found. "What's this?"

"A new eftpos card." Danny pointed to the bottom of it. "I opened a new account today and put some money on it for you."

"Why?"

"I wanted to say thank you for what you got me for my birthday. I love the new clothes."

"You do know that is how birthdays go, right? People buy you shit because it's your birthday."

Danny chuckled. "I know that but what you did for me was beyond just the presents. You made me feel like a new person with the makeover and…" he began to blush. "And you made me a man that night and I can't thank you enough."

Levi nodded, glancing down at the card in his hand. "How much is on it?"

"Five hundred dollars."

Five hundred dollars didn't mean much to Levi but with his allowance gone it was going to help. "Cheers, buddy. Thanks."

"Your welcome." Danny stroked Levi's leg. "And maybe I could start putting more money on it each week if you wanted to make things official."

Levi raised a questioning brow. "Official?"

"You know… be my boyfriend." Danny smiled at him as he tickled the hairs on Levi's leg. "I'd be a really good boyfriend and would give you everything I could. I'd take you out for dinner. To the movies. We could even go away for holidays together."

"I'm not a whore, Danny," Levi said flatly. He considered shoving the card back in Danny's face but decided his need for cash outweighed his moral outrage.

"Gosh no. That's not what I mean at all." Danny looked frazzled. "I know this is only a sex arrangement but I'm hoping you might be open to more at some stage and when you are I want you to know that I am the kind of man who can take care of you the way you deserve to be taken care of."

"Riiight."

"I'm not saying we have to start dating right this second but surely it is something we can look at later down the track, right?"

"Brothers can't be boyfriends."

"Brothers aren't supposed to have sex but we are."

"I know but…"

"You do want to keep having sex with me, don't you?" Danny gazed at Levi with concern.

Levi stared into his brother's worried eyes, willing his mouth to say no but he couldn't bring himself to dishonour the arrangement. Danny's dominance over him was in his veins—and leaking out his arse—and too powerful to disobey. "If you want to have sex then I will keep having sex."

"Then why not make us official? It only makes sense."

Rather than try and explain to Danny the definition of no-strings, Levi took a different approach. "I think you're forgetting that you will be moving away to university soon and I bet you anything you will meet some pretty girl and you'll fall in love."

"But I'm already in love," Danny said bluntly. "I'm in love with you."

Oh fuck. "But that doesn't change the fact you are moving away for uni next year."

"Then you could come with me. Or I could stay here and study. I don't mind."

Levi had not expected this kind of problem. He was not in the business of dating guys, and certainly not one he was related to. It was fucking lunacy on Danny's part to think they could ever be in a relationship. *But is it a problem or an opportunity?* He hated himself for thinking that but it was true. With his allowance cut off, and his mother straying from the marital bed, Levi knew his cushy lifestyle was in serious danger of being over. Rather than tell Danny *forget about it*—like he knew he should—Levi's survival instinct kicked in and he said, "I'll think about it."

His response put a smile on Danny's face that could probably be seen from space. "That's so awesome!"

"I haven't said yes yet. Just that I'll think about it."

Danny nodded smugly. "You're gonna say yes. I can tell."

Not if I can help it. Levi crawled off the bed and collected his clothes, desperate to go empty his body of liquid shame. He managed to get halfway to the door when he heard Danny say "Bongo drums."

Levi spun around. "What?"

"Bongo drums." Danny rose to his knees on the bed, smiling deviously. "I wanna play the bongo drums again."

"But... but you just came?"

"I know but I wanna do it again." Danny tugged on his deflated prick. "You can suck me until I get hard again."

Levi was furious, ready to fire off an arsenal of nasty words back at his horny stepbrother. But he didn't. He couldn't. The power of his own submission was too strong. He dropped his clothes and skulked his way back to the bed and put Danny's dick in his mouth and sucked.

CHAPTER 20

Hey cum bucket! Have you been wanking non-stop thinking about massaging my dick with your mouth? LOL

Dwight's eyes bugged in shock and then anger and finally disgust. He dropped his son's cell phone like it was riddled with disease. It bounced off the couch and onto the floor with a loud thud. He left it there.

This was the first chance he'd had to check Josh's cell phone since he'd called Levi on it in private the day before. When he'd checked Josh's message history straight after Levi had hung up on him there was no incriminating evidence of any homo nonsense but today was a different story.

"I am going to fucking kill you, Soggy!" He began pacing the lounge of his hotel suite, wishing he was back in New Zealand so he could throttle Levi. Josh's text, even with the LOL attached, was enough to confirm Levi had been telling the truth in the video call. "How can you be so fucking stupid, Joshy."

What was more troubling was the use of cum bucket. Dwight had drawn that on Levi's back with the intention of showing Josh just what kind of faggot Levi was. *A used one.* But instead it was being used as a nickname for Christ's sake. It was safe to say that his plan had backfired. Backfired in a big way.

He sank his butt down onto the couch and propped his bare feet up on the small wooden coffee table. He swiped an angry hand through his hair, muttering curse words under his breath. Now that he had seen evidence of what Levi was up to, Dwight felt it essential to do something about it and try and put a stop to it before his son did something he might regret. Josh was too trusting for his own good. He saw the best in people and was blind to dirty tactics used by snakes like Levi Candy. Dwight knew exactly how things would go if Josh made a habit of sticking his dick in Levi's mouth, eventually Levi would turn the tables, encourage Josh to be the one sucking and at some point Josh's arse would find itself the recipient of Candy cock. Dwight refused to let his son be fucked by Levi who he knew without a doubt would take pictures of the occasion and post them to his blog for the world to see.

"I can't let that happen. No fucking way is that happening." He thought hard about what he could do. There was the option of showing Josh the website but Dwight wasn't sure if Josh would believe the blog belonged to Levi. Nowhere on the blog were there any pictures of Levi's face, the boy's identity was well-hidden for the most part, and it wasn't like Dwight could force Josh to sit down and scroll through each erotic story and the hundreds of pictures of men pissing their pants and God only knows what else just to prove it was Levi.

Not a father son moment I want.

Dwight knew it was hypocritical to be angry at Josh for showing an interest in other men, no matter how innocent or minimal his curiosity may be. But it did fucking irk him. Josh was his mirror image and supposed to be the quintessential red-blooded male out there bagging hot birds and leaving a trail of Stephenson spunk in his wake as he conquered the world. His accomplishments would be

Dwight's accomplishments, and Dwight did not need or want Josh accomplishing a love of dick. Dwight had always secretly hoped that Josh's exploits would somehow make up for his own wayward tastes.

He glanced down at his feet resting on the table, remembering how great it had felt to watch Levi kneel before him and kiss them. That had been a moment of pure adrenalin watching someone who thought of himself as high and mighty reduced to pressing his lips to the dirt on the soles of Dwight's feet. It was almost as hot as when he'd watched his cock slide inside Levi's virgin arsehole that first night when he'd forced the boy into giving up the goods in exchange for silence about his blog.

It wasn't often he experienced such a tight heat strangling his girth but Levi had been plenty tight and plenty hot. Dwight was sure he'd never been as hard in his life as he was when he was fucking Levi and playing with his tight little balls. The memory almost brought on a fresh erection but just as he felt his cock pulse and begin to stiffen it died a sudden death when the images of Levi submitting were replaced by his son being fucked by Levi.

Fuck off! Dwight slapped his face to shoo the image away. He turned his head and looked towards the door of Josh's room. He could hear the distant echo of running water from the room's en suite. Josh would be out soon and probably suggest they go to the beach or wander down to the shops. Dwight wasn't in the mood. He was going to struggle to even look Josh in the face with the Levi issue on his mind. He set his brain back to the task of trying to think of a solution, something that would put an end to Levi's nasty plan.

Then it hit him.

I couldn't do that though...

Or could he?

But that would be fucking insane.

Or would it be genius?

If he could do what his mind was suggesting then he was pretty damn sure that it would not only destroy Levi's plan to seduce Josh but it could also destroy Josh and Levi's friendship. A slow smile spread on Dwight's face as he imagined how distraught Levi would be. It was a big risk and would mean sacrificing some pride but maybe, just maybe, it would be worth it to get Levi Candy out of the picture once and for all.

He began nodding to himself. He could do it. He *would* do it.

As he waited for Josh to get out of the shower, he rehearsed what he was going to say, choosing his words carefully. He played out the conversation in his head several times until he was sure that it would bring about the desired result—the destruction of Levi Candy.

Ice doused Dwight's veins when he heard the soft slap of Josh's feet coming towards the lounge, and he suddenly forgot all the words he'd just rehearsed.

Seconds later, Josh entered the room with nothing but a towel wrapped around his trim waist. He coughed up a friendly smile and wandered over to the kitchen where he pottered about in the fridge and grabbed himself some chilled water.

It's now or never.

While Josh had his back turned, Dwight began rubbing his eyes and sniffling.

Josh spun around. "Dad. Are you okay?"

Dwight sniffled again. "I-I'm fine."

"I can tell something's upsetting you. Just tell me what's wrong?" Josh padded over to the couch and sat beside him. "Is it about your house? I told you can stay with me until you can find a new place or until the insurance company pay you out to build again.

"It's not that. Well… it's not just that."

"What is it?" Josh's eyes brimmed with concern.

Dwight looked up at the ceiling, blinking and sighing for dramatic effect. "You don't want to be bothered with your old man's problems."

"Your my dad, of course I want to know if something is bothering you."

Dwight let a sickly pause clog the room before he continued. "Nobody knows but I have actually been seeing someone recently and I thought everything was going good, ya know? But I just found out they've been screwing around on me."

"Cheaters are the worst." Josh gave Dwight's back an affectionate rub. "I know it will hurt now but trust me you're better off without her."

Dwight swallowed deeply and whispered the fatal blow. "It's not a her. It's Levi."

CHAPTER 21

The air was warm but the ground looked so cold and lonely, menacing even. Levi lifted the spade he was holding and thrust it into the dirt, slicing the earth open like a scalpel cutting skin. The moon was bright but beneath the foliage of the trees he could barely see a thing, the only light on offer was the torch app on his mother's cell phone that she was holding and aiming at the ground.

He was grateful for the dark though. Not just because it hid them as they dug up his father's corpse, but because it meant his mother couldn't spot the misshaped lump in the seat of his pants. Before leaving the house to pick his mother up, Levi had shoved tissues in his briefs to soak up Danny's swimmers which kept leaking from his well-abused hole. They'd played the "bongo drums" another three times since the first session, resulting in Levi's arsehole becoming a creamy lake of Candy DNA. What Danny lacked in length he more than made up for in sperm, Levi thought.

Sex could do weird things to a person, and Danny was proving to be no exception. The kid had gone from mild-mannered good boy to a demanding little shit in the space of a few hours and orgasms. Not only had he demanded Levi service him later when he returned home but he'd also had the audacity to say, "When you come home tonight, I want you to tidy up your room."

"You want me to clean my room?" Levi had almost laughed right in his face.

"Yes. It smells of dirty socks. I don't like it."

Fuck what you like. It's my bedroom you little wanker was what Levi had wanted to say but instead he had just nodded and walked away. The kid was fucking dreaming if he thought he could boss Levi around like that. Sexual demands were one thing, but Levi wasn't about to change the way he lived in his own bedroom just to suit some teenage neat-freak.

He began sweating up a storm as he dug up his father's grave. He considered himself pretty fit but he definitely wasn't used to this sort of manual labour. His mother offered now and then to take a turn with the digging but each time Levi just shook his head and told her he had it under control. That was about the extent of their conversation. He was too mad at her to say anything else. Even when he'd picked her up outside The Community and she had asked why he was driving the Porsche he barely said more than a few words to her.

He used the silence to think about Danny's offer of a relationship. He had never considered the possibility of dating another guy, and certainly not one who was related to him. The whole suggestion was crazy, taboo and downright fucked-up but Levi was not prepared to rule it out just yet.

Like the sex, any relationship between them would have to remain a secret but maybe it could work for a little while? Shit, he was already letting the dork fuck him so why not throw in a few dinner dates and kisses and cuddles? It didn't have to last forever, Levi reminded himself. Just until Mark gave him his allowance back. *That might never fucking happen now thanks to her.* He discreetly gave his mother the evils.

He stopped digging for a moment so he could scratch his butt and wipe the sweat off his brow. He looked down at the hole which was now over two feet deep. "How bloody deep did you and Shay bury him?"

"You must be close," his mother replied. "It didn't take as long last time because there were two of us and Shay is very strong."

"What's that supposed to mean?" Levi hissed.

"Just that Shay was a bit more used to hard work than you are." She giggled. "Don't worry, darling, I still consider you my big strong boy."

Levi rolled his eyes. "Very funny." He reached around and scratched his butt again.

"You've been doing that every two minutes," His mother commented. "I'm starting to wonder if you have worms."

"I don't have worms. I'm just itchy, okay." He glared angrily at her. "So just fucking drop it."

"Settle down. It was just a joke."

"How am I supposed to be calm considering what it is we are here doing. If you hadn't noticed but now is not the time for stupid jokes."

"Why are you being so titchy with me?"

"I'm not being titchy with you."

"Yes you are. You've barely said a word to me since you picked me up."

Levi knew he should drop it and just continue digging but the words flew out of his mouth before he could stop them. "How long have you been fucking Johan?" His question was met with a wall of silence so he said it again. "I said... How. Long. Have. You. Been. Fucking. Johan?" He was shocked with himself for speaking to his mother like this but he was beyond angry. He wasn't just angry with her, he was angry with himself for his own stupid behaviour with Danny. He needed to let some of it out and he didn't care who it was aimed at.

"Don't talk like that to me," she growled.

"Let me rephrase it then. How long have you been intimate with a man's dick that isn't your husband's?"

Her hand suddenly whirred through the air and connected with his face in almighty slap.

He rubbed his burning cheek, dazed. "Sorry," he mumbled.

"So you should be," she said sternly before softening her tone. "Sorry if I hurt you."

"It's okay. I deserved it."

"Yes you did." She stared him down. "When did you find out about Johan?"

"That's not important. I just want to know why the hell would you risk everything for some aging hippy."

"Johan is not some aging hippy."

"I don't care what he is, Mum, but you do realise how fucking stupid you're being?"

He half-expected his mother to slap him again but she didn't. "Love makes us do stupid things, darling. Surely you know that?"

He supposed he did. He'd behaved like a fucking idiot when he'd dated Sophie, going out of his way to please her and embarrassing himself with over-the-top gestures. "I don't mean to pry but I need to know if it is serious?"

"We are in love, so yes, it is serious."

"Is this why you have been telling me I should be standing on my own two feet? Because you plan on leaving Mark?" Levi gulped, scared of what her answer may be.

She pursed her lips. "I've only said that because I think it is time for you to do so. You are nearly twenty-one, Levi. You can't go through life relying on Mark's money to take care of you."

Levi looked across the shallow grave separating them and stared into his mother's hazel eyes. "I can't believe I am about to stick up for the knob but surely you can see that Mark is a WAY better catch than Johan." He stared at his mother waiting for her to agree with him. "Mark's rich, I guess you could say he isn't ugly, and while I do think he is a major tool, like really major, I have to admit that he treats you really well, Mum. Much better than Dad ever did."

"Mark is a wonderful man but I don't know if I have ever loved him the way he loves me. I certainly care for him a great deal but not love in the true sense of the word."

"But does being in love with him even matter? We have such a good life."

"For a long while I wasn't sure if being in love with him mattered either. Mark is an excellent provider and after the hell your father put us through that was all I was worried about. I wanted to make it up to you for how badly I had failed you as a mother."

Levi was still mad at her but he felt obliged to tell her she was wrong. "You never failed me. You've always been a great mum."

"Thank you, darling, but we both know that isn't true. I can't say I knew the kind of stuff your father was up to but I'd be lying if I said I didn't know something was wrong. That you weren't hurting." The pain in her voice was very real. "A mother's job is to protect her children and I didn't do that. I was too lost in my head, worried about my own problems to focus on protecting you like I should have. That's why when Mark came along, trying to sweep me off my feet, I decided to give him a chance and just hope to fall in love along the way because I knew that he was a man who could give us both a better life."

"So what you're saying is you regret marrying him?"

"Not at all. Mark has given us a better life. I just never managed to fall in love like I hoped I would."

"And now you want to leave?"

"I haven't made any decisions yet. Even if we do end up separating, which I'm not saying will happen, I'm sure Mark would let you stay living with him if you wanted to. He knows it is your home."

Levi scoffed. "No he won't. He fucking hates my guts."

"Mark doesn't hate you, Levi."

"Yes he does."

"I don't think you give him enough credit. Mark is a good man."

"If you think he is so good why the hell are you cheating on him?"

"Because I don't control my heart any more than you can control yours."

Levi sniggered. "I don't have one. This arsehole made sure of that." He rammed the shovel into the dirt like he was stabbing his father all over again.

"You shouldn't say stuff like that."

Levi ignored her comment and reverted back to the issue at hand. "You said yourself that I have to be prepared to learn to stand on my own two feet which would insinuate you believe Mark will cut me off. So what is it, Mum? Mark the lovable stepdaddy who will look out for me, or Mark the man who throws us both out on our arses when he finds out about the affair. I know which one I think it is."

She let out a frustrated sigh. "I can't see the future, Levi, so I have no idea what Mark will do but I do know he doesn't hate you."

Levi decided to keep his mouth shut for fear of saying something he shouldn't. He'd already earned himself one slap, he didn't want another. He carried on digging, focusing on the job at hand, ignoring the burn of blisters forming on his hands. After about fifteen minutes though, he dropped the shovel in the hole when a chilling realization gut-punched him.

He looked across at his mother. "It isn't here, is it?"

She stared into the freshly dug hole where the body should have been. "I don't think so."

"And you're sure this is the right spot?"

"Absolutely certain."

Levi was too. He remembered the spot well because of the misshaped tree that stood beside the grave. Its trunk had a hollow in it and was unmistakable. Easy to find if they ever had to come back. Which was the reason he assumed Shay had chosen it.

Shay...

Levi's mother must have been thinking the same thing. "Do you think Shay moved it?"

"Obviously. Who else could it be?"

"Fucking hell," his mother cursed. She never swore which made it so much more shocking. "Why on earth would he not tell one of us? He should have told one of us."

"Because he's a fucking moron," Levi said.

"If only he was still around so we could ask him."

"Do we need to though?" Levi asked. "If it isn't here then we don't need to worry about it."

"We need to worry about it because who's to say he didn't just bury it somewhere else in the valley."

Levi hadn't thought of that. "Fuck."

"You told me Scott thinks he is still alive, right? Do you think that is true? Or do you think Ameesh was right when he said Shay was... no longer with us."

"Scott's the one who is right," Levi said. "Not Ameesh."

"How can we be sure though?"

Levi had no intention about telling his mother about how he'd seen a video of Shay naked and suspended in some sex dungeon, but he owed her the truth that Shay was still alive. *Well, according to Demon Dave he's still alive.* "He's not dead," Levi said. "Even though he probably wishes he was."

"What are you saying?"

"I'm saying Shay is alive."

"So you know where he is?" Her face lit with hope. "You could go see him?"

"I don't know where he is." Levi took a shuddering breath. "But I know someone who does."

CHAPTER 22

Levi stretched in a useless effort to loosen his knotted back muscles. Digging for a body that wasn't where it was supposed to be had taken its toll. He raised an arm and sniffed his damp armpit. He definitely needed a shower. But first, he had to reply to Demon Dave's invite. He didn't want to respond but he knew he didn't have a choice. He sat down on his bed and used his phone to sign into his blog to reply to Demon Dave's last message.

Hi Dave,

If the offer still stands then I would be keen to meet with you to talk about an arrangement. My latest story hasn't done as well as I thought so I am definitely open to any suggestions that might help me out. It would also be good to catch up with Shay again. It's been a while since we last "hung out" LOL

Levi

He didn't see the point in signing it as Candy Boy. It was obvious this Dave person knew who he was so why pretend otherwise. With a rolling tummy, he pressed send and braced himself for whatever came back. He half-expected Dave to reply immediately but no response came.

Mind you, it was just after midnight so Levi figured the guy was probably in bed.

As he took himself to the shower, Levi's mind haunted him with the last time he and Shay had been face to face. It hadn't been pleasant. It had been fucking awful.

He thought about his comment earlier to his mother about how he didn't have a heart. That wasn't true. He had loved Sophie romantically. He loved his mum as you do with family. He also loved Josh and Peach as the great friends they were. But there was one person he had loved in all three of those ways. Shay Jacobs.

But six months ago, the rebel with a heart of gold had killed Levi's love and had the audacity to laugh at him while doing it. Levi had written a story about that day and posted it to his blog under the name Twisted Candy. Nothing particularly twisted happened in the story, just a quick rundown about a rather dull almost-seduction. The twisted part was what he'd left out.

Candy Boy prided himself on telling the truth. But that didn't mean he always told the *whole* story.

∞

"Where is he?" Levi muttered as he paced the front porch. His palms leaked sweat like blood pouring from a bullet wound. He wasn't usually this nervous when he met guys but today was different. Today he was meeting the one guy he had lusted after for years. Shay Jacobs: Levi's former babysitter and childhood hero.

He had spent a ridiculous amount of time choosing something to wear, and in the end had settled on a pair of black jeans and a black shirt. The shirt was a short-sleeve polo his mother had bought him for Christmas the year before. It was actually one size too small so each time he raised his arms the shirt would ride and show off the small trail of hair below his belly button. The payoff though was how the tight fit hugged his pecs and biceps, flattering his physique tremendously.

Levi had arranged the meet four days earlier, after his mother told him that she and Mark would be leaving on Thursday to fly to Adelaide for a winery tour. It was out of the blue, like most of their holidays were, and Levi decided to seize the opportunity to do something he'd been trying to do all year—add Shay Jacobs to Candy Boy's list of stars.

It was the fifth time Levi had tried to arrange to catch up with Shay in as many months. Shay usually had something on though—drugs probably—but this time he had surprised Levi by saying he was free to catch up and that he would swing by Friday after work.

Two years had passed since they'd last seen each other, and it seemed a bit sad that someone who was once considered part of the family had become such a stranger, but Levi knew that was sometimes how life worked. Their lives didn't complement each other like they used to. Part of the reason for their lack of contact was because they no longer lived in the same area but a bigger part of their lack of contact was down to Shay's growing drug habit and his frequent stints inside jail. He wasn't the kind of person you could invite around for dinner in this part of town without raising a few eyebrows.

Just before Levi was about to give Shay a call to see if he was still coming, the rebel with a heart of gold pulled up across the street in his rusted-out white van. He climbed out of the vehicle with a small backpack in tow, and slowly crossed the street. His strides were slow but long, eating up the surface of the road with bad boy nonchalance.

Goddamn, you're hot!

Unruly black hair. Creamy coffee skin. Piercing blue eyes. He seemed a tad thinner than when Levi had last seen him, but he still had a good body on him by the looks.

Especially that arse. Levi wasn't much of an arse man but Shay Jacobs had a great arse. Even in the baggy jeans he had on, you could tell he was the owner of a beautifully firm and perfectly shaped backside.

Shay waved erratically as he came up the driveway. He was still dressed in his work clothes: dusty work boots, mucky jeans and a green t-shirt that had his name badge pinned just below the logo of his employer; Brixton Building Supplies.

As he climbed the front steps, his pillowy lips parted with a friendly smile. "It's so fucking good to see you, LP."

Shay had called Levi LP for as long as Levi could remember. It stemmed from the titular character in what was probably one of the few books Shay had ever read *The Little Prince*. According to Shay he imagined The Little Prince's lovable laugh to sound exactly like Levi's had as a small child and that if he never heard it again it would make him sad. It had always made Levi's heart swell with pride knowing that something as simple as the sound of his laughter was able to make Shay happy.

"It's good to see you too, man." Levi went to shake Shay's hand.

Shay looked at Levi's outstretched hand like he was offering a dog terd. "Fuck the handshake. We're whanau and whanau hugs."

It was true, they were whanau. *Family*. They may not have shared the same blood in their veins but they were bonded by the shedding of it.

Shay wrapped Levi up into a bear hug, smothering him with the stench of sawdust and sweat. When the hug ended, Shay took his work boots off at the door and followed Levi inside to the guest lounge.

"You have a real nice place, LP. Much better than you and your mum's old place," Shay commented, rubbernecking as he tried to take in as much of the plush surroundings as possible. "This place must be worth a fucking fortune."

"Have you not been here before?" Levi asked, despite knowing damn well Shay hadn't.

"Nar, bro. This is my first time."

"Did you want me to show you around?"

"Nar, nar. It's okay. I'm here to see you. Not your flash as house." He laughed.

"Did you want a drink?"

"Whatcha got?"

"Whatdaya want?"

Shay grinned. "Don't tell me you have a bar in this joint?"

"Pretty much. My stepfather has a huge collection of alcohol down in the basement. He could probably start his own nightclub," Levi joked. "Which is kind of fucked up because he hardly ever drinks."

"Just grab me whatever's easiest."

Levi went down to the basement and fetched them some of the scotch Mark kept for entertaining. There was so much down there that Mark wouldn't notice if Levi swiped any.

When he returned to the lounge Shay was sat down on one of large patchwork couches, his legs spread wide as he jerkily tapped his left foot on the floor. The grey socks he had on looked sad and wounded, holes on the heel of each foot. Levi grabbed them a tumbler each and then poured them both a glass. As he walked over and handed Shay his drink, Levi discreetly trickled his sight down to the bunched material around Shay's crotch. A primal urge coursed through his veins and he had to use all his strength not to reach out and touch him.

Levi was about to take a seat beside Shay on the couch but decided against it, choosing to sit on one of the arm chairs instead.

"This ain't too bad, LP." Shay chugged back a hearty mouthful like he was drinking a cheap beer. "Not too bad at all." It was better than *not too bad*. The amber liquid was very old, very smooth, and very fucking expensive. "So where's the rest of the whanau?"

"Mum's in Australia with my stepfather at the moment."

"Gutted. I was hoping to catch up with Jenny while I was here. Your mum is such an awesome lady. I wish she was my mum." Shay took another swig on his drink and sniggered. "Actually, maybe it's a good thing she isn't my mum because if she was she'd still be breastfeeding me."

Levi humoured him with a laugh.

"Sorry. I know you must get sick of people going on about how hot your mum is but damn... Brixton went ugly overnight when she moved away."

"That's not true. You're still there."

"Aww. Thanks." Shay rubbed the side of his twitching face. "But I don't think this old mug will win a beauty contest any time soon."

"I reckon it would," Levi said, his tummy squirming with nerves from being so bold.

"Speaking of good-looks, you've turned into quite the stud, haven't you?"

"What? This old mug?" Levi mimicked Shay by rubbing the side of his face.

"Don't play humble, LP. I bet you have all the honeys after you."

"I suppose so," Levi said, sounding more arrogant than he intended to.

Shay laughed and raised his drink. "Tu meke, bro."

Levi fetched his phone out of his pocket and quickly snapped a photo of Shay sat on the couch. He always liked to get a picture of Candy Boy's playthings before things got heated. There was a beauty attached to the difference between the relaxed nature of a guy chilling out in one shot and in the next on his hands and knees earning dollars with a dick in his mouth.

"What the fuck?" Shay grumbled as he covered his face, albeit too late to avoid his face being captured in the photo. "Did you just take a picture?"

"Yeah."

"What'd you do that for?"

"It's been so long since I seen you I wanted to grab a picture."

Shay raked an angry hand through his hair. "Could you try bloody asking next time?"

"Sure. Sorry. Won't happen again." Levi shot him an apologetic smile as he put his phone back in his pocket. If Levi wasn't so damn horny then he might have been taken aback by Shay's surly response to having his picture taken but he was too focused on what Shay's mouth would look like at the end of his dick.

Shay calmed down a little. "Sorry. I shouldn't have snapped at you, LP. It's just that I'm not used to having my picture taken unless I'm down at the station getting booked." He laughed, trying to break the tension he'd just caused. "Anyway, tell me what the hell you've been up to since I last saw you?"

For the next thirty minutes or so they just say there talking utter shit, remembering days gone by when they used to be neighbours. Even with the warmth of eighty-year-old scotch working to loosen his muscles, Levi was still edgy and wondering how the hell he would veer the evening to where he wanted it to go.

As the minutes whirred on, and Shay hogged the conversation with exaggerated mannerisms, Levi began to see just how on edge he was. The guy just couldn't stay still. He would be halfway through spitting out a stupidly fast sentence then randomly stand up, tug at his clothing, and walk around the lounge in erratic circles before sitting back down on the couch and tapping his foot up and down like a jackhammer.

He's on more than just alcohol, Levi thought.

Shay being pinged out was disappointing but it was hardly surprising. The little Levi had seen of Shay since leaving Brixton, Shay was nearly always off his face on something. It seemed a shame that his former babysitter had graduated from a recreational drug user to a fucked-up addict but, like so many guys in Brixton, it carried an air of inevitability about it.

"Do you still catch up with Scott Morris?" Shay asked. Before Levi could even respond, Shay launched into a random story about Scott's best friend Fergus. "Don't get me wrong, I like Fergus, I really do, but he totally takes Scott for granted. Always staying at his house for free and never giving him a cent towards anything. Now I know mates are supposed to help each other out but there comes a point where you gotta be thinking this guy is just taking the piss, right? Well, that's what I think…"

Shay went on and on about the freeloading Fergus while Levi nodded along and pretended to be listening. He used the opportunity to eye the bulge between Shay's legs, wondering if the lumps he could see were from Shay's dick and balls or just flattering folds of denim. He figured it was a bit of both.

Shay suddenly laughed, a quiet, soft sound that made Levi quirk his lip in response and ask, "What?"

"Nothing." Shay grinned, playing coy. "Nothing at all."

"Obviously you find something funny."

Shay downed a mouthful of his drink then rocked back in his seat. "What's funny, LP, is the way you've been staring at my cock for the past five minutes." He laughed again, apparently much more aware than Levi had given him credit for.

Levi's tongue got stuck to the roof of his mouth. Panic ruptured through his veins and he began to blush but what Shay said next was both surprising and calming.

"It's a free world. You can look all you like." Shay blatantly adjusted his bulge. "I just like to know when somebody is trying to stare at my dick."

"And if I was?"

"Then I would offer to change the way I am sitting so you can have a better view." Shay laughed.

Levi laughed too, then asked, "Are you into guys?"

"Nar, man. But I don't care if you are."

"Oh..."

"And are you?" Shay waggled his eyebrows. "Into guys that is?"

Levi paused for a moment, studying Shay's face to make sure a confession was safe. "Sometimes."

Shay grinned. "So you like the best of both worlds, aye?"

"That's probably the best way to put it."

"Guess it's good to cover all your bases, aye," Shay replied so casually that anyone would have thought Levi had just made a comment about the weather.

"Have you ever fooled around with another guy at all?" Levi asked.

It was Shay's turn to pause, studying Levi's face. "I suppose so."

"You suppose so?"

"You know what us guys are like when we're younger." Shay saw the way Levi was staring at him and wanting a more detailed response. "Okay. If it will make your horny heart happy I will share the short history of my brief foray into faggotry."

Levi chuckled. "Cool."

"When I was at high school me and my mate Logan Middleton used to fool around a bit. Nothing serious. Just curious teen shit. We'd sneak out to an old woodshed behind his house and look at dirty magazines together and toss one another off. He tried to fuck me one time but it hurt too much so I made him pull it out." Shay slapped his knee and laughed. "I'm sure everyone in Brixton must have heard me fucking squeal that day. It hurt like a motherfucker so we stuck to handys after that. That homo shit stopped though when we both got girlfriends and didn't need each other's helping hand anymore. Then when I was eighteen, I got absolutely fucking wasted at a party up in Auckland one night and let this gay couple take turns blowing me, and then one time a few years ago I had threeway with a married couple and the guy rimmed me while I fucked his missus." Shay smiled and nodded. "And that's it."

Holy fuck! Levi was impressed by the blunt honesty Shay had shared. "That makes me think you might be into guys just a little bit."

"Nar, bro. Not at all. I enjoyed each experience but it's not the kind of thing I go looking for. I just live for the moment, you know?"

Levi nodded. It made sense. It also presented the perfect opportunity for him to strike. "Would you be keen to add a new experience to the list?"

"Are you saying what I think you're saying?"

"Probably." Levi smiled wickedly.

"I'm really flattered, LP, you really are a handsome dude, but I don't think it's a good idea."

"Why not?"

"Because you're like my little brother. It would just feel wrong." He glared at Levi. "Don't you agree?"

Shay was right. It would feel wrong. But that was probably what made the whole scenario so damn hot in Levi's mind. But it went deeper than that. Deeper than Shay's attractive physique, rebel charm and his alluring X factor. Shay had been the one person in his life who'd always been honest and shared his knowledge like a wise elder. It had been Shay, not Levi's father, who'd taught Levi how to shave, how to impress girls, and pointers on fingering and fucking. And for Levi, who enjoyed emasculating his male partners, there was nothing hotter than the idea of emasculating the man who had taught him how to be a man.

"What if I gave you an incentive?" Levi reached a hand down to his shoe and pulled out the money he had hidden in his sock. He fanned the notes out and lay them on the floor in front of his feet.

"Fucking hell," Shay muttered. He put his drink down on the coffee table, just a little too hard. The table shook. "How much is that?"

"Four-hundred."

"And is that for me?" Shay asked as he raised a jittery hand to scratch at his fuzzy cheek. "If I agree to fool around?"

Levi nodded. He'd never offered to pay that much before but Shay was worth it.

"Oh, bro. This is a tough one." One side of Shay's mouth curled into a smile. "I love pussy... but I also love money."

They regarded each other with neither hostility or kindness, but the gaze they shared was long. After a moment Shay placed his palms together and let out a long sigh. "So what would I have to do to earn that?"

"You would get naked, let me take some pictures, wank in front of me, suck me off. And maybe some other stuff."

"Other stuff? Do you mean fucking?"

Levi had never wanted to try anal, worried it was a step too far, like somehow it would take him from sometimes bi to full-on homo. But if there was anyone who could make him dip his dick in a forbidden pond then it would be Shay. "I wasn't thinking about anal but I could be into that."

"What were you thinking of?"

Levi hesitated, embarrassed to share with Shay what he wanted. Usually it didn't matter because he didn't give a fuck what his whores thought.

"Just tell me, LP. Ain't no shame in it." Shay grinned. "Is it kinky?"

"You could say that."

"Ain't nothing wrong with a bit of kink, bro." Shay waggled his dark eyebrows. "Let your freak flag fly is what I say."

"I like to have my feet rubbed and told how hot I am."

Shay's tone stayed jovial and noncommittal. "An ego rub with a foot rub, aye?"

"Yeah." Levi chuckled.

"What else?"

Levi cleared his throat, trying to sound confident with his kinkiest request. "I'd also be keen to watch you piss your pants." Watching the guy wet himself was always Levi's favourite part. He would have his fun with pictures and touching first then let the guy put his clothes back on before giving the order for them to piss their pants. They always look a little broken when he gave the instruction, like they had hoped he'd forgotten about it, but Levi never forgot. It was the part of the hook-up that gave him the biggest rush of power.

Shay's lips pouted ever so slightly, and he blinked slowly. He definitely looked uneasy about the thought of wetting himself. He put his head in his hands, running his fingers through his dark hair. He stared at the money by Levi's feet like he was lost in deep thought. The moment stretched out like the horizon until finally he raised his face and met Levi's gaze. "If you can promise me that this will stay between us then you have yourself a deal, LP."

"Awesome."

"You really have to PROMISE that you won't tell ANYONE about this. Not a soul. The last thing I need is for everyone to know that I did homo shit for cash." His lips quirked. "And pissed myself."

"I promise. Whatever happens here today stays between us."

"Cheers, bro. I trust you."

Levi's dick was making its presence known, stiffening at the realisation that Shay Jacobs, his childhood hero, had just agreed to become his whore. Every time a guy agreed to sell himself was a thrill but this time was worth more than all the others combined. He leaned forward and picked up the cash and put it in his pocket.

"Whatcha doing with the cash, bro?" Shay balked. "I thought that was for me?"

"It is for you. I'm just putting it away until we're finished. Then I will hand it over."

Shay gave him a doubtful glance but relented with a nod. "So how does this work, LP?"

"You can start by taking off your shirt."

Shay pulled his T-shirt off, mussing his black hair. He shook his head and squinted an eye at Levi as if asking *now what?*

Levi was too transfixed admiring Shay's chest to respond. His pecs were dusted with just the right amount of hair. It narrowed and tapered down the centre of his chest, briefly widening over his toned stomach, before narrowing again and disappearing under the belt of his jeans.

Shay smirked. "I take it you like me with my shirt off?"

"Yeah, man. You look hot." Levi smiled at him. "How tall are you?"

"Five-eleven."

"What size are your feet?"

"Size twelve. Why?"

"No reason." Levi jotted the answers down in his mind so he could use them later when he wrote the story. "And how big is your cock? When erect?"

"I dunno. I've never measured it before." Shay must have spotted the *don't talk bullshit* look in Levi's eyes because he very quickly added. "It ain't small if that's what you're wondering. If you can get me hard then we can measure it together if you like."

"I like the sound of that." Levi thumped the floor with the heel of his foot. "Come stand here."

Shay's steps were more like a crawl as he went and stood right in front of Levi. He had a goofy grin on his face but it was clear he was nervous.

Levi's eyes remained fixated on Shay's torso before dropping down to the raggedy jeans covering his lower half. His need to touch him was so strong that it wobbled his equilibrium. Without fully realising what he was doing, Levi reached out and closed his hand over Shay's denim-covered crotch. He gave it slow, rhythmic squeezes, exploring the bulge and plump ridges of Shay's cock and balls.

Unexpectedly Levi whimpered—not a fag-whimper, just a guy-groan that escaped from his throat. He didn't intend it. It just happened. The whole realisation of whose cock he was groping had just pushed his buttons a little too hard.

He then pulled the metal teeth of Shay's zipper apart, and stuck his hand inside to get a better feel. The heat of Shay's balls emanated into his palm, triggering another bolt of lust to course through his body. He used the pad of his thumb to stroke the outline of Shay's flaccid dick. Not being able to help himself, he pulled his hand out and brought his fingers to his nose and sniffed. His nostrils were whacked with the smell of stale sweat and a small trace of dried piss. The pungent smells were not pleasant but Levi's cock still hardened knowing it was Shay's cock responsible for the thick scent.

"You're a brave man, LP," Shay said, smirking. "My nuts need a wash."

"They do," Levi agreed but that didn't stop him slipping his hand back in the gap of Shay's jeans and fondling him some more to get another whiff on his fingers. "Now take your pants off," Levi whispered.

Shay gave a slight nod and his hands dropped to his belt which he unclicked, dropping his dirty jeans to his knees. He hunched over, wobbling as he did so, and tugged the jeans over his feet and removed his smelly socks.

You really are stunning.

Barefoot in just tight black briefs, Shay stood there with his arms folded and an edgy grin on his face. His breathing was uneven and his body trembled. He was nervous. Nervous as fuck.

"Stand still," Levi said, retrieving his phone from his pocket. "I wanna take some pics."

Shay exhaled and fell still.

Levi began snapping picture after picture, starting at Shay's long feet and working his way up to his stubbled face.

"No one else will see these, aye?" Shay asked.

"They're just for my eyes," Levi lied before asking, "Turn around. I wanna get some of your other side."

"Some might say my best side," Shay joked. He turned and wiggled his bum.

Levi humoured him with a light laugh, snapping a series of shots of Shay's perfectly shaped behind. He yanked the briefs down to expose Shay's buttocks. They were dusted with a very light sprinkling of hair but still looked delicious. Levi surprised himself once again when he leaned forward and gave each cheek a sloppy kiss and hungry nip.

Shay chuckled. "Somebody's keen." He pulled his briefs up and turned back around to face Levi's lust-filled gaze.

"Take them off," Levi tugged on the elastic waistband of Shay's undies. "I need to see this cock of yours. I've been wanting to see it for years."

Shay chuckled, gently pushing Levi's hand away. "What's the rush? If you've waited that long then what's the harm in waiting a little longer?"

"I'm paying good money so I expect to see your dick."

A flicker of anger rolled in Shay's eyes but it quickly went away. "I'm just saying that we have all night, don't we? So what's the rush?"

Levi figured Shay had a point. What was the harm in waiting a little longer? "Okay. But you can start kissing my feet now."

Shay squatted down in front of him, and removed Levi's shoes and socks. His shaky fingers began stroking the arches of Levi's barefeet, smiling as he did so. "This is so weird. I used to play with your feet when you were little, remember?" He proceeded to pinch Levi's toes. "This little piggy went to the market. This little piggy stayed home. This little piggy—"

"Stop that. You're making it weird."

"Sorry, LP. But this whole thing is weird for me."

Levi exhaled heavily, making his annoyance known. "Look, maybe we should just forget it. If I'm paying for a guy to be my whore then I expect him to do whore stuff." Levi was amazed how harsh he spoke. To Shay of all people. But it did the trick. Shay wanted the money too much.

"Nar, man. I can do this." Shay raised Levi's left foot and began licking it slowly, caressing the sides gently. "You're the man with the money." Another long lick. "I'm the whore."

Fuck yeah. Levi loved hearing him say that.

Shay ran his tongue in between Levi's toes, drawing each one into his mouth and sucking it like a cock. When he was finished with the first foot, he lowered it gently to the floor, then grabbed Levi's other foot and pressed it against his face to give it the same treatment.

Levi was so overwhelmed by the footsy bliss that he didn't even mind Shay wasn't mouthing words of praise like he had requested. In fact, he was so lost to desire that he hadn't even tried recording Shay's moment of shame. It felt that fucking good. But as good as it felt, he wanted to take things to the next level.

"Take my pants off," Levi whispered.

Shay stopped sucking on his toes. "What's that?"

"Take my pants off."

Shay didn't back away but his gaze was extremely wary. He gave a slight nod and his hands climbed to Levi's waist and began unbuttoning his pants. Once they were undone, he took hold of the cuffs of Levi's jeans, and slithered them off. Before being told what to do next, Shay pressed his lips to the inside of Levi's thigh, kissing and nibbling. "I can't wait to have my first cock in my mouth." *Kiss. Kiss. Lick.* "I bet a man like you has such a sexy cock too." *Kiss. Kiss. Nip.* "Bet you can't wait to fuck my face and make me your bitch, aye Little prince... or should I say *big prince.*"

It was as if he knew Levi's fantasies and was repeating them back to him, including some Levi didn't even know he had.

"You got all this money now and you can just fuck me how you like. Treat me like dirt. It's what I deserve though." Shay's lips ghosted over the outline of Levi's bulge. "Imagine how hot it would be ramming your big rich cock in my rent boy arse. I bet you know how to fuck like a real man too."

Fuck me! You are amazing! Levi grabbed the back of Shay's head and shoved him into his groin, loving the feel of Shay's rough stubble scraping against his inner thighs. "Lick my nuts, bitch. Show me how much of a cheap slut you are."

Shay let out a series of sexy little groans, licking the material covering Levi's balls and throbbing boner.

Every dirty lick drew pangs of desire from Levi's balls until he was so worked up he thought he might spill his load.

Shay raised his face, his half-lidded gaze burning into Levi's eyes. "You wanna fuck me, LP? Show me how much of a cheap slut I really am?"

Levi was breathless. All he could do was nod.

"Good shit. If I'm gonna be made a faggot then it may as well be a real man's cock I take up my arse." Shay smirked and gave Levi's erection one more kiss. "Let me just grab a rubber from my bag, big boy."

And that is where Twisted Candy the story ended. Just with the added white lie of Shay not being able to find a rubber so they had agreed to call it a day. But it was only half the story...

Levi tried settling his lewd breaths as he watched Shay crawl seductively on his hands and knees to his backpack sitting on the couch. Fucking Shay hadn't been part of the plan, but if Levi was ever gonna try anal with a dude then it made sense to try it with someone who had such a sexy arse. "You are so fucking hot, Shay. I can't believe this is finally—" Levi's heart sank to his toes.

What the fuck!!!

"Party's over, faggot," Shay said, wielding a handgun that he'd pulled out of his backpack.

"What the hell are you doing, Shay? Put the bloody gun away."

"Nope." Shay shook his head.

Now that he'd had a moment to settle his initial fright, Levi suspected it was nothing more than a water pistol in the drug-fucked idiot's hand. "Look, Shay. Just fuck off home and we can pretend like tonight never happened. You're obviously off your fucking nut right now."

"What makes you think that?" Shay grinned.

"Because you're pointing a water pistol at me for starters, you fucking moron."

Shay turned the gun towards the wall and pulled the trigger. *BANG.* A bullet fired, ripping through the wallpaper.

Levi scrambled backwards in his chair. "What the fuck, man! Why the fuck do you have a real gun on you."

"For protection from predators like you."

"I'm not a predator."

"Yeah you are. You're just like your dad was. A dirty fucking pervert who will rape Brixton boys to get his jollies."

The words hit harder than any bullet could. "I'm nothing like my father."

"Yeah you are. You and him are exactly the same. Fuck, you may as well be the same fucking person."

Levi hated how similar Shay's twisted spiel sounded like the bullshit Lucky used to say. "I am not like my dad. You know that."

"You've both tried fucking me. But neither of you sick fucks ever managed to seal the deal." Shay laughed. "Your mother's just the same. The only difference is she succeeded."

"You're lying."

"No I'm not. Ask her. I pumped her with jizz every day for over a year. Every fucking day we were at it like rabbits when your father was out at work and you were at school." He chuckled darkly. "She couldn't get enough of my big brown dick."

"I think you're confusing my mum with your sad slapper of a mother."

"My mum is a slag. I ain't denying that. But at least she owns it and doesn't go around pretending she's something she's not."

"Mum would never sleep with you."

Shay nodded, smiling. "She did, Lp. She did plenty."

Something about the nasty glint in Shay's eyes curled Levi's stomach. Not because what he was saying was cruel but because it looked like he was telling the truth.

"Why are you doing this?" Levi asked. "I'm your friend."

"You're not my fucking friend. Friends stay in touch."

"It's not like I haven't tried to stay in touch."

"Oh really?" Shay rolled his eyes. "We haven't seen each other in how long?"

"I've rung you about five times this year to ask to hang out and you said you were too busy every time. Except this one."

"You wanna know why I keep cancelling on hanging out with you? Because I knew you'd pull a stunt like this. People talk, LP. Not loudly but there are whispers going around Brixton about the pretty boy in the red Porsche giving guys money for jobs. Sex jobs."

Oh my God... Levi gulped.

"So if I were you I would stop going out to Brixton to try and find cheap trade. If you wanna be a faggot then be a faggot with your own kind."

Levi was torn between fear at having a loaded gun pointed at him and hearing Shay such hurtful things.

"And back to the whole 'hanging out' bullshit. Whenever you rang, you only ever called up and asked to hang out at my place. This is the first time you've invited me here. The first time in seven fucking years!" Shay let out a cruel laugh. "What's that about, aye? You and your slut of a mother suddenly think you're too good to have my brown arse in your house or some shit."

Levi shivered with fury. "Maybe we don't invite you because you're a drug-fucked thief. How can we have someone visit who will turn up high—which you are right now—and who will probably steal our shit when we aren't looking so you can then sell it to support your drug habit."

"That's where your wrong. I would never steal from youse."

"Yet you came here with a gun?" Levi scoffed. "That tells me otherwise."

"Oh, I will be leaving with money today. That 400 you owe me for what we just did."

"Fuck off. You're not getting paid for pointing a fucking gun at me."

"If you don't hand it over then you're gonna get a bullet."

Levi held his nerve. "You won't shoot me. You couldn't kill me."

"You're right. You're the murderer. Not me." Shay grinned deviously. "But I would shoot you in the cock. It won't kill you but it would make you hand over the money."

"No you wouldn't."

BANG! A bullet got fired right into the carpet, inches away from Levi's feet.

"FUCK!" Levi jumped in the air, scrambling out of his chair and tumbling onto the floor.

"Stop where you are, cunt, or the next one does go right in that stinky little dick of yours."

Levi's heart was pounding like a stampede. He remained seated on the floor beside the chair, clutching his crotch.

"It's a bit rich of you and your mum to hold my addiction against me when it's you two who are to blame for it," Shay said.

"Why are we to blame?" Levi asked as calmly as possible.

"Because I had to chop a dead man's fucking hands off and use plyers to pull his fucking teeth out of his head, all so I could help you ungrateful pricks. How the fuck am I supposed to get through that sort of twisted shit without a little help? Hmm?" Shay shook his head. "Sometimes in bed at night I can still hear the cracks of his teeth being ripped out and the noise his bones made when I sawed through his wrists. Meanwhile you and your mum are here living the high life, swanning about like nothing fucking happened. Not me. I don't have money to take my mind off all that shit. All I have is drugs, so don't fucking lecture me about that."

"We all suffered that night, Shay. Not just you."

"Fuck off, you didn't suffer," Shay snapped. "Yeah, you might have killed the fat fuck but it was more by accident than anything."

"It wasn't by accident. I killed him to save you. And what about all the other things I went through?"

"You mean being your daddy's plaything." Shay laughed. "You didn't suffer. You fucking loved it. You loved it so much you're doing it to other guys now. So don't tell me you suffered."

Levi's heart squeezed in malice. He wished so much he was made of metal so he could get up and beat Shay to a bloody pulp.

"Anyway, LP. I think it's time you give me my money. 400 I believe." Shay knelt down and threw Levi his pants. "Get the money out and give it to me."

Levi fished through the pockets with jittery fingers, pulling the notes out and handing them over.

Shay stuffed the cash inside his underwear then tilted his head as he gazed at Levi with a depraved smile. "You know... I feel bad taking your money without finishing the job."

"It's fine. J-Just go."

"Oh, don't be like that, LP. I'm a firm believer in giving the customer what they want."

"Please, Shay. Just go. I won't tell anyone. Just take the money and leave. Take anything you want."

"Settle down, LP. I'm not going to hurt you if you promise to do what I say." He aimed the gun at Levi's crotch.

Levi shuddered. "What do I have to do."

"Take your shirt off and lay down. That's all. Lay down and close your eyes."

"I don't want to do that, Shay. Please."

"LAY THE FUCK DOWN!" Shay screamed, a vein throbbing in his temple.

Levi yanked his shirt off and swiftly laid down on the floor, ramming his eyes shut

"That's it. Good boy."

Levi lay shivering in fear as he heard Shay's footsteps get closer until he must have been standing beside Levi's head.

"Now. I want you to keep your eyes closed. If you open them, I shoot your cock off. Simple as that. Got it?"

Levi nodded; his trembling arms pressed up against his side like a corpse in a casket. Everything went eerily quiet for a moment until he heard Shay groan.

"Here it comes, LP. What you asked for."

Here's what come? Levi's internal question was answered with a heavy stream of piss splashing over his nose and mouth. *You dirty fucking cunt!* He tried wriggling his face to the side to avoid the warm waterfall of filth.

"Keep your fucking face still, or I shoot."

Levi grimaced, holding still as he received a steamy face wash.

"Open your mouth," Shay ordered. When Levi didn't, Shay screamed the order. "OPEN YOUR MOUTH!"

Oh God. Levi opened his mouth and Shay's piss went straight in, hitting the back of his throat. There was so much of it, it kept filling and filling until eventually it filled his mouth and spilled past his lips down his cheeks and pooled onto the carpet.

"Swallow. Swallow it."

Levi curled his hands into fists, and gulped it down, grimacing as the foul and bitter taste slid down his throat and fed his belly. He coughed and spluttered but Shay just kept pissing on him, hosing his chest and soaking his cock and balls. The warm torrent slowly became less heavy and slowed to a trickle and eventually just a few drops which Shay shook onto Levi's drenched face.

Shay laughed hysterically. His footsteps then headed back towards the couch. "You can open your eyes now, LP."

Levi wiped his face and opened his eyes, staring down at the piss-spattered surface of his body. He looked over to the couch where Shay was putting his jeans back on.

"Oh, man. I can't believe you drank my piss, bro." Shay sniggered. "That's just fucking feral."

"It's not like I had a choice."

"We always have a choice, bro."

Levi scowled, trying to block out the strong taste of piss staining his mouth.

Shay very casually threw his t-shirt on and sat down on the couch. "Before I go, I'm gonna go over a few rules, okay?"

"What rules?" Levi grumbled.

"You are to never come to Brixton cruising for boys to pay for sex. It's fucked up and I won't have it."

"What's fucked up is what you just made me do."

"I'm still the man with the gun, LP, so be smart." Shay waved the weapon at him. "So like I said; no cruising for Brixton cock anymore. And if you don't want me telling people about you and your love of drinking piss then I expect money put into my bank account next week. I will text you my account details."

"I'm not paying you anymore money."

"Yes you will, because if you don't I will tell everyone. And I do mean everyone."

Levi's patience and fear had run out. He was done being held hostage. "Tell everyone in Brixton, I don't care. Who gives a fuck what they think. You're all a bunch of fucking losers anyway."

"Maybe so, but I bet you care what all your Flyer mates think of you."

"You don't even know them."

"You'd be surprised. You're not the only little rich boy who comes to Brixton looking for drugs." Shay scratched his cheek, his foot jerking about. "And I won't stop there. I will go on every Fitzroy Flyer social media page and write comment after comment about how much of a sexual predator you are. How your mother is a slut who likes to sleep with younger men."

"No one will believe you."

"They'll believe me because pretentious gits like you lot live for that sort of drama. They love to see their own ripped to shreds. And I'll rip you fucking good." Shay chuckled to himself. "Imagine it. Ladies' man, Levi Candy, outed as a dick-smoker and filthy little piss pig. You know they'll lap it up. Just like you lapped up my piss."

Levi seethed at Shay's blackmail but he knew there was little he could do. Not even Peach could save him from that level of gossip if it got out. "How much money do you want put into your account?"

"I think 200 will be fine. But I'll let you know if I need more." Shay threw the gun and his dirty socks in his backpack then rose to his feet. He cast Levi a mockful glare. "I hope you get that carpet cleaned before your mum gets back from her holiday. It fucking stinks."

"Fuck you."

"No thanks." Shay laughed and scurried away barefoot.

Levi was numb. He sat in the dampness of what Shay had done to him, breathing in the rank scent of piss. He tried to comprehend how his plan had gone so spectacularly wrong. He couldn't work it out. But what he could work out very fucking easily was that Shay Jacobs was dead to him.

CHAPTER 23

After he'd finished having a shower, scrubbing off all the sweat and dirt from his trip to a valley of death, Levi spent the next hour tidying his room. He gathered up all his dirty clothes and took them to the laundry before taking all his dirty cups and plates to the kitchen. He even vacuumed the floor and lit incense sticks to rid the room of its sweaty sock smell. By the time he was finished it was spotless. He couldn't remember the last time his room had been this clean. He tried telling himself that his late night cleaning frenzy had nothing to do with Danny's demands. *Yeah right,* his inner voice threw back sarcastically.

Levi glanced at the time on his phone. 2 a.m. Was it too late to go see Danny? It probably was but the boy had asked to be serviced one more time before Levi went to bed and Levi felt compelled to grant his wish.

As his feet stepped in the direction of Danny's bedroom, Levi felt like a mere witness to his body's movements. Ever so gently, he pushed the door open, stepping inside the boy's bedroom. It was cast in a soft yellow glow coming from a small bedside lamp, no doubt left on to guide Levi in his subservient chore.

Danny was out to it, sprawled out on his back, his face turned to the side and buried in a pillow. A thin, twisted white bedsheet covered his crotch and very little else.

Levi knew he should just turn around and leave, but he couldn't. He felt compelled to fulfil the order he had been given. *Here goes nothing,* he thought.

He crossed the room and sunk to his knees beside the bed and gently kissed Danny's ankle.

Danny stirred awake, groaning. He rolled over, opening his eyes. He gave Levi a groggy smile. "Fancy seeing you here."

Levi gave a tilt of his head, too ashamed to speak.

Danny threw the sheet off like he was on autopilot, exposing his genitals. Just the sight of them made Levi's still-tender hole twitch.

"You can give me a blowjob if you want," Danny said, his voice still sleepy.

Levi gave his answer by clambering onto the bed and positioning himself between Danny's open legs. He looked down at the young cock that knew him intimately. He hovered his mouth above it, then scooped it between his lips, sucking and slurping hurriedly. He tugged on Danny's nuts, plumping them in his palm. He needed the young gun to get hard quickly. Once he'd been filled with his stepbrother's load then Levi could go back to his own bed.

Danny moaned affirmatively, approving of the way Levi sucked his dick. His hands lowered, stroking Levi's hair, twirling his fingers. "That feels so good, baby."

Don't call me that!

Once Danny was erect, Levi slurped his mouth free. He spat in his hand and rubbed the saliva down his crack, lubing his arsehole. He straddled Danny's waist, grabbed the base of Danny's cock, and guided it into the tight ring of his arsehole. His hole slowly stretched open as he fed himself the boy's curved five inches, until eventually Danny was fully sheathed.

"Can I make a request?" Danny asked.

Levi nodded.

"While I'm fucking you, instead of groaning like you do, can you try and sound a bit different?"

Levi frowned. "Different how?"

"I dunno. Maybe try sounding a bit more girly."

Levi found the request odd. But it was his duty to obey. "Okay. I'll try."

Danny started slowly, fucking Levi very gently, stroking Levi's arms. After a few minutes though, Danny changed his rhythm and his hips began to pump at a steady rate, his cock widening Levi's passage as he fucked him like a boss. The boy was owning his power. He gripped Levi's dick, tugging him in time with his fucking.

With each stroke of Danny's cock, the pitch of Levi's voice went up. His masculinity slipped away and he allowed himself to sound like a needy little girl.

"Fuck me, Danny! Oooo, I need it! Oooo, I need you inside me! Oooo, take what's yours! You own me!"

"I'm taking it, baby. I'm taking it."

Sliding up and down in small, controlled bounces Levi realised he wasn't in any pain—his arsehole had adapted to the shape of Danny's cock. *He's tamed my body.*

Erotic, dirty sounds filled the room, and within a couple of minutes Danny groaned as he fed Levi another hot batch of cum.

"Oh, Danny. Thank you. Thank you so much." Levi's girly voice was mangled with pure gratefulness.

Danny kept jacking Levi's cock, his furled fingers squeezing with dominant intent, demanding Levi also lose his load.

With the combination of Danny's vice-like grip wrapped around his cock and the erotic feel of the boy's plentiful ball juice deep inside arsehole, Levi cried out an ultra-feminine squeal as his cock heaved several arching ropes of cum through the air to land with splattering results across Danny's stomach and chest. Levi looked down at the puddles of cum covering his stepbrother's torso, feeling bad for a split-second until he realised Danny was laughing at him. "What's funny?"

"You."

"Me?"

"The noise you made when you ejaculated was so... so girly."

"You told me to sound like that," Levi said defensively.

"Don't be angry. I wasn't laughing in a nasty way. I was laughing because it was so cute." Danny pouted and made kissy noises. "It was actually quite sexy."

"If it was sexy you wouldn't have laughed," Levi grumbled.

Danny just smiled, stroking Levi's sides. "You're even sexy when you sulk, did you know that?"

"Cheers." Levi scrunched his face up as he raised his arse, letting Danny's slippery cock slide out of his flooded orifice. As he put his clothes back on he felt uneasy from the way Danny stared at him with such loving eyes.

"Did you want to spend the night with me?" Danny asked.

"Not tonight." Levi hesitated. "Unless that's an order?"

"It's not an order. You can sleep in your own room if that's what you prefer. I don't want to abuse my power."

"Thanks, buddy." Levi smiled. "By the way, I cleaned my room like you wanted me to."

"Did you really?"

Levi nodded. "I did it just before I came in here."

"A proper clean or just a Levi clean?"

"What's a Levi clean?"

"Not a proper clean."

Levi laughed. "You're a dork. And yes, it was a proper clean."

"I'm impressed," Danny said, laying back with his hands behind his head. "I must be a good influence on you."

"You reckon?"

"I do. If we dated imagine what else I could help you achieve. You might even find a job."

Levi rolled his eyes. "Don't you start."

Danny laughed. "You know what they say: responsibility breeds character and self-sufficiency breeds confidence."

Levi's heart kicked his ribs. He stared at his stepbrother intently. Pale skin. Inky black hair. Sleepy blue eyes.

No way. No fucking way!

Levi suddenly realised who Danny reminded him of. It was someone from his past *and* his present. It was so obvious now. How had he not worked it out sooner? With a sense of curdling unease, Levi waved Danny goodnight and walked back to his own bedroom where he tried to go to sleep with the hideous knowledge that although it was his stepbrother's seed inside him, it was his stepfather he was attracted to.

His daddy.

Fuck…

EPILOGUE

Three months earlier

"Five guys have died trying to escape from here," said Dion. "Apparently they used their blankets as a rope, just like in the movies, and then jumped over the fence and into the river. But they all drowned while trying to swim away."

Shay lit a cigarette and peered over the edge of the rooftop garden they were standing on. He stared down at the unforgiving concrete of the outdoor patio four floors below. His eyes then skimmed to the fence line acting as a barrier to the sixty-foot cliff that dropped off into the fast-moving river running behind the property. "Were they trying to escape or kill themselves?" He was only half-joking.

Dion shrugged. "Dunno. Either way they all died."

Shay enjoyed a tall tale as much as the next guy but this just reeked of pure bullshit. Life here was challenging but it wasn't unbearable. "So you're saying that five guys were so dumb they tried escaping from a place they could actually ask permission to leave from?"

Dion paused. "Um..."

"And not once after five people died has anyone considered blocking off access to the rooftop?" Shay shook his head and laughed. "Who told you this story?"

"Brayden."

"Brayden talks more shit than we leave on dicks."

Dion grimaced, laughing. "Eww. Speak for yourself."

"So what else did Brayden tell you about these dead dudes?"

"He said that on a full moon their spirits climb up the cliff and then scale the wall of the building to try and get back inside where it's warm." There was a noticeable shiver to Dion's voice.

"Brayden's only trying to scare you," Shay said. "You shouldn't listen to him."

"He didn't scare me," Dion said defensively. "I don't believe in ghosts."

Shay inhaled on his cigarette. "Good for you."

"What about you? Do you believe in stuff like that?"

"I'm Maori, of course I believe in spirits. Just not ones made up by Brayden."

Dion shot him a funny look. "You're Maori? Since when?"

Shay smiled. "Since I was conceived, doofus."

"But I thought you were Lebanese."

Shay laughed. "Yeah, cos there are so many Lebanese guys in New Zealand who talk like this," he said in his laidback Maori accent.

Dion blushed, smiling. His eyes were set so deep in his face that they seemed to shut altogether when he smiled, which he did often. He was tall and thin, nineteen years of age, with sandy-coloured hair and a harmless pleasant look. He was sweet, and trusting, and had a naivety about him that made him seem childlike. A nice contrast to the other two *pets* living in the building with them.

There was Kane. A twenty-four-year-old tatted badboy with a shaved head and a permanent scowl on his face. Based on appearances, Shay had assumed when he arrived that Kane with his six-two frame and bulging inked biceps would have been the alpha male of the bunch but that title, surprisingly, belonged to the youngest member of the house, Brayden.

Eighteen-year-old Brayden was a nasty little fucker who loved to crow on about how good he was at everything. He was also a vain little bitch who spent too long in front of the mirror styling his blond hair to look like he'd just rolled out of bed before taking just as long choosing which pair of skate shoes to wear for the day.

"So you really believe in ghosts?" Dion asked.

Shay nodded. "I sure do. My Nan taught me all about spiritual stuff."

Shay's nan had been a deeply spiritual woman, a Maori elder who claimed to sense tapu a mile away. Whenever she would enter a house you would know if she thought the place was good or not, if she sensed any negativity she would usually sigh and say something like, "This place could do with a spring clean from Jesus." If it was really bad she would complain about the smell or appear to become lightheaded.

The closest she ever got to fainting from a house's evil was when Shay had asked her to help cleanse the Buttwell family home. Levi's story about a nasty naked boy covered in stickers hadn't felt right, so Shay had asked his nan if she could bless the house, which she gladly did. Shay had arranged to sneak her in the house when Barry and Jenny were both out for the day and it was just Levi home. Shay's Nan had made Shay take Levi next door for the afternoon. When she returned from the cleansing, she confided in Shay that Lucky was gone but evil still lived there. Shay hadn't known what she meant at the time but in hindsight it seemed pretty clear she wasn't talking about anything supernatural; she had been talking about Barry Buttwell.

Dion's voice pulled Shay out of his trip down memory lane. "Is your Nan still alive?"

Shay shook his head. "Nar, bro. She passed away last year."

"Oh, I'm sorry."

"Thanks. She was an awesome lady my nan."

Guilt cut at Shay's heart as he remembered how he'd skipped his grandmother's funeral to score drugs before going to smoke up with his girlfriend at the time and spending the next three days fucking and puffing. Just one of many things he'd done while under the fog of addiction that he now regretted.

It fell silent for a moment until Dion asked, "Do you think Brayden and Kane will be back soon?"

"Who knows."

"They didn't look happy about today's job."

"Nar, they didn't."

Shay exhaled heavily, releasing a white plume of nicotine smoke. He looked out into the distance and admired the scenery. Forested ranges, gorges and valleys carved by a deep-green river and even a mountain in the far-off distance. The rooftop garden provided a stunning view and was one of the few good things about this place, Shay thought. But it wasn't just the view that made coming up here for a smoke worthwhile, it was also because this was the only place in the castle—that's what they all called it—that you could be without being watched.

They might have been living in the middle of nowhere but were always being watched, even when they were alone. Every room inside this crazy-looking building was monitored with cameras. You couldn't even take a shit without big brother watching. The footage was probably jerked off over, he thought, or sold online to some sick fuck who got off on that sort of shit.

It was unnerving and downright wrong but he'd agreed to this, signed away his freedom and right to privacy for the chance to earn big dollars—and save himself from being killed.

Getting fucked in the arse wasn't exactly a straight boy's dream job but you sort of got used to it after a while. The boredom, however, that was impossible to get used to. They were locked inside 24/7 with no contact with the outside world which meant no cell phones or internet. Their world was confined to the strange building he and Dion were currently standing atop of.

Before coming here Shay had never seen anything like it. A tall, wide funnel-shaped concrete structure decorated with numerous curly yellow slides that ran down the side of the building, cutting in and out of the walls to the different floors and rooms. These slides were used by the pets as a faster alternative to the stairs, enabling them to get downstairs in a hurry if they had a client waiting for them. There was an elevator running from the basement to the rooftop but only Dave and Sione had access to that with their swipe cards. Most of the rooms in the castle, and the old farm cottage at the front of the property, required one of those cards to gain access.

From a distance the castle probably looked like a stubby cock with knobbly yellow veins, Shay thought. He couldn't be sure though, he'd arrived here in the back of a van in the middle of the night, blindfolded the whole way after being collected from the rehab facility. He had only been permitted to remove the blindfold once he was taken inside, and what he saw as he found himself standing in the middle of an empty dancefloor blew his mind.

Inside the castle was a gigantic mirrored wall that ran from the ground floor all the way to the rooftop, slicing the funnel-shaped building into two sections. On one side was a barely-used entertainment area with a large stage and drinking bar. You could stand on the dance floor and look all the way up to the ceiling—four floors above. The open-air space of this half of the building was huge and showed off the castle's impressive height.

The other side, behind the mirrored wall, housed four different levels. On the ground floor, directly beside the entertainment area, was a maze of rooms and private stalls used for sex with the customers referred to as the *upstairs clients*. Even though it was on the ground floor they were called upstairs clients because *downstairs clients* referred to the men who paid to fulfil much darker fantasies in the basement— a part of the castle Shay had yet to explore and prayed he never had to.

The next level up, the first floor, housed a gymnasium, a small library and a classroom where the pets would go for weekly lessons on how to be better at their job. These lessons were patronizing and stomach-curling and sometimes frightening. Each boy had free access across most of this level, and they were expected to use the gym daily to keep in shape.

The second floor was more restricted in regards to access because it contained Sione and Dave's private quarters. Sione seemed to live at the property permanently acting as a caretaker of some sort. Dave though, he came and went as he pleased. Also on this level was Doctor Harten's office and medical room. The pets would see the doctor once a month to have blood tests done and then be probed and prodded in degrading fashion by a man who looked like he enjoyed it all a little too much.

The third—and top—floor was where the pets all lived together in their own penthouse apartment. The open plan living area was humungous and they had three bathrooms to share between the four of them. None of the windows opened so they relied on air-conditioning to keep them warm in winter and cool in summer. Thankfully access was granted to the rooftop where there was ample seating and planter boxes they could use to grow their own fruit and vegetables. Not that they needed to grow their own food. Groceries—and plenty of them—were provided each fortnight from Sione's trips to town. Which town that was, Shay had no idea. None of the pets had a clue where the fuck they were.

The first week Shay arrived here following his stint in rehab was arguably quite fun if he were being honest. He hadn't been expected to work with any of the clients, and aside from having Sione take him through a few induction tutorials about what his role would involve, he was free to do as he pleased. He roamed everywhere he could without a swipe card, using the crazy slides to search the different levels of the castle, exploring his new home with wide-eyed wonder.

When week two arrived, and he had his first "lesson" before tending to his first client, the fun was over. Shay quickly realised he was expected to work hard for his money. He went to bed that night with an ache in his arse he worried would never go away. It did fade but there always seemed to be another guy arriving the next day who would make the ache return. From day one Shay had been told that if it ever got too much for him then he was welcome to leave but if he did leave then he wouldn't get a cent of the money that was left owing to him and he would have to pay back the deposit he'd been advanced. That was not an option for Shay.

The *ding* of the elevator sounded behind them.

Running a hand through his wavy black hair, Shay turned around to see Dave appear in the opening doors of the lift. The older man stuck out like dog balls with what he was wearing; a ghastly Hawaiian shirt, a pair of pink shorts, and green crocs. Dave was the perfect example of why not to judge a book by its cover. Regardless of the older man's habit of wearing camp shit and calling everyone "sunshine" he wasn't some soft creature whose mouth coughed out limp lisps, he was a rugged fucker whose still surprisingly fit build paid homage to his past life as a bouncer and professional boxer. At nearly sixty he could still take down a man half his age with his calloused meaty mitts.

Dave's gaze circled like a hawk, finally coming to rest on Shay and Dion. "Howdy boys. How's my two favourite pets doing?" he asked in his trademark gravelly drawl.

"I bet you say that to all the boys," Shay replied cheekily, purposely not using the word pet, despite pets being exactly what Dave considered them to be.

Dave laughed. "Only when I have my two favourites standing in front of me."

"Are we really your favourites?" Dion asked.

"Of course, sunshine. You and Pinky light up my life."

I hate that fucking name!

Out of all the pet names he could have been given Shay couldn't believe he'd been landed with such a faggy one. Sure, he was doing a faggy job but why couldn't he have a cool pet name like Dion who had been christened as Ace. Even Brayden and Kane's names weren't as bad; Twitch and Jock. But nope. Shay had been given Pinky for Christ's sake.

Dave wedged his menacing presence between them. "I thought I'd better come tell you boys to get showered soon. You both have medicals today."

"Oh goody," Shay groaned sarcastically.

Dave chuckled. "It sounds like Pinky isn't a fan of his monthly check up?"

"Not really," Shay admitted.

"I understand you are still new here so it will take a bit of getting used to," Dave said.

"I don't think I'll ever get used to some dude ramming two gloved fingers up my nono."

"Up your what?"

"My butt," Shay translated.

"We arrange these medicals because we care about you boys and are looking out for your best interests." Dave ruffled Shay's hair, like one would do to a dog. "I make sure I take care of my pets."

If you really cared about us then you'd make your clients wear protection, Shay thought.

The clients were allowed to bareback them if they paid extra—which some of the men were happy to do. So far Shay had avoided the STD bullet but he felt like he was in a game of Russian roulette and it was only a matter of time before he was hit with something. He just hoped it wasn't anything serious.

A taut silence fell between the three of them as Dave rubbed his crotch. Shay may have been the new kid on the block but in his short time here he'd already experienced the raw hunger of Dave's desire.

Shay and Dion swapped each other a nervous look. He knew they could both sense what was coming, and that they both probably hoped it was the other who would be chosen to fulfil the horny old man's needs.

Don't choose me. Don't choose me. Don't choose me.

"Ace…" Dave's voice hung in the air menacingly.

"Yes, sir?" Dion replied in a shaky whisper.

"On your knees, sunshine. Daddy's dick needs a good clean."

Thank fuck for that! Shay's mind sang in relief.

Dion obliged, dropping to his knees and unzipping Dave's shorts to haul the man's fat cock out. Dave's flaccid tool was a big veiny monster and the skin of its helmet was blemished like it had a birthmark. It also looked unwashed and smelly. If it did smell, Dion didn't seem to mind, he slurped his lips over Dave's limp meat like he was sucking chocolate from a straw.

"Mmm," Dion moaned as he suckled, and Dave echoed it above him.

"Thatta boy, Ace... thatta fucking boy." Dave rubbed the back of Dion's neck and slowly sawed his cock in and out of the boy's mouth. "Now play with my balls a bit."

Dion dragged Dave's shorts to his knees, tugging the man's testicles as he continued to deepthroat Dave's hardening meat.

Shay masked his unease of what was happening right beside him by throwing his gaze towards the horizon, focusing on the hills and river while he tried to block out Dave's wild grunts and Dion's gagging slurps.

Dion wasn't gay but he always followed Dave's commands. All the pets did. Shay also did what he was told to do but he lacked the erotic enthusiasm the other pets displayed. It had taken him a couple weeks to discover why the other pets were so keen to please their crusty master. It was so they could try and earn the dubious honour of an overnight stay in Dave's private room. On account of Dave only staying here one or two days a week, invites weren't given out that often, but when they were, the chosen pet would have a smile so big anyone would think he'd just scored a date with Mila Kunis.

To get an answer to what Shay considered misguided smiles, he'd asked Dion why they were all so keen to spend the night with Dave.

"Because he lets you watch Netflix and he even lets you use his laptop to look up any type of porn you like."

"He does fuck you though, right?"

"Usually."

"That so doesn't sound worth it to me, bro" Shay had replied.

"Nar, man. It's totally worth it! He lets you have whatever you want for dinner. I had crayfish and scallops last time he let me stay, and you can eat as much junk food as you like—all night! And you're allowed to sleep in late."

To pussy-deprived straight boys two seasons behind in their favourite Netflix shows, falling asleep with Dave's baby batter inside their battered behind probably seemed a sacrifice worth making if it meant you got to jerk off to straight porn and fall asleep with the taste of gummy bears in your mouth. But perhaps the biggest attraction of winning the sleepover was the chance to have a decent night sleep in a proper bed.

It seemed crazy that although the pets shared such a large apartment, they didn't actually have their own bedrooms. What they had instead was what Dave liked to call *the bitches box*. The bitches' box was a cube-shaped contraption built of transparent red, blue and yellow glass bricks. It was suspended from the ceiling from inside the *other* half of the building where it dangled like a giant strobe light above the dancefloor. Shay wasn't afraid of heights but he didn't like knowing he was sleeping in a dangling cube a hundred feet above a concrete floor.

To access the bitches box you had to crawl through either a hole in the wall of the apartment's lounge or another hole found in one of the three bathrooms. From these entry points you would crawl inside winding tubes, up and down and all around in zany circles, before you finally came out the other end into the bitches' box. It was almost as if it had been designed to add humiliation to their ordeal by making them crawl and climb like children at a playground just to go to bed. The inside of the dangling glass cube contained wardrobes for their personal clothes, four skinny mattresses and a pile of blankets. The skinny mattresses on the hard glass floor and the echo of each other's snoring inside the cube did not gift the best night's sleep. But that was probably the point. This way Dave got his pets desperate to *win* a night with him. Just like Dion was doing right now.

"Oh, Ace, you are so good to your daddy."

"Mmm." Dion garbled back. "That's because I love your big dick, sir."

Dave chuckled. He pulled his spit-soaked rod from Dion's mouth and began slapping it across the boy's face. Not gently either.

The slap-slap-slap of dick on face was impossible for Shay to block out. He glanced down and watched Dion stick his tongue out to try and catch the hefty cock-whacks Dave was giving him. Dave's dick was now fully-erect; seven-and-a-bit inches of vein-riddled unforgiving flesh.

Dave gave his manhood three hard yanks and he yelled to the sky as he sprayed Dion's face with thick, creamy, white ropes of cum. Dave panted, grinning as he looked down at the cum canvas he'd created. Dion went to wipe his face clean. "No," Dave growled. "I didn't say you could clean it."

"Sorry, sir."

Dave hauled his shorts up and put his cock away. He turned to Shay. "Clean him up for me, Pinky."

Shay's tummy turned. He gave his master an obedient nod. He joined Dion on his knees and began to lick the boy's face clean of Dave's gooey jizz, swallowing the bitter man butter into the pit of his stomach until it was all gone. Before he pulled away, Dion tilted his open mouth towards Shay's, sticking his tongue inside Shay's mouth. At first Shay was shocked but he accepted his friend's warm tongue, sharing with him the taste of Dave's cum.

"Good boys." Dave looked down at them like a proud father. "I like it when my pets play nice and get along."

They finished the kiss then slowly stood up.

"Before I forget," Dave said. "I have some good news for you, Pinky. I've been talking with the powers that be and we have decided your talents are wasted on a tier one contract and we would like you to start working with clients in the basement."

"Oh…" A shadow of alarm passed over Shay's face that went unnoticed.

"Yep. I thought you might be surprised to be offered a promotion so quickly but you have proven to be very popular with the customers and many are requesting your services be provided downstairs as well."

He knew what his answer was and he knew Dave wouldn't like it. While the other pets never spoke about what happened in the basement, Shay suspected it involved a lot more than sloppy blow jobs and getting fucked.

"I'll get Sione to bring up a new contract after lunch for you to sign." Dave smiled at him. "I think you will be very pleased with the new amount we have offered you."

"I can't accept it," Shay whispered.

Dave blinked. "What's that?"

"I can't sign the new contract?"

"Why not?"

Shay took a deep breath. "Because I don't want to."

"What the fuck do you mean you don't want to?"

"I'm not trying to be rude or nothing, sir. It's just that I'd rather keep doing the job I'm already doing."

Dave let out a humourless laugh, staring at the ground. When he raised his dark eyes back up, they revealed the true monster in the man. He stepped forward, his sour breath wafting with ill intent all over Shay's face.

"You've been a good boy up till now, Pinky, I strongly suggest you don't test my patience. It doesn't end well for pets who do."

"It' not that I'm not grateful, I just don't want to work in the basement."

"This isn't about what you want, this is about what our customers want."

"No," Shay said firmly.

"I think now would be a good time to remind you not to forget your place, *Pinky*." Dave said Shay's pet name with nasty disdain. "You signed a contract, remember? You and your little brown pecker belong to me for the next twelve months, so when I offer your arse a promotion then you will accept it."

This was the part where Shay was supposed to say *yes sir* but the rebel in him refused to bite his tongue. "And if I don't?" he challenged.

"Oh, Pinky, believe me when I tell you that you are fucking with the wrong man right now. I can be one nasty fucker when I wannabe."

Shay didn't doubt it.

"Just sign the bloody contract, Pinky," Dion said in a stressy whisper.

"Stay out of this, Ace," Dave snapped. He took a slow step backwards, his monstrous gaze not leaving Shay's blue eyes. "Pinky needs to have a long, hard think about what he plans to do. It's him who will face the consequences."

Everything went quiet and the tension-heavy ten seconds of silence that followed felt like an eternity.

Finally, Dave said, "I am going up to Auckland tonight and I won't be back until Friday. We will discuss this then." On those surprisingly calm words, he walked away and left Shay and Dion alone.

"That was stupid, Shay. Really fucking stupid. You never say no to Dave. Never!" Dion glared at him, his eyebrows wrinkled in worry. "You have to sign that contract."

"It's not like he can kill me if I don't."

"I wouldn't be so sure about that."

Shay laughed but Dion looked deadly serious. "You need to chill out, bro. Dave won't do shit. I know a thing or two about breaking the law, and while this place is rather creative when it comes to playing by the rules, they do actually have a rule book."

"You say that but you just licked his cum off my face," Dion said.

"And your point?"

"Dave makes his own rules and he expects us to play by them."

Shay looked down towards the river that had claimed the lives of Brayden's fictional spirits. The ominous vibe Dave had left hanging in the air began to toy with Shay's brain, and a very small part of him began to question if maybe Brayden's story had an element of truth. He quickly shook away the ludicrous thought and reminded himself it was just Brayden talking shit.

"I'm not signing that contract," Shay said firmly.

"You know we get paid extra for working in the basement, right?"

"And what sort of twisted shit does he make youse do down there to earn that extra money?"

"It depends... but I'm pretty sure they'd go easy on you to begin with."

"And what's easy when it's at home?"

"Maybe some bondage. Maybe the milking machine."

"The milking machine?"

"It's where they tie you up and hook your willy up to this tube that pumps out all your cum."

"Fuck that! I'm not letting some bastard treat me like I'm a human cow. That's just sick." Shay shook his head vehemently. "Trust me, Dion. They will never put me down in that basement. Mark my words!"

To be continued...

ABOUT THE AUTHOR

Zane lives along the rugged west coast of New Zealand in a pink shack with his gaming-obsessed flatmate. He is a fan of ghost stories, road trips and nights out that usually lead to his head hanging in a bucket the next morning.

He enjoys creating characters who have flaws, crazy thoughts and a tendency to make bad decisions. His stories are emotionally-charged and don't shy away from some of love and life's darker themes.

Printed in Great Britain
by Amazon